Jane Godman writes in a variety of romance genres, including paranormal, gothic and romantic suspense. Jane lives in England and loves to travel to European cities that are steeped in history and romance—Venice, Dubrovnik and Vienna are among her favorites. Jane is married to a lovely man and is mum to two grown-up children.

Also by Jane Godman

Discover more at millsandboon.co.uk

ENTICING THE DRAGON

JANE GODMAN

MILLS & BOON

First Published in Great Britain 2018
by Mills & Boon, an imprint of HarperCollins*Publishers*
1 London Bridge Street, London, SE1 9GF

Enticing the Dragon © 2018 Amanda Anders

ISBN: 978-0-263-26684-9

49-0718

MIX
Paper from
responsible sources
FSC™ C007454

This book is produced from independently certified FSC™ paper to ensure responsible forest management.

For more information visit: www.harpercollins.co.uk/green

Printed and bound in Spain
by CPI, Barcelona

This book is dedicated to my new grandson, Harry.
Welcome to the world, little one.

Chapter 1

It didn't matter how many ways Hollie Brennan looked at the information on her laptop screen—the same pattern emerged every time. Only too aware of the problems the evidence posed, she had reviewed it over and over. Her faith in the computer program should have been absolute. She had been the person to devise it, and she had done it with just this sort of scenario in mind. It was used by fire investigators all over the country. Now she was doubting the information it was giving her. Instead of trusting it, she had gone back to basics. As she drank her early-morning coffee, the table in her small apartment was littered with maps, scribbled notes and scrawled diagrams.

She had even woken with a start at three in the morning, tearing herself away from her dreams of enchantment and mystery, before jumping out of bed to double-check one of the locations. But no. She had been right all along…which meant, no matter how crazy it sounded, she had to take this to her boss.

You have to listen to what the data is telling you, even if it appears bizarre. It was part of her introductory talk to trainee fire investigators. On this occasion, she was finding it increasingly difficult to take her own advice.

The streets were clear as she drove toward the office. This was one advantage of being up and about so early. She was half listening to the radio, her mind tuning in and out of the news stories, when the first bars of a rock ballad caught her full attention. It was the latest release from Beast, one of the biggest bands in the world. It was also, on this particular morning, the ultimate irony. After listening for a few moments, Hollie switched the radio off.

On arriving at the office, she was pleased to see her boss's car was already in its designated parking space. There was a joke among the agents at the Newark Division of the FBI that, since no one ever saw her come or go, Assistant Special Agent-in-Charge Melissa McLain might actually spend the night there.

Hollie didn't subscribe to the same view as her colleagues. ASAC McLain was a professional, but she wasn't an automaton. Maybe it was because of Hollie's unique role within the Bureau, but she had been granted occasional glances beneath the steely mask. They had even, now and then, gone out and gotten mildly tipsy together. No, McLain was human, and she was mightily pissed about their inability to catch one of the most prolific and deadly arsonists to come the Bureau's way.

On reaching the third floor, Hollie knocked on McLain's office door and waited for the abrupt instruction to enter.

"I come bearing caffeine." She held up the carton

from her boss's favorite coffee shop. She knew from experience that stopping on the way into work to purchase the strongest, largest espresso worked well in two ways. It softened McLain's mood slightly, and it meant she was forced to look up from her desk and focus on Hollie while they talked.

"It's never good if you have to bribe me." McLain removed the lid from the carton and closed her eyes as she inhaled.

"Not only is it not good—" Hollie sighed as she sipped her peppermint tea; the coffee had been tempting, but she needed a clear head for this conversation "—it's so weird I don't know where to start."

"How about the beginning?" McLain's direct gaze didn't allow for hesitation.

Okay. Deep breath. "You know I like rock music?"

A corner of McLain's mouth lifted. "I'm more of a classical fan myself, but I won't hold your musical preferences against you. Is this going anywhere?"

"Bear with me. About a week ago, I was looking at dates, hoping to get a ticket for Beast's next tour. They're like gold dust." *The facts. Stick with the facts.* "Anyway, there was a sidebar on the webpage, showing all the places they'd toured in the last few years. And it got my attention."

"Because?"

Hollie reached for her file of paperwork. "Because, in the last four years, the places Beast has toured are the towns the Incinerator has targeted. Our random arsonist is not so random, after all."

McLain's brows snapped together. "Let me see if I've got this straight. You're saying our arsonist set his fires in the same towns that this rock band tours? Does he do it at the same time?"

"Typically, the fires take place the day after a Beast concert. Sometimes two days," Hollie said. "But there's more. Once I found the link, I did some checking into Beast's international tours. Guess what?"

McLain took a gulp of her coffee, some of her customary poise deserting her. "Our guy has a passport?"

"It looks that way. In the four years we have been hunting the Incinerator, Beast has traveled to Europe, Australia and Asia. I checked with the police in each of those countries, and during each Beast tour, there were classic Incinerator fires in every location. Generally, the intervals between the international concerts and the fires were longer. Often they were weeks apart. But they always happened."

"Damn."

Hollie took her maps out of her file and placed them on the desk. "There's a problem."

"No, don't give me problems." McLain groaned. "Not when you've just given me the closest thing we've ever had to a breakthrough in this damn case."

Hollie pointed to the two maps. "This is a map showing the location of every Incinerator fire. This one shows every place Beast has toured. The two match up every time...except for recently." She pulled in a breath. Now for the hard part. "The last three Incinerator fires were set in towns that were *not* the location of a Beast tour."

McLain muttered a curse under her breath. "Why have you brought me this if you've already disproved your own theory?"

"Because there is another link." Hollie drew her electronic tablet from its case. "I reasoned that the Beast link was too strong to be overlooked." She brought an image of the band up on the screen. "This guy is the lead singer, Khan. He got married recently and the birth of his baby daughter twelve months ago coincided with the band's decision to take a break from touring. During that time, the other members of the group have done some solo projects."

Sensing McLain's impatience, she played a brief recording of the group. On the screen, dense smoke rolled like fog from the stage. Within it, colored strobe lights danced in time with the drumbeat. Giant LED screens at the rear of the stage projected alternating images of roaring fire, close-ups of snarling animals and Beast's logo, a stylized symbol resembling three entwined number sixes. At the side of the stage, explosions went off at random intervals, shooting orange flames high into the night sky.

Beast was a fire-storming force of nature, but McLain appeared unimpressed. "Why do I need to see this?"

"I want you to look at this guy." Hollie zoomed in on the front of the stage. Tall and muscular with his dark red hair drawn back into a ponytail, the man she indicated was all burning drama and flickering movement. Even on a screen, it was clear that the air around him sizzled into life as he timed the sweeping arc of his hand on the guitar to the explosions at the side of the stage. As they watched, he gestured in the manner of a conjurer, igniting a flickering blue blaze along the front of the stage.

"Looks like he enjoys playing with fire. Who is he?"

Hollie ended the recording. "Torque. Lead guitar."

The reason I wanted that Beast ticket. It was hard to explain her feelings about a man she had never met. Luckily, she didn't think McLain would require the additional information.

"You can match him to the other three Incinerator locations?"

Hollie nodded, withdrawing a third map from her file. "I tracked each individual member of Beast to find out what they have been doing during the past twelve months. Torque did a solo tour of small venues around the Midwest. We wondered why the Incinerator had changed his targets from big cities to small towns? It's because Torque did."

McLain leaned back in her chair, gazing at the ceiling for a moment or two. "You know what this means?"

Hollie nodded miserably. She was one step ahead of McLain. She'd already made the connection her boss was about to voice.

"We either have a crazed fan who is setting these fires as a tribute to his favorite, fiery rock star..."

"Or Torque is the Incinerator."

There were things Torque missed about touring with Beast. He enjoyed traveling. Since distance was meaningless to him, he particularly relished journeying across continents and oceans, although he found conventional means of reaching his destination restrictive. After twelve months of seeing his bandmates only occasionally, he could honestly say he was missing them. Even though they could collectively, and individually, bring him to a point where it felt like his head was about to explode, they were his friends. Too much alpha-maleness in one place was usually the problem. On their tour bus Beast was a cocktail of testosterone and shifter genes that meant one wrong look, or a word out of place, and the vehicle was in a constant state of near combustion.

Strangely, it was Torque, the fieriest member of the

group when performing, who often acted as the peace-maker offstage. Alongside Ged Taverner, their manager, Torque could defuse a situation with his calm manner and quiet good humor. When Khan, the lead singer, and Diablo, the drummer, were engaged in one of their snarling exchanges, most people stood back. Torque was the one who got between them and made them back down. That was probably something to do with shifter hierarchy.

There were plenty of things he didn't miss about being on the road. Torque hated being at the mercy of someone else's schedule, and touring felt like the ultimate restriction on his freedom. Food was always a problem when the band was on tour, both in terms of quality and quantity. Torque ate meat, and plenty of it. Well-done red meat. Everywhere he went, it was the same story. It didn't matter what country he was in, or what the establishment was. There was always an assumption that he would want salad, or bread, or some other trimming. The only accompaniment he wanted with his meat was more meat. Flame-grilled until it was black. No one ever understood that.

The other disadvantage to touring was the lack of privacy. There had been a time in the past when confidentiality wasn't an issue, when finding wide-open spaces away from prying eyes was easier. Now, of course, technology presented its own set of problems, taking surveillance to a whole new level. It meant he had to constantly stay one step ahead. But Torque was an expert at keeping secrets. He had been doing it for a very long time.

Unlike some of his bandmates, Torque had no problem with the rock-star lifestyle. Late nights? Parties? Groupies? He could handle anything fame threw his way. Yes, there were aspects of his life he didn't care to share with his fans, but he had learned how to strike a balance. And having billions of dollars at his disposal... well, that helped him maintain the life he wanted. It helped a lot.

He thought about that as he stood at the edge of his private beach, looking out across Pleasant Bay. When they weren't touring, the other members of Beast were based in New York, close to their recording studio. Torque owned an apartment in Manhattan, but this was his home. It had nothing to do with the celebrity lifestyle and everything to do with his personal needs. He didn't want glamour. This tucked-away, luxury Maine property had a perfect addition for anyone seeking the sort of isolation Torque needed. From where he was standing now, he could just about see the outline of his own secluded island.

Maybe it was thinking about his bandmates that had done it, but he was feeling restless. Having his own retreat was all very well. It was here when he needed it, but on this particular evening, his need for company was stronger than the desire for solitude. It was a short walk into the town of Addison, and the regulars in the Pleasant Bay Bar didn't get starstruck by the presence of one of the world's most famous men. A few were fans and asked about tours and forthcoming albums. Others clearly had no idea who he was...and didn't care. Torque found this as refreshing as the beer.

The route from his house into town was one of his favorite walks. The dramatic coastline, with its craggy rocks and wild waves, was on one side and soaring pine forests on the other. It was a landscape from another time, making Torque think of days gone by. Of knights and maidens and heroic deeds. When humans looked beyond the veil of possibility and believed in magic.

It was still early and the Pleasant Bay Bar was quiet. The contrast as he walked from sunlight into shade made him blink. His eyes were extraordinarily sensitive, but they took a moment to adjust. The background music was a country ballad—*definitely not one of ours*—that suited his mood. Yes, this had been a good idea.

A couple of regulars were engrossed in a card game and didn't look up as Torque approached the bar. Another guy, whose name he couldn't remember, nodded a greeting. A few others didn't even turn their heads. Since there was no sign of Doug, the bartender, Torque leaned on the bar, content to enjoy the atmosphere. It was the complete opposite of many of the places he visited with Beast, lacking the crowds, the noise level, the darkened corners and gimmicks. Torque's moods were mercurial, but right now laid-back and quaint was what suited him.

Doug appeared from the storeroom at the back. "That's about it." The words were addressed over his shoulder to the woman who followed him.

As she emerged fully from the room and Torque got a good look at her, he had the feeling of time standing still. Dressed casually in jeans and a white linen blouse, she was of average height and slender build…and everything about her took his breath away. She had thick golden hair that bounced on her shoulders, an impudent, button nose and full ruby-red lips. Aware that he was staring, and that his interest was being returned by a pair of huge emerald-green eyes, he roused himself from his trance.

"Hi, Doug." He winced at a greeting that felt lame,

mainly because he hadn't withdrawn his gaze from the bartender's companion.

Doug didn't seem to notice. "The usual?" He held up a tankard and Torque nodded. "Did I tell you I'm finally taking that leave of absence so I can go travelling? This is my replacement..."

The woman at Doug's side gave Torque a shy smile. It made him want to leap across the bar to get closer to her.

"Hi, I'm Hollie Br..." She caught her breath, bringing a hand up to her throat with a nervous laugh. "I'm sorry. I've been a fan of yours forever. That's why I can't even remember my own name. I'm Hollie Brown."

That's why I can't even remember my own name? Ten minutes later and Hollie could still feel the blush burning her cheeks. How to blow her cover before she even got started. One look from Torque's unusual eyes and she had almost blurted out her real name. Not that he appeared to have noticed. He was still glancing her way every now and then, but the looks he was giving her didn't seem suspicious.

He seemed... Now that she gave it some thought, she wasn't sure how he seemed. Bemused? That might explain the tiny crease at the corner of his mouth when he stared at her. Nervous? How was that even possible? This was a man used to performing before thousands, even tens of thousands, of adoring fans. What was there about this situation that could possibly make him experience the same fumbling awkwardness she was feeling? Even so, his hand shook ever so slightly as he raised his glass to his lips. Most of all, Torque's expression was that of a man about to step over a boundary into the unknown. It was fear and excitement in equal measures.

Was it possible she was projecting her own emotions at this first meeting on to him? When she told him she had been a fan forever, it was the truth. Her love of Beast had always centered on Torque. For someone as grounded as Hollie, her adoration of a rock star had always been a slight annoyance to her. It almost felt out of character, like something she should have been above. And that starstruck sensation when she had gone to their concerts and seen him onstage? *So not me.* Even though he had been a speck in the distance, the pull of attraction had been so strong it had brought tears to her eyes.

To come face-to-face with her idol in these circumstances was the ultimate irony. To feel that same attraction up close, while under pressure to do her job…no wonder she was having trouble thinking straight. As she performed the routine tasks behind the bar under Doug's supervision, her stomach was churning and her hands were clammy.

Hollie had never worked undercover, and once McLain had decided to place Torque under surveillance, things had moved fast. Checking out the area around his home, local agents had come back with information that the owner of Torque's favorite bar was a former cop. If they could get someone in there, right up close to their target, just for a few days… Someone who could observe a celebrity rock star without arousing his suspicion…

"Have you ever worked in a bar?" McLain's sharp eyes had narrowed as she studied Hollie's face.

"I had a summer job when I was studying…" She had caught the trend of her chief's thoughts and trailed off. "No way." Blatant insubordination was not her style, but this was out-and-out crazy. "You need an experienced undercover agent."

"I need someone who knows the Incinerator. You've worked this case from the start, Hollie." Things were serious when McLain used her first name. "You understand everything about our fire starter." McLain had flipped over a sheet of paper. "This John 'Torque' Jones. You also know about him. This is highly sensitive. If we screw this up, the press will be screaming harassment of a superstar and the Incinerator case will become public property. No one else can replicate your intuition about this. I want you to get up close to Torque and find out if there's a chance he's our guy."

Get up close to Torque? Hollie was twenty-eight years old, but that instruction still made her heart rate soar as if she were nineteen and attending her first Beast concert. She told herself those words had nothing to do with why she was here. She was a professional. Catching the deadly arsonist whose trail of destruction had led to billions of dollars' worth of damage and more than twenty deaths was all that mattered. That was why she had agreed to McLain's request. For the next few weeks, she wasn't Agent Hollie Brennan, Chief Fire Investigator. Instead, she was Hollie Brown, bartender.

As she felt Torque's eyes following her, she thought back to her eighteen-year-old self. How often had she gazed at the image on the cover of *Fire and Fury*, Beast's most successful album? It depicted the band in evening dress, all of them looking glamorous as hell and slightly debauched, as though the shot had been taken the morning after a heavy night. While the others were pictured leaning against a whitewashed wall, bow ties hanging loose and hands thrust into dinner jacket pockets, it was always Torque who drew her gaze.

In the picture, he was apart from his bandmates, half sitting, half lying on a set of stone steps. With his flame-red hair tossed over one shoulder, bronzed skin tones and long legs encased in daringly tight black pants, he could have been a fashion model. The black top hat he wore was tilted low, its shadow concealing the upper part of his face, but his beautiful mouth and chiseled jaw were visible. His hands were raised as though his long fingers were strumming an invisible guitar. It was a stunning, iconic image.

The man who tilted his empty glass toward her now with a raised brow wore torn, faded jeans and work boots. His black T-shirt clung lovingly to his biceps and emphasized his dramatic coloring. Even in everyday clothing, Torque was breathtaking. Even with his features that looked like they had been lovingly carved by the hand of a master sculptor, it was still his eyes that drew her attention. Just when they appeared a nondescript gray, the light caught the multicolored moonstone flecks in their depths, making them shimmer like opals in sunlight.

Those eyes watched her again from beneath heavy lids as she refilled his glass. "What brings you to Addison?"

Keep it simple. That was what the veteran undercover agent who had given her an intense induction course had told her. Vince King had coached her in every aspect of the role, going over and over what she needed to know until she was word perfect. *Stick to a short, basic story and don't elaborate.*

"I like Maine. I thought it would be a nice place to spend the summer." She smiled. "Don't worry. Although I'm a fan, I'm not a stalker."

She'd seen his smile on her TV and laptop, on the pages of magazines, on the huge LED screens at the back of the stage at concerts. Now she was experiencing its full force across a distance of a few feet. As her knees turned to Jell-O, she gripped the edge of the bar to keep herself upright.

"Good. I don't want any more of those."

So Torque had a stalker. His words implied there was more than one. Could the Incinerator be an obsessive fan? Torque was well-known for his fiery onstage antics. Were the arson attacks a sick tribute?

Or was Hollie, already a Torque fan herself, now feeling the hit of his attractiveness close up, reluctant to accept that he could be the man they were looking for? Whatever the truth turned out to be, she needed to take care. She had come here to unmask a fire-wielding killer. After only minutes in Torque's company, she was already in danger of getting burned.

Chapter 2

Days of yore. Torque liked that phrase. It was all-encompassing, conjuring up images of chivalrous knights in armor on white chargers, maidens in distress and, of course, the obligatory dragon who terrorized the neighborhood by demanding a regular blood or virgin sacrifice.

Except legend didn't always get its facts straight. Sometimes the maidens did the rescuing, the knights were the ones who terrorized and the dragons were in charge of chivalry. To Torque, *yore* was more than just a nostalgic word for describing a bygone era. It summed up a time when the veil between worlds had been thinner. When the line between magic and mundane was blurred. When mortals had accepted the evidence of their hearts and their souls. Science had brought humankind a long way. Its benefits were far-reaching, but it had closed down many of those instincts. People looked with suspicion upon the very things that had once sustained them. Witches were cast out, charms and spells were frowned upon, alchemy faded into insignificance.

And dragons? What of those unique creatures who, most people would say, had only ever existed in legend? Even the believers, the humans who truly wanted dragons to have been real, would shake their heads sadly and mourn their loss, holding on to them through their games, paintings and stories.

It was better this way, of course. The last of the true dragons had died out five hundred years ago, spending his last days on a remote island in the South China Sea. Now only the dragon-shifters—a unique breed of half human, half dragon beings—remained. If the world ever discovered their existence? Torque clenched his jaw hard. *Not on my watch.* He had no desire to end his days in a cage, poked and prodded in the name of research. Even worse would be to become an exhibit in the name of entertainment, paraded and ogled like an elephant in a circus.

Torque was a dragon-shifter, but he no longer bore any responsibility to the others of his kind. His leadership had been brought to an abrupt end and the world had moved on from the days of dragon clans and oaths of fealty. He was the last of his kin. The mighty Cumhachdach had been wiped out by powerful magic, his own life saved only because the sorceress who killed his clan had chosen to torture him by keeping him alive. There had been a time, once... He shook his head, clearing it of any lingering thoughts as he unfurled his huge wings and took to the skies. Once might as well be never. These days, his only loyalty was to himself.

He swooped over his private island, blending easily with the night sky. As he flew lower over the dense forest, his scales changed color to match the tones of the trees. Camouflage was the dragon version of invisibility. Had he ventured into a city skyline, he would have become concrete gray. When he passed over an ocean in daylight, he was the exact blue of the waves below him and the sky above.

Torque's eyes scanned the landscape, homing in on a tiny creature moving in grass and the tilt of a bird's wing many miles away. His ears isolated individual sounds, locating rustling leaves and human voices along the coast. Dragon senses were the keenest of all, but on this night he was distracted by his human emotions. Feelings he barely understood were pulling at the edges of his consciousness, forcing his attention away from the beauty of the landscape.

After centuries of being alone—and liking it that way—he had felt something deep inside him stirring. And he knew why. All it had taken was a pair of green eyes, a shy smile and an enticing figure. It wasn't as if he lived a hermit's life as a human. He was a rock star. Temptation came his way and he didn't turn it down. Beast worked hard and played harder. Although the dynamics had changed now that Khan, lead singer and former party-animal-in-chief, had become a happily married man.

Torque knew why his emotions were in turmoil. The Pleasant Bay Bar's new employee had shaken him so much he couldn't think of anything but her. Hollie Brown was undeniably good to look at, and she had admitted that she was a fan. A plume of white smoke rose from his nostrils into the night sky as he snorted. He encountered fans all the time. His head wouldn't be turned by nothing more than a pretty face.

No, this was about something deeper and far more

dangerous. Throughout the many centuries of his existence, Torque had never considered the possibility of taking a mate. Dragons mated for life and so did shifters. Fortunately, his mortal persona wasn't bound by the same constraints. When it came to his sex life, Torque preferred to be guided by his human genetics. They had served him well…up to now.

Now, suddenly, his instincts were telling him things were changing. It was crazy on so many levels. He knew nothing about Hollie. But he knew everything he needed. As soon as he had looked into her eyes, he had recognized two things. The first was that she was his. As if that wasn't earth-shattering enough, the second was that she wasn't who she claimed to be.

So, let's take a second to analyze this… My mate just strolled into town. And she's lying to me.

It wasn't the best start to a long-term relationship. And he had to accept that his instincts must be wrong. Because Hollie couldn't possibly be his mate. She was *human*. Dragons and humans? How could that ever be a thing? Other shifters could take humans as mates. It was rare, but when it happened, the humans could choose to become converts. That meant they could take the bite of their mates and be transformed into shifters themselves. Although it was a huge commitment, Torque had known of a few occasions when it had happened.

Not for dragons. To maintain the purity of the dragon bloodline, the option to convert a human mate didn't exist for them. A dragon could have a relationship with a mortal, but it could only ever last as long as the human's lifetime. They could never truly be fated mates.

Even supposing he decided to initiate the whole "mates for your lifetime" conversation, he couldn't picture it going well. *I'm a dragon...* He just couldn't see it working as a first-date conversation starter.

Normally, Torque looked forward to these nighttime flights. Maine wasn't Scotland, the dramatic land of his birth, but the scenery wasn't entirely dissimilar. Tonight, his heart wasn't in his exercise routine. He had a feeling those green eyes and that shy smile might be responsible for his apathy. Something about Hollie had reminded him of the past. Yore. In those days there had been a creed, a code of honor, and she had reawakened it within his breast. Although nothing about their encounter had led him to believe Hollie needed his protection, Torque's senses were on high alert. *If* she had been his mate—and that was one hell of a big if—and *if* there had been a looming danger, back in the day he would have been beneath her window, watching over his lady while she slept. Simpler times, easier solutions.

Circling the bay one last time, he landed on a slope close to the trees. His huge claws gripped the soft ground, gouging deep into the grass. Folding his wings close to his body, he shifted quickly back to his human form. Naked, he stretched his limbs, enjoying the sensation of the cool air soothing his heated flesh.

He had left his clothes in the boat and he shrugged them on, weighing up whether to spend the night on the island. The little cabin in the trees was basic, but comfortable, and he kept the refrigerator stocked in case he decided to stay over. But he needed Wi-Fi if he was going to check his emails for details of Beast's forthcoming tour. And he wasn't sure the isolation of the island suited his current restlessness.

Torque could have easily rowed the distance across the bay, but he liked the soft chug of the motorboat. Although he enjoyed the peace of the bay from the skies, now he was seeing a different view. This time—the hours between midnight and dawn—the old witching time, was when that veil between worlds was thinnest. When it almost seemed there was still a hint of the old magic in the air.

His inner dragon was a creature of contrasts, craving wide-open spaces when in flight but seeking solitude when grounded. The cinematic depictions of dragons living underground, guarding their hoards of treasure, were an exaggeration, but he liked enclosed spaces. Out here, on the water, he felt small and alone. Un-dragon-like. It wasn't unpleasant, but it challenged his shifter senses. And speaking of senses...

He tilted his head, trying to figure out what was different. As he neared the wooden jetty in front of his mainland home, he caught the first whiff of smoke. It was delicious and woody. The scent of burning called to his dragon the way catnip affected a kitten. Except something was wrong. The scent was out of place and the night sky over the town shouldn't be lit by a golden glow.

Leaping out of the boat, Torque broke into a run as he realized what was happening. The Pleasant Bay Bar was on fire.

Hollie's room was tucked away at the top of the old building. Doug had been apologetic about it. "I don't know why the boss suddenly changed his mind about letting me go traveling. Don't get me wrong—I'm glad he managed to find a replacement—but the short notice meant I didn't have much time to get this room ready."

She had assured him that the room was fine. And it was. A little on the small side, but it was clean and comfortable. Since she wasn't going to be in Addison for long, it hardly mattered. There was no point finding an alternative. Once Torque left Maine to go on tour, she would be returning to Newark. This was somewhere to sleep, to use her laptop to record her notes, to call in to McLain and to gather her thoughts.

Ah, her thoughts. They should be all about the job she had come here to do, shouldn't they? But they weren't. She was totally shaken by how much the encounter with Torque had affected her.

You are a twenty-eight-year-old FBI agent, for heaven's sake. You cannot still have a crush on a rock star.

It didn't matter how much she reproached herself, how hard she tried to concentrate on typing up her notes, half her mind remained firmly fixed on a pair of shimmering eyes and a very disturbing smile. Torque's mouth had lingered in her imagination as she drifted off to sleep. The disturbing, but pleasant, fantasy of feeling that full lower lip against her own had been achingly real...

The dream came quickly and she tumbled into it, welcoming it like a familiar friend. She couldn't remember a time when she hadn't experienced this slumbering adventure. It was warm, comforting and thrilling all at the same time.

Her sleeping self approached the giant creature. The beautiful red-gold dragon lay still, his breathing deep and rhythmic. A faint thrumming issued from his chest, and wisps of smoke curled from his nostrils, but she knew his inner fire would be subdued in slumber. His powerful hind limbs and huge coiled tail were tucked beneath him, and he slept on top of his hoard. His precious gems and jewels were scattered all around him, their brilliance dulled by the light of the cave.

When dream-Hollie approached, the dragon's eyes

opened as if a switch had been flicked. Smoke poured from his nostrils, and there was a sound of scales sliding over coins as he shifted position. Keeping his wings tucked in tight, he lifted his head to gaze at her. Hollie raised a hand to touch his face...

She came awake abruptly, angry that her dream had been interrupted. Her annoyance dissipated fast as she realized what was happening. Hollie had been in too many fire simulations not to recognize the real thing when she was thrust into the middle of it.

Subconsciously, when she arrived at the Pleasant Bay Bar, she had done what she always did and checked out the fire safety systems. The bar itself had been fine. As a business, it needed to comply with industry standards. When it came to an escape route, her bedroom was not ideal. It had only one door and a small window high above the street. She hadn't realized, when she checked those things out on her arrival, that she would be putting them to the test quite so soon.

Smoke was already filling the room. Sliding from the bed, she found the T-shirt she had taken off when she undressed and tied it around the lower part of her face. Crawling commando-style in order to stay low, she made her way across to the door. Just as she had feared, one touch told her everything she needed to know. The wooden panels were hot beneath her fingertips. It meant the fire was raging on the other side of the door.

Although the window was her only escape route, she already knew it wasn't going to be easy. She was two floors up and there was no fire escape. A thirty-foot drop onto concrete faced her. *Break the glass and make some noise.* That was about the best plan she had as she crawled her way back across the room.

This was no coincidence. That thought hammered

through her mind as the toxic smoke stung her eyes. The stench of synthetic carpet burning and electrical wiring melting made her gag. Above the roar of the fire, she could hear the whine of a smoke alarm. But it hadn't done its job. It hadn't warned her in time. It was a discordant thought, one for which she didn't have time. She spent her life fighting fire, but this one was personal. This one was meant for her.

As she reached the window, the noise level changed. There was sound that could have been a roar of fury and the door came crashing in. *That shouldn't happen.* Hollie knew how fire behaved. Although it could be unpredictable, it didn't kick down doors. Through the choking haze, she saw a tall figure, framed by shimmering tongues of fire.

It's too late. I've inhaled too much smoke...now I'm seeing things.

She sank helplessly to the rug, her eyelids drifting closed as the flame-haired figure strode toward her. She was swept up into strong arms...or maybe swept away on a tide of unconsciousness. It was impossible to tell which as she felt the searing heat on her exposed skin and through her lightweight pajamas.

Opening her eyes, she gave a horrified gasp. She was in Torque's arms, and he was advancing toward the door. He was purposefully carrying her into the source of the fire. Desperately, she squirmed against him.

"Keep still." His voice was different. Authoritative, slightly rasping. "If you move as we go down the stairs, I can't protect you from the flames."

This couldn't be happening. This man—one of the most famous rock stars in the world—couldn't seriously think he could get them down that blazing staircase. *I am about to be killed by my celebrity crush. Either that or I really am hallucinating.*

Unable to fight, she was helpless to do anything except press her cheek into the hard muscle of Torque's chest as he stepped into the flames. Her job made what was happening so much worse. Hollie had seen too many burned bodies, had attended too many coroners' inquests on people who had died in agony. This was a first. She had never come across a case in which someone had willingly walked through a blaze.

Yet, as Torque slowly made his way down the stairs, the strangest thing was happening. She could feel the heat of the flames, but it was like getting too close to a roaring coal fire. She was uncomfortable, but she wasn't being incinerated. Wrapped tight in Torque's arms, she had the strangest feeling that *he* was the source of her protection. But how could that be? It was like he was fireproof. She caught glimpses of what was going on around them. Flames were licking at his arms and shoulders, catching the long length of his hair and dancing gleefully like a halo around his head. Torque was on fire…but he didn't flinch.

As they neared the final step, one of the ceiling beams gave way with a weary groan. Orange cinders rained down on Torque's head as he reached up a hand and caught the blazing bar. Still holding Hollie tight against him with his other hand, he gave a grunt that sounded like it was half pain, half annoyance as he thrust the beam aside without breaking his stride. Two more steps and he was kicking open the door that led them into the street.

Her last memory before she passed out was of those moonstone eyes glowing bright with concern as he placed her gently on the grass.

* * *

Hollie slowly opened her eyes, hoping she'd been dreaming, fairly certain she hadn't. Her throat felt like she'd drunk a glass of chopped razor blades and her nose itched unbearably. Her eyes streamed with the effects of the smoke and she smelled disgusting. Lifting a hand, she could see thick black grime coating her skin. When she tried to sit up, everything ached.

A strong arm slid around her waist, and although she wanted to question its source, she was too grateful for the support. Leaning against a broad shoulder, she eased into a sitting position.

"What…?" The word came out as a feeble croak, followed by a coughing fit.

"I got you out before the blaze took hold of the staircase."

They were far enough away from the burning building to be safe from any explosions or debris, but she could still feel the searing heat of the blaze. When she tilted her head to look at Torque, he took away what was left of her breath. With his hair streaming in the breeze and his eyes glittering with that strange intense light, he appeared otherworldly.

Around them, a fire team bustled into action and paramedics approached. Hollie might be feeling the effects of the smoke, but her memory was clear. Torque was lying about what had just happened. He hadn't rescued her *before* the fire took hold. Like a comic book hero, he had carried her right through the heart of the inferno. And he was untouched, completely uninjured by the fire he had just walked through.

They should both have been incinerated. Instead, apart from the effects she was feeling from the smoke inhalation, they were unscathed. And Torque ap-

peared… She searched for the right word. *Invigorated.*
Perhaps it was the adrenaline rush of the rescue, but he
appeared energized, his former laid-back manner replaced by restless, flickering presence he presented onstage. Almost as if the fire had entered his bloodstream.

I am hallucinating.

As a paramedic knelt at her other side and placed
an oxygen mask over her nose and mouth, Hollie tried
to get to grips with her new, alternate reality. An existence that included a superhero rock star. A man who
could walk through fire. How the hell was she going to
explain *this* to McLain?

"My laptop." Her attempt at an exclamation was muffled by the mask.

"Pardon?" Torque leaned closer as he tried to hear
what she was saying.

"All my clothes, my purse, my cell phone, my laptop…they were all in that room." Her voice was still
a painful rasp, but she managed to get the words out.

There was nothing left of the top floor of the Pleasant Bay Bar. The roof had fallen in and bright orange
flames were shooting into the night sky. It was a pyro-
technic performance of epic proportions, almost as if
the fire itself was celebrating.

Hollie's professional senses got to work, weighing up
what had happened. The fire must have started in the
upper part of the building. Was it an arson attack? It was
too soon to say. But it was an awfully big coincidence
that Hollie, the person who was here to investigate the
Incinerator, had almost died in a fire. The second thing
Hollie noticed was that Torque had gotten here before
the emergency services.

He had saved her life, and from that, she might assume he wasn't the Incinerator. Unless the rescue was a

huge double bluff, designed to throw her off the scent? As she turned her head back to look at him again, she had the oddest sensation of her world tilting off balance. Was Torque the Incinerator, and was he capable of such cunning? If he knew she was here to investigate him, had he planned to set a fire and save her from it, thereby lulling her into a false sense of security? Her heart wanted to rebel against such an idea, to tell her he wasn't behind such deviousness, but her training and her experience warned her to be wary.

Hollie had been part of the team hunting the Incinerator for four years, wondering how the daring arsonist had set increasingly elaborate fires and escaped without injury. She didn't know how Torque had walked through those flames and emerged unscathed. If she hadn't seen it for herself, she wouldn't have believed it was possible. All she knew for sure was, she had to find out more about this phenomenon and whether it was linked to their inquiry.

The paramedic removed the oxygen mask. "How does that feel?" The woman had checked her over and found no injuries. The only concern was the effects of the smoke.

"I'm fine." Hollie knew better than anyone what the health risks were, but she could feel her lungs returning to normal. "I don't need any further treatment." She bit her lip. "I just don't have anywhere to go."

"You can stay at my place." Torque's breath was warm on her cheek.

His words triggered a world of conflict inside Hollie. She was here to investigate him. Staying in his house was certainly one way to keep a closer watch on him. It was also a good way to put herself in danger. She could almost hear McLain's response. Outraged caution followed by an insistence that she get her ass back into the office immediately would probably be the mild version.

Hollie's own internal warning system appeared to be broken. In spite of everything, her heart's initial reaction to his offer was a leap of joy. Common sense refused to prevail, but maybe that was because her choices were seriously limited. It was the middle of the night, she was coated from head to foot in foul-smelling ash, she could barely open her eyes and she sounded like a donkey with asthma. The only clothes she possessed were these once-pink, now-black pajamas. Even if she'd had the strength to get to her feet, she didn't have her ATM card to draw the cash to get herself home…

With a sound that could have been a laugh, but was closer to a sob, she rested her head back against Torque's chest. It was a very comforting place to be. "Thank you."

Chapter 3

Torque showed Hollie to one of the luxurious guest bedrooms. He explained that there were toiletries and towels in the bathroom, and brought her a pair of his sweatpants and a T-shirt.

"They'll both be too big, but until I can get to a store in the morning, it's the best I can do."

She plucked at the front of her grimy pajama top with a grimace. "Anything will be better than this."

"You're sure you'll be okay on your own?" He realized how that sounded and held up his hands in a backing-off gesture. "Not that I'm offering to help you shower."

She attempted a laugh, but it ended on a cough. "I'll be fine."

Her bravery and resilience astounded him. She should have died in that fire. Did she know that? Even if she hadn't figured it out, she must be experiencing a profound sense of shock, yet her courage shone through. When he first saw her, Torque had been drawn to her because of her looks. Seconds later, he had taken the whole never-meant-to-be, fated-mates hit. Now her spirit and strength attracted him just as powerfully as her physical characteristics.

Overcoming a fierce desire to pull her into his arms, he left her alone. But the urge to protect her remained strong. Torque never slept well. The same sorceress who had stolen his liberty and wiped out his clan had once cursed him with her trademark insomnia spell.

Yeah, Teine, the fire sorceress…what a charmer she had turned out to be.

Taking up a position just outside Hollie's bedroom window, he sat on the grass with his back against the wall and his long legs drawn up so he could rest his forearms on his bent knees. From this angle, he could make sure she was safe and watch the sun rise over the bay. Not that he was in any mood to admire the beauty of his surroundings. His mind was wholly occupied with Hollie and what had just happened.

· Being a rock star brought many privileges Torque's way. This beautiful house with its sweeping grounds and its dramatic views, his island, his fast cars and faster motorbikes…any material thing he wanted was his for the asking. But there was a dark undercurrent to his fame, one at which he had already hinted to Hollie. There were always a few fans whose admiration spilled over into obsession. Enthusiasts who thought they owned him because they knew his face and read every article and interview about him.

Even among a band of big characters, Torque attracted more than his fair share of obsessive fans. Ged, his manager, put it down to Torque's fiery onstage personality. "They see you as Beast's torchbearer. Even though Khan is the ultimate showman and Diablo has the dark, brooding looks of a Hollywood leading man, you stand out because the photographers love to catch you surrounded by fire."

Ged knew who Torque was, of course. The man who had rescued him from the centuries-deep spell cast by Teine was also the man who had given him a new lease on life as a musician. It was a strange life choice, but one that worked. Torque was the only dragon-shifter in the band, but he was among equals. Tiger, jaguar, snow leopard, wolf...his bandmates were all shifters who had been rescued by Ged. Their manager was a businessman by day, a were-bear who saved damaged or endangered shifters by night.

No matter how knowledgeable Ged was, Torque wasn't sure he bought into the torchbearer theory. It wasn't just that he got *more* contact from obsessed fans than his bandmates. The contact he did get was on a crazier level. Ged called it stalking, but Torque wasn't sure letters and emails fitted that definition. No physical contact was made—he had never even gotten a disturbing phone call—no harm had ever been done to him or his property. And being a shifter in a human world, he found it difficult to know what to do about that. Determined to maintain their anonymity, shifters steered clear of the mortal forces of law and order. Since Torque's obsessive fans had, so far, limited their activities to strange confessions and occasional threats, he had done his best to ignore them.

Until now. He had a feeling tonight represented a crossed line. Because some of the confessions were very specific. Torque was the person who played a burning guitar. He walked through a wall of flame. He raised a hand and, like the conductor of an orchestra, coordinated a series of perfectly timed explosions along the edge of the stage. And he attracted a small group of people who were unashamed and fanatical about their love of fire. People who looked up to Torque because they sensed something in him that appealed to their fixation. For those very few, it was an infatuation that bordered on worship. They believed he was a fire-god and they offered him their devotion...whether he wanted it or not.

Not. His expression twisted into a grimace of distaste as he tossed a pebble toward the shimmering water.

Being a shifter meant that two parts of him lived in harmony inside one body. His inner dragon didn't just need fire, it defined him. Sizzling through his bloodstream alongside his mortal DNA. But he was also part human, and that side of him reined in his fiery self. He knew what flames could do. He didn't worship fire, he respected it. While it excited him, it didn't arouse him. He could play with its force without pressing the destruct button.

Some of the messages he got suggested his followers—he used the word even though he disliked it—were unable to display the same restraint.

"If anyone gets hurt, I won't be able to stay quiet." That had been his ultimatum to Ged when the tributes first started coming. "That's my deal breaker."

"You think it isn't mine?" Ged's reply had reassured him. "If we find out any of these crazies has actually gone beyond the letter-writing stage, we'll do something about it."

As far as they could see, the madness had stayed on paper. It was wild and disturbing, but harmless. Tonight had been far from benign. Tonight, Hollie had almost died. And no matter how hard he tried, Torque couldn't separate that event from his obsessive fan mail.

His intuition about the fire at the Pleasant Bay Bar scared him. For several reasons, it filled him with more fear than anything he had ever known. First, it meant he was being watched. It was a possibility he had never considered. He wanted to be more intuitive, to be able to say with absolute certainty that he would know if a malignant presence was tracking him. But he didn't. He was a creature of legend and mysticism, but hunches and premonitions evaded him. His dragon instincts were all sizzling energy and action. He left the finer detail to others.

All he had was an uncomfortable feeling in the pit of his stomach that Hollie had been targeted. She was the change, the common denominator. From the moment he first set eyes on her, Torque had been in free fall, as if he had given up control of his emotions. They no longer belonged to him; they were the property of a woman he barely knew.

If he was right, someone else knew what had happened to him in that instant. Someone else was aware of the profound effect Hollie had on him. That person had witnessed their meeting in the Pleasant Bay Bar... and he, or she, clearly didn't like it. It shook him to consider that an observer could have known the impact Hollie had on him. It had been devastating to Torque himself, but he had fooled himself he had hidden it well. It seemed his acting abilities weren't as good as he believed.

Even so, no matter how many times he reviewed that scene, Torque couldn't find anything out of the ordinary about it. Apart from Doug, there had been only a few regulars in the bar. While he didn't know any of them well, he couldn't picture any of them as a demented pyromaniac or a jealous stalker.

His thoughts turned to Teine, the sorceress who had fallen in love with him. When Torque didn't return her feelings—*because, let's face it, she was evil as well as crazy*—she had destroyed his clan and imprisoned Torque in an enchanted cave. He would be there now if it wasn't for Ged. But Teine couldn't be the person responsible for the fire. She was dead.

Dawn had sneaked up on him and the rising sun was a huge golden disk in the cloudless sky hovering over the silhouette of the trees. Torque knew from centuries of experience that darkness wasn't the enemy. Nightfall merely provided a cloak for evil deeds. Even so, daylight offered a return to normality. Stretching, he got to his feet.

Within his nighttime reflections, he had been skirting around the central issue. When Hollie awoke, she would want to discuss the fire and Torque would need to make a decision. How much was he prepared to share with her? About his suspicions…but also about his feelings?

Hollie opened her eyes slowly, leaving her dreaming world behind. The images had been even more vivid than usual. She had clambered onto the dragon's back, clinging to his muscular neck and pressing her cheek to his scales as he soared over a landscape that was wild, restless and angry. High, towering hills were slashed through with steep valleys and dark, eerie lochs. As they flew, the weather ranged in untamed moods from soaring discontent to blazing sunshine with no thought of moderation between. Although there was no exchange between them, she knew this was *his* land and she loved it for that reason.

As wakefulness dragged her from her slumber, she knew she was in a strange place. Even so, she felt a curious sense of comfort, as though she was wrapped in a protective cloak through which no harm could penetrate. As memories of the previous night came flooding back, her feeling of well-being dispersed. By the time she was fully awake, she wondered how she could possibly have felt even a trace of security.

Not only did her intuition tell her she had been the intended victim of a targeted arson attack, she needed to call it in. McLain's reaction was going to make the flash point of that fire look like a failed firework.

Oh, and I have no belongings. No clothes, no money, nothing...

That wasn't strictly true, of course. When Hollie called McLain, her boss would be able to get her out of Addison within the hour. She could walk away from this undercover job and be back in her own apartment later that day. It would be the safe, sensible thing to do. With every fiber of her being, she did *not* want to take the safe, sensible option.

Ever since the Incinerator first came to her attention, Hollie had felt a personal connection to him. She always thought of the arsonist as male, but she couldn't pinpoint why. Until now, her role had never been hands-on. She was a scientist. Her colleagues called her a geek and she accepted the name with an element of professional pride. It had taken a lot of hard work to reach this level of geekery, one where she was called upon to give talks to experienced fire investigators on the science behind the blazes they studied.

Hollie's inclusion in the Incinerator task force was an

indication of the seriousness with which the FBI took the case. She was one of six senior agents assigned to the investigation into possibly the most prolific and dangerous arsonist the agency had ever come across. Her expertise included fire behavior, analytical chemistry and the use of technology to enhance fire scene investigation. She used those skills to enhance and support the team.

The Incinerator's legacy was the stuff of nightmares. He was a daring exhibitionist who didn't care about the loss of life as well as the damage to property. The current death toll was twenty-one, but that didn't include the information Hollie had gleaned from the other countries. Her colleagues had still been processing the details of the new cases when she left the field office to come to Maine. There had been a sense of urgency about starting the undercover operation because Torque would soon set off on tour.

Her thoughts were interrupted by a soft knock on the door. She scrambled into a sitting position.

"Come in." Her voice had benefited from the few hours of rest. Although it was still croaky, it sounded almost normal and at least she could speak without coughing. She wished she could blame smoke inhalation for the way her chest constricted and the breath left her lungs in a sudden rush as the door opened. But no. That was the Torque-effect.

He remained close to the door, studying her face. "I want to say you look better, but you're way too pale."

"Shock." Hollie made a movement to brush the hair back from her forehead and was surprised to find her hand shaking. Her lip trembled. "I'm sorry…"

He was at her side in a single movement. Although Hollie's current role kept her away from the action, her

early training had brought her in contact with the sur-
vivors of fire. She knew she was suffering the classic
aftereffects. The extreme physical impact of the shock
was receding, but the emotional trauma still had her
in its grip.

For an instant, Torque hesitated as though he had
encountered an invisible barrier. His expression was
guarded, and even in her distress, Hollie took a moment
to wonder what was going through his mind. Then he
appeared to shrug aside whatever doubts were assail-
ing him. Sitting on the edge of the bed, he drew her
gently into his arms.

As she leaned her cheek against the warm, solid muscle of his chest, Hollie spared a fleeting thought for the
rules of undercover work. She guessed this probably
broke several of them. Possibly it smashed them all into
tiny pieces. As Torque's arms tightened around her, the
trembling that had gripped her began to subside. Rules
were fine if things were going according to plan. Any
plan of Hollie's was ash blowing across Pleasant Bay
in the early-morning breeze.

After a few minutes, she lifted her head and attempted a smile. The expression in Torque's eyes was
even more disturbing than the aftereffects of the fire.
It was probably best to avoid any close contact in the
future. Professional distance. That should be the new
plan. Reluctantly, she drew away from him. Some new
intuition told her he was equally unwilling to let her go.

"It was just…you know…"

"I know." His lips hardened into a thin line, indicating he was well aware that the fire was no accident.
Suggesting that he wasn't responsible? *Don't make as-
sumptions.* "You don't need to explain. It was a horrible experience, and recovering from it will take time."

Her brow furrowed, the unspoken questions hanging in the air between them. Torque must know what she wanted to say. He had walked through a blaze as though his flesh was fireproof. More than that. He had somehow used his body to form a protective barrier between Hollie and the flames. She didn't need her years of study and hard-earned qualifications to tell her he had defied the laws of science. He could pretend it hadn't happened, make up a story that he had arrived before the blaze took hold. They both knew it wasn't true.

"You saved my life." The huskiness in her voice wasn't entirely due to the smoke damage. "I don't know how you did it. I know you didn't get there before the fire took hold—"

"Some things can't be explained. Your perception and mine are different." He got to his feet, bringing any further discussion of the subject to an abrupt end. "I need to go out and stock up on some provisions. I'm not used to having a houseguest." His smile dawned, swift and dazzling. "I'll get you some clothes, as well, although I don't claim to be an expert in women's fashion."

Hollie laughed. "I'll be glad of anything I can wear with dignity. Your sweatpants fall down when I walk."

"There is one important thing we need to talk about."

"There is?"

"Underwear." Torque rummaged in the drawer of the bedside locker and produced a piece of paper and a pen.

Hollie placed her head in her hands. "I can't believe I'm sharing my bra size with the man I've worshiped from afar for most of my adult life."

Torque's face changed from laughter to seriousness, his eyes darkening to a slate-gray color.

"What is it?"

He shook his head. "Just that expression. *Worshiped from afar.* It makes me uncomfortable."

She waited for him to elaborate, but he switched the conversation to practicalities. Pointing her in the direction of the kitchen, he explained that there was fresh coffee already made and the toaster could be temperamental.

"I won't be long." She sensed he wanted to say more, almost as if something was troubling him. Whatever it was, he shrugged it off and headed toward the door.

"Can I make a call?"

"Of course." The moonstone glitter was back in his eyes. "My God, I never gave it a thought. Your family..."

"I don't have any family. I'm an only child and my parents are both dead. But I have a friend who looks out for me." Although it was stretching a point to call McLain a friend, it was the best explanation she could come up with. "She can be a bit of a dragon, but she worries."

Torque's rich, warm laughter poured over her. When she raised questioning brows, he shook his head. "There are worse things than having a dragon to watch over you."

When the call went straight to voice mail, Hollie's stomach did a bungee jump. This was the secure line Vince King had set up when she went undercover. McLain was her designated handler. The agreement was that she would be available on this number 24/7. Hollie had memorized the number so carefully she was actually able to recite it in her dreams. Her nondragon dreams. Voice mail was not an option.

Maybe she had gotten one of the digits wrong. Taking a steadying breath, she ended the call without leaving a message. Slowly, deliberately, she tried McLain's number again. And got the same bland voice mail message once more. Panic gripped the back of her neck like a mugger's hand.

Breathe. Think. After a moment or two, the mists cleared from her mind and some of her usual calm returned. She was letting the Incinerator get to her. Somehow she was making this about him, turning it into something personal. There could be a dozen reasons why her call wasn't connecting. There could be a fault with McLain's cell phone. A signal problem here in Torque's house.

She ignored the little voice that tried to tell her those arguments weren't plausible. Even so, she wasn't in any danger. If she wanted to, she could walk out of Torque's home right now. Okay, she was barefoot and she would have to hold up his sweatpants with both hands, but the point was, she wasn't a prisoner. She could go to Addison, get in a cab and get the hell out of here. Getting back to Newark wouldn't be easy, but she could do it. No one was after her. There was no reason to look fearfully over her shoulder...

The thought immediately made her cast a fearful glance behind her. *No.* She wasn't going to do this. She had no proof that the Incinerator had set fire to the Pleasant Bay Bar, no proof that anything had happened to McLain. Her imagination was working overtime as a result of shock. Pure and simple.

Her cell phone had died in the fire, taking all her contacts with it, but there was someone else she could call. It wasn't part of the undercover protocols they'd agreed, but things had already veered so far off script she'd lost sight of the original plan. One colleague calling another wasn't against the rules. There were other problems attached to calling Dalton Hilger, but they were personal. And they were in the past, she reminded herself. Her history with Dalton was something she preferred to forget. Unlike his cell phone number, which, for some strange reason, was imprinted on her brain.

She knew he hadn't changed it. Dalton was one of the agents on the Incinerator task force and she'd called him just last week to check some minor details. Her businesslike approach always jarred with his wounded pride. Five years ago, ending their brief relationship had been difficult. Even now Hollie always finished a conversation with Dalton feeling like she'd kicked a puppy...which was why her finger hesitated for a moment over the call button. But she trusted him, and that was what she needed right now.

"Hilger." The word was a hoarse mumble. A glance at the clock confirmed it was still early. Dalton wasn't a morning person and Hollie guessed she'd just woken him on an off-duty day.

"Dalton, it's Hollie." Sliding open full-length glass doors, she carried the phone and her coffee out onto a terrace that ran the length of the house. Torque had a rock-star view over the bay and she sank into a cushioned chair, drinking in the stunning vista.

"Hey, Hols." He yawned loudly down the phone. "McLain briefed the team that you were away on some Incinerator-related business."

"I am, but I need to get in touch with McLain and she's not answering her cell phone."

He yawned again and Hollie could picture him. Tall and handsome, with brown hair that never quite did what he wanted it to, endearing in so many ways...*just not right for me.* Unfortunately, only one of them had been able to see that.

"McLain's away."

"What do you mean '*away*'?" The word came out as an undignified squeak and prompted another coughing fit.

"Damn it, Hols. Could you warn me next time you plan on squealing like that? I have very sensitive ears."

"Where has McLain gone?" She regained enough control over her voice to infuse a warning note into it.

"How would I know? She's the boss. She doesn't share her itinerary with me."

Hollie's mind was racing. This was all wrong. No matter how urgent McLain's business might be, there was no way she would have left Hollie without a contact. So what should she do now? Share her suspicions that McLain's absence was linked to the Incinerator and the fire at the Pleasant Bay Bar? She knew how preposterous it sounded inside her own head. Trying to explain it to someone else, even someone she trusted as much as Dalton? *Not happening.*

Unprompted, her thoughts turned to Torque. Maybe her perspective had become skewed when he walked through fire for her. It had certainly added another layer to the whole mystery. She faced a stark choice. Do the sensible thing. Tell Dalton about the blaze at the bar and end her undercover status here and now. Or play with fire—the analogy brought a grim smile to her lips— for a little longer.

There was more. It was something she couldn't define. Hollie was gripped by a powerful conviction that she *needed* to be with Torque. It wasn't to do with him; it was about her. She had no idea where it was coming from, or why it had taken such a powerful hold. Maybe it was that old crush, or the shock of the fire. All she knew was she had never felt anything so strongly.

Torque was the link to the Incinerator. She was sure of that. Did Torque know it? If she walked away from him now, she might never find out.

"Are you still there?"

"Yes." She drew a breath, ignoring the pain in her lungs as well as the misgivings. "When McLain gets back I need you to give her a message. Tell her my cell phone has been damaged, but I'm fine and I'll keep trying to call her."

"Okay, but I don't know when I'll see her." To her relief, Dalton didn't appear to have picked up on anything unusual.

"Can you get me a number for Senior Special Agent Vince King in the New Haven field office?" If she couldn't speak to McLain, she needed guidance from the agent who had prepared her for this undercover assignment. McLain had brought King in from the other field office, citing his years of experience. He was also skilled in offering support to rookies like Hollie. She had a feeling she wouldn't like his advice, but she should at least hear it.

"Sure." Dalton was silent for a few minutes. When he spoke again, Hollie could hear a note of bemusement in his voice. "No one of that name in New Haven."

"Are you certain?"

"Hundred percent."

She wanted to insist he go back and check again, but she knew Dalton wouldn't make a mistake over something like that. His attitude could be casual, but that was deceptive. He was razor-sharp at all times, one of the best agents she knew. Could she have got it wrong?

She was sure those were the details McLain had given her... The feeling of discomfort intensified.

"Hey—" the casual way Dalton said the word alerted Hollie to the fact that there was nothing casual about what was coming next "—I may be able to get us tickets to see Beast. Some guy I know has contacts. Not quite front row, but not bad."

Not quite front row. It summed up her feelings about Dalton. She hadn't realized it until now, but she wanted front row. Actually, she wanted center stage. The thought coincided with the sound of a car pulling into the drive. "I'm not sure when I'll be back, but thanks for the thought."

She ended the call with that familiar feeling of guilt tugging at the center of her chest. It didn't matter how often she told herself Dalton was a grown man—*he's five years older than me*—with a successful career, and a wide circle of friends. He always managed to make her feel as if she had blighted his life.

Six months. That's how long we were together. It was fun, but it didn't set my world on fire. Speaking of which...

She turned her head as Torque walked into the kitchen carrying a variety of bags. He wore a sweatshirt she had seen him wearing in dozens of photographs. It was copied by fans around the world. Black and red, with an oversize hood, it had an image of a burning guitar on the back.

"I have food and clothes." He nodded at the phone in her hand. "Was your overprotective friend reassured?"

"I couldn't get in touch with her."

He stepped onto the terrace. "What will you do now?"

"I don't know." Her voice sounded hollow as she

tilted her head to look up at him. She had come here to investigate him, had known him barely a day, so why did keeping secrets from him suddenly feel all wrong? And why did the thought of leaving him feel worse?

"In a few days, I need to join the rest of the band for the start of our tour."

Hollie bit her lip. "I understand—"

"I don't think you do." His lips curved into a smile, the one that warmed her insides and left her feeling slightly breathless. "How would you like to come with me?"

Chapter 4

Hollie looked tired and confused as she sat at the kitchen counter sipping coffee and nibbling at a pastry. She had showered and her blond hair was still slightly damp. Torque had done a good job of estimating her size, so at least she now wore sweatpants that stayed up and a pale gray sweater that suited her coloring and clung deliciously to her curves. Despite her pallor and the dark circles under her eyes, he couldn't drag his gaze away from her face.

"I can't just tag along on your tour." Ever since he had made the offer, there had been an underlying emotion about her that he didn't understand. It was like she was being torn in two different directions. He wished she'd just tell him the truth about who she was.

"Why not?" He leaned against the counter, just close enough to breathe in her warm, soapy scent.

"Because…" She flapped a helpless hand. "What

would people think? They would assume I was a groupie, or something."

"But you're not. Anyway, why does it matter what other people think?"

She laughed. "That's so *you.*"

He shrugged. "Can't help being me."

"Torque, I don't want to seem ungrateful—"

He cut abruptly across her protests. "Where else will you go?"

Hollie hesitated and he got the feeling there was a lot she wasn't telling him. He wanted to explain to her that he didn't care. No matter what secrets she was keeping from him, he would fulfill his duty. She was his mate and that meant he had an obligation to keep her safe. But if he told her that, he would have to reveal a whole lot more. Like how he knew she wasn't safe. And how he had the ability to protect her. From *anything.*

"I don't know." The words were barely a whisper... and clearly a lie.

"Would you feel better if you had a job to do?"

"What do you mean?" Her brow furrowed, but he could see a glimmer of interest in the green depths of her eyes.

"My manager is forever telling me to get myself a personal assistant. I'm offering you the position."

"But you don't know if I'm qualified." Hollie appeared torn between laughter and incredulity. "And do all your bandmates take their PAs on tour? Because that sounds to me like one crowded tour bus...if that's still how you get around."

"My job offer, my rules. And yes. We use a bus. It gets a bit crazy, but I'll be there to look after you. Do you want the position or not?" He leaned over and took one of the pastries, biting into it as he watched her face.

Laughter shook her slender body as she gazed up at him. "I'll take the job. Although I can't help thinking you made it up just to give me something to do."

"You won't say that when you see my emails and letters."

Hollie shook her head. "Touring with Beast? This was my wildest fantasy when I was in college."

Before Torque could answer, the intercom for the electronic gates buzzed and he went to answer it. He pressed a button and an image of a man in uniform filled the screen. "Yes?"

"Jackson Kirk, Fire Investigation. I was told by the paramedics who treated Ms. Brown that she was here. I'd like to speak with her."

"She is here. But the decision about whether she's ready to speak with you is hers." He looked over his shoulder at Hollie, who sat up straighter, nodding her agreement.

Torque pressed the release button on the gates. When he opened the front door, Kirk was striding up the path. Torque got the impression the guy's shrewd, dark eyes were assessing him, the house and the grounds as he approached. Kirk held out an ID badge and Torque stepped aside to let him pass. He led Kirk through to the kitchen and introduced him to Hollie.

"The fire was started deliberately." It wasn't a question. She calmly stated it as a fact.

"How did you reach that conclusion?" Kirk asked.

"Because you're here."

Torque watched Hollie carefully as he made more coffee. Where she was concerned, his senses were finely tuned and his protective instincts were razor-sharp. He didn't need intuition to tell him her behavior was…unexpected. Until now, he'd had no dealings with victims of fire, but he didn't imagine they were the ones who usually led the conversation with a fire investigator.

"Was the point of ignition at the turn on the staircase?"

Kirk blinked. "Uh…yeah. Looks that way." He reached into his top pocket, drawing out a small notebook. "Although there were two other ignition points. One inside the bar and one in the storeroom. That's not always an indication of arson, but there were signs of a break-in."

Hollie appeared to be storing that information away. "How did he get in?"

That was it? That was her calm, collected question when faced with the information that a guy had broken in and set light to the staircase that led to her room? *Who are you, Hollie Brown?*

"Pried open a window at the back." Kirk nodded his thanks as Torque placed a coffee cup in front of him, indicating the cream and sugar. "The guy must have checked the place out in daylight, or risked using a powerful flashlight. That window was the only one large enough for him to climb through."

"You won't know what accelerant he used until you've run tests, but he would only have had what he could carry. I don't imagine there was anything in the bar he could use?"

Kirk flipped through his notes. He looked like a man who had come unprepared to an interview. "No. The staircase burned ferociously and it's been difficult to establish what happened there. My initial investigation suggests he stacked an absorbent, flammable substance—probably something he found in the bar, such as newspaper—at each ignition point before pouring his accelerant over it. He doesn't seem to have made any attempt to make it look like an accident."

Hollie nodded. "A professional torch."

Torque's lips twitched. *A professional torch? Oh, Hollie. Are you seriously proposing we keep up the pretense that you arrived in my local bar by chance?*

Kirk appeared not to notice the slip. "Looks that way. Which means we have to consider whether you were the target."

"Is there any question about that?" Torque asked. "If that fire was deliberately started on the staircase when Hollie was upstairs, it seems obvious that she was the intended target."

"We're right at the start of the investigation. It looks likely a crime was committed. We don't yet know whether that crime was arson or attempted murder. Which is why I'm here." Kirk turned back to Hollie. "Can you think of any reason why someone might do this?"

The hesitation was infinitesimal. If Torque hadn't been observing her so closely, he would have missed it. Or maybe it was because he was already so disconcertingly in tune with her emotions. "No."

"No recent breakup?" She shook her head. "Stalker? You haven't noticed anyone following you? No one who calls and then hangs up?" A shake of the head followed each question. "Nothing at all you can think of that has been out of the ordinary?"

"None of those things." It was just the wrong side of evasive. "Will you report this fire to anyone?"

Kirk frowned. "I'm the investigator. Who would I report it to?"

Hollie reached for another pastry, but seemed more intent on crumbling it into pieces on her plate than eating it. "I wondered if there was a database—" she waved a vague hand "—or something."

"Don't worry. I know how to do my job." Kirk finished his coffee. "Will you be staying here? With Mr.—?" He raised an inquiring brow.

"It's just Torque."

Kirk's glance managed to convey his disapproval of rock stars with long hair, big houses and unconventional names.

Hollie drew his attention back to her. "I'll be traveling and I lost my cell phone in the fire."

"You can reach us both on this number." Torque might not be the most organized person in the world, but he had succumbed to Ged's insistence and always carried a supply of his manager's business cards. He handed one of these to Kirk.

Kirk made a note of his own number on a page of his notebook and tore it out. He handed it to Hollie. "If you think of anything—"

"I'll be sure to get in touch."

Torque escorted Kirk to the door. "She seems to be taking it well." The investigator jerked his head back in the direction of the kitchen. "Most people would be shaken up after an experience like that."

"Shock affects people in different ways." Privately, he agreed with Kirk. Hollie seemed more intent on conducting her own investigation than on providing Kirk with answers.

He watched Kirk walk away, making sure the electric gates were closed behind him. His steps were uncharacteristically slow and deliberate as he returned to the kitchen. Hollie turned her head to look at him, smiling as he approached, and his heart lurched.

Everything about her enthralled him. The tendrils

of gold hair blowing about her face in the breeze from the open window. The faint blush on her cheeks as his gaze lingered on her face. Her scent, the aroma of *her* that he could smell beneath the vanilla and pine tones of the soap, made his inner dragon growl with lust. She was his mate. He wanted to sweep her up into his arms, take her off to a cave somewhere and show her what that meant.

The big green eyes scanning his face brought him crashing back down to earth. They were big green *human* eyes. Nothing about wanting Hollie made sense. Yet, from the moment he first saw her, she had become the most important thing in his life. Wanting her was something he would just have to fight. Not easy when all he wanted to do was grab her and growl out the truth. *Mine.*

Even so, it was torture. Exquisite but agonizing. How was he going to cope in even closer proximity to his mate?

"You look fierce." Hollie's smile wavered.

He laughed. "You have no idea."

Hollie was annoyed that she'd allowed her professional instincts to show through in the meeting with Jackson Kirk. She wasn't very good at this undercover thing. Her real self kept fighting to be let out.

She decided to tackle the subject head-on with Torque. "I suppose you're wondering what that was all about."

After Kirk left, they were seated on a bench in the garden, overlooking the wide sweep of the bay.

"I guess you'll tell me when you want me to know."

His gaze was steady on hers and she suddenly felt guilty. This man had saved her life, taken her into his home, bought her new clothes, offered her a job...and she was deceiving him. She was as convinced as she could be that he wasn't the Incinerator, that she could trust him, but her training told her instinct wasn't enough. Proof. That was what she needed. Until she had it, she should probably be wary of him. Instead of constantly wanting to get nearer to him.

"Torque..."

"Hollie." That glittering gaze held hers. "It doesn't matter."

The words jolted her, the sincerity in his tone almost knocking her off her seat. The message was clear. He understood that she was keeping secrets from him... but he didn't care. What *was* this? Everything about the situation she was in felt bizarre, yet she wasn't unnerved. It was somehow right. More right than anything she had ever known.

Needing to lighten the mood, she turned her attention to the job she would be doing. "Tell me about the tour."

"We're touring east to west, starting in New York, which is our base."

When Torque started to explain who the individual members of the group were, Hollie laughed. "You are talking to the girl who bought your first album and was hooked from day one."

"So you know all about us?"

Although Hollie still felt tired, the events of the previous day had receded. It was almost like a bad dream that had happened to someone else. There were things about the fire that nagged at the edge of her consciousness. Jackson Kirk had appeared unaware of the FBI database, but maybe he didn't feel it was necessary to discuss it with her. As far as he was concerned, she was a member of the public, not an expert. He didn't know she was the person who had devised the complex information system. It was the means by which the Bureau collated information about all fires and cross-referenced it with their existing records.

It frustrated her that she knew so much more than Kirk did. Although it appeared Hollie herself was the target of the fire at the Pleasant Bay Bar, she was even more convinced that Torque was the key. If she could discover why that was, she would be able to find her way to the Incinerator.

Then, of course, there was the issue of McLain's absence. That worried her most of all. But she had to have faith that her boss knew what he was doing. In the meantime, Hollie would continue to do her own job. She had decided to do that, even though every professional instinct told her she was wrong to remain undercover. Although the Incinerator had turned his attention to her, she felt safe with Torque. Safer than she'd ever felt in her life.

She was aware of him watching her, and pulled her attention back to his question. "Does anyone know all about you? For one of the most famous bands in the world, you guys have been incredibly successful at keeping yourselves private."

He was partly turned away from her and she studied his profile as he looked across the bay toward a small island. His gaze lingered there for long, silent moments before he turned back to her. Those unusual eyes glowed as he smiled. "I guess we just enjoy being enigmatic."

"How did you meet?" It was one of the things that had always interested her. The band kept their biographical details to a minimum. "I know Diablo is Native

American, Khan is from India, Dev comes from Nepal, Finglas is Irish and you…you like to be mysterious."

Torque held a hand over his heart in mock hurt. "I'm a child of the world. Wherever I lay my well-worn beanie, that's my home. As for how we met… Ged brought us together."

Ged Taverner was the mystery man of rock. Beast's hugely successful manager, he was the puppet master, the Svengali, behind the legend. The thought that she would soon be meeting him, and the members of the band, seemed unreal. Everything since she had arrived in Addison seemed unreal.

Except Torque. He was her new reality. Since they weren't touching, it must be her imagination that made her think she could feel the heat of his body warming her through her clothing. His eyes had a hypnotic effect on her. Once she stared at them, she couldn't turn away. And his lips… *Oh, dear Lord. Don't get me started on those lips.*

"Don't look at me that way." His voice was low. Not quite a whisper, almost a growl.

"What way?" She could no longer blame the smoke for the huskiness in her own tone.

"Probably the same way I look at you."

She edged closer. "Like you want me? Because that's how I feel about you."

"Hollie…" Although he said her name like it was made for his lips, he remained still, his hands splayed on his thighs.

"Oh." She let out a shaky sigh, slumping down in her seat. How could she have got this so *wrong*? "I see."

"No." He rubbed a hand over his face. "No, you don't see. Hollie, this can't happen."

"Torque, the only reason I can see why nothing can

happen between us is that you *don't* want me." When he turned to look at her, the raw agony on his face told her everything she needed to know. Her desire for him— her *craving* for him—wasn't one-sided. "Or if there's someone else in your life?"

He leaned forward, placing his head in his hands. When he started to laugh, there was no humor in the sound.

"What did I say that was so funny? *Is* there someone else in your life?"

Torque straightened, and the desolation in his eyes tugged at her heart. "I suppose there is, but not in the way you think." He caught hold of her hand and raised it to his lips. "Trust me. This way is better."

He got to his feet and Hollie watched him as he walked away. *Better for whom?*

Two days later, Hollie opened her eyes wide as she reached the rooftop terrace of Torque's New York apartment. Turning in a full circle, she took in the iconic views, the private pool, the sauna and the hot tub.

"I'm starting to think I died in that fire and this might be heaven." She turned to look at Torque. "You do know I may never leave?"

"You haven't started on that paperwork yet." Although he kept his voice light, the thought of Hollie staying in his life sounded just fine to Torque. If they could close the door on the rest of the world for eternity, that would be okay with him. He had grown used to her company with frightening speed. And if he could shut out everything else, he would be able to keep her safe from the person who had started that fire, from anything that might harm her. It was so damn hard. He would go to the ends of the earth for this woman…but he couldn't tell her that.

Ever since the conversation in his garden when Hollie had confessed to wanting him and he had turned her down—*like an idiot*—they had been tiptoeing around the subject. The attraction between them burned brighter with every passing minute. They were just doing their best to ignore it. Which was somehow making the whole situation even more tense.

Torque felt like he was living in a constant state of arousal. He was intoxicated by Hollie, drinking her in until his senses were filled with her. Unable to concentrate on anything else, he was barely aware of the practicalities of the forthcoming tour. Much to the annoyance of his manager.

"I have to go out in about an hour to a rehearsal." He grimaced. "Ged isn't happy. He thinks we haven't spent enough time together before we hit the road."

They headed back down the stairs into the open-plan living space. Although this place was incredible, it never quite felt like home to Torque. He had given a designer free rein with the decor, and the end result was stunning. The white and chrome furnishings were comfortable as well as classy, with everything chosen to make the most of the views. Even so, it had always been just a place to stay. He had only ever had one home. The mountains of Scotland had been forged in fire around the same time that the Cumhachdach dragon clan was born. Now the closest thing he had to a home was the house in Maine.

"How important is it to rehearse? Don't you already know your songs and each other really well?" Hollie asked.

"We do, but we have other people onstage with us.

Backing musicians and singers, some dancers. And our special effects are always evolving."

"Nothing will ever beat the display you put on a few years ago in Marseilles." Her eyes shone with excitement. "The one where it looked like wolves stormed the stage."

"You liked that?" Although Torque smiled at her enthusiasm, he remained wary. The band had done its best to cover up what had happened in Marseilles. In reality, there had been a genuine werewolf strike during one of their concerts. The band had all shifted in response and fought off the attackers. Caught on film, they had been forced to pass the whole thing off as one of the greatest special effects displays ever. They had succeeded, but they were constantly trying to cover up the reality.

"Liked it? It was incredible. I only wish I'd been there to see it in person. The atmosphere must have been amazing."

"You could say that." He decided a quick change of subject was in order. "Anyway, this week will be intense. It's always hard work just prior to the start of a tour, but Ged is right. He always is. The rehearsals are necessary."

Her gaze scanned his face. She was getting good at reading him. Just not too good, he hoped. There were many hundreds of years of secrets he didn't want to reveal. "I'd always wondered what made Ged so important, but when you speak about him, I can see it. It goes deeper than affection, doesn't it?"

It was a scarily perceptive comment. Ged was the glue that held Beast together, but he was so much more. He was the reason they existed. Each member of the band owed his life to the giant bear-shifter. "Yeah. Ged is a good guy." Such an understatement.

Hollie shook her head. "Do you ever *stop* being enigmatic?"

He laughed. "Only long enough to get coffee. But first, let me show you to your room."

There were four bedrooms, each with its own dressing room and bathroom. Hollie held up a small gym bag. "How will I ever fit all my stuff in?"

"We have to get you some new clothes."

"Torque..." She groaned. "That was *not* my way of trying to get you to purchase me some expensive new things. You've given me a job. I can buy my own clothes."

"That reminds me, we didn't discuss your salary. And I should probably see about giving you an advance—"

She dropped her bag and marched toward him. Reaching up, she placed a hand over his mouth. The action started out as a joke, but it violated their unspoken "no contact" rule. As soon as her fingers touched his lips, heat blazed from the point of contact through every part of his body. He saw Hollie's eyes widen and knew she was feeling it, too. So much more than attraction. It was their own firestorm and they were helpless against its power.

And...he wasn't quite sure how it happened, but his hands appeared to have developed a life of their own. His intention had been to move her gently but firmly away. Instead, his unruly body disobeyed him as he gripped her waist and pulled her closer. Now what was he supposed to do? With her parted lips so achingly close, there seemed to be only one solution to his dilemma.

As Hollie swayed closer, the temptation to kiss her grew into a necessity. Every reason why this was a bad idea had just flown out of his head when they were interrupted by a buzzing noise.

Hollie blinked as though she had been roused from a trance. "What was that?"

"It's the concierge. I'm expecting a delivery."

She sighed, resting her forehead briefly against his chest. "Then I guess you have to go." The disappointment in her voice almost undid his resolve.

"Come with me." He took her hand. "This is for you."

Hollie quirked an inquiring brow in his direction, but followed him without comment. When he opened the door, the uniformed concierge handed Torque a small package. Once he had tipped the doorman and closed the door again, he gave the box to Hollie.

"It's a cell phone."

She turned the carton over in her hands. Her expression was hard to read, but Torque was caught up in that swirl of conflicting emotions coming from her once again. She was feeling regret and sorrow. *Why, Hollie? What's bothering you?*

"You are such a good man." When she raised her eyes to his, he caught a glimpse of tears before she blinked them away.

"Tell me." The words were out before he knew he was going to say them.

"Pardon?" He knew she'd heard him.

He shrugged the question aside. Now was not the best time. "Nothing. You need a way to keep in touch with your overprotective friend."

"If she's taking calls." She placed a hand on his shoulder and pressed her lips to his cheek. "Thank you, Torque."

To hell with restraint. Her warm, soft mouth felt perfect on his skin, and just for a moment, he let it happen. Allowed himself that one, tiny indulgence.

"While I'm out you can try and contact her." He grabbed his jacket, turning back as he reached the door. "Be careful."

Her brow wrinkled. "About calling my friend?"

"Until Kirk gets in touch to say the guy who set fire to the bar has been caught, you need to be careful about everything."

She looked sweet and vulnerable—and so incredibly beautiful—that it took every ounce of self-control he possessed to walk out the door.

Chapter 5

Hollie took the new cell phone through to her bedroom. Her feet felt heavy, the sensation slowing her down, and she kicked off her shoes in an attempt to make herself comfortable. It didn't work. Her discomfort wasn't physical. Torque had been so generous, and asked nothing in return, not even an explanation. She hated taking advantage of his kindness. Sometimes she wondered if she should just tell him everything, but even though they had grown closer, there were still those nagging doubts attached to him. She was as sure as she could be that he wasn't the person who had tried to kill her, but there was still a mystery surrounding the night of the Pleasant Bay Bar fire. No matter how many different ways she looked at it, no matter how many explanations he gave about timing, Torque should not have been able to walk through those flames.

If she was honest, she'd admit there was another

reason for her reluctance to tell him the truth. Once Torque knew she had deceived him, things wouldn't be the same between them. It was unlikely they could continue the way they were. When she examined her motives, this was the strongest. She didn't want to leave Torque and this enjoyable bubble in which they were living. It was that simple.

She wondered if he was aware of the Incinerator's activities. The arsonist had received some press attention, but because the attacks were geographically so far apart, there hadn't been the same sensationalism as if he was operating within a smaller area. And McLain had done a good job of keeping the details out of the public eye.

The thought of the chief made Hollie eager to call her. Surely by now McLain would be back in her office and everything would be right with the world? They would clear up the issue about Vince King and Hollie would persuade her boss that sticking with Torque was a good idea. If that didn't happen? She frowned. It had to happen. She wasn't giving up on this now. As she set up the new cell phone, she tried to analyze what *this* was. Was it still the Incinerator investigation? Or was it something new, something to do with the unbreakable ties that bound her to Torque? By the time she had completed the setup process, she still hadn't decided.

When she tried McLain's number, her hands were shaking. Because she already knew what the outcome would be. Sure enough, she got the same voice mail message as last time. Bowing her head, she took a few deep breaths.

Okay. There were other ways to contact McLain. Trying the field office, she got through to the main telephone operator. "I'd like to speak to Assistant Special Agent-in-Charge McLain, please."

"I'm sorry, the ASAC isn't here right now. We're not sure when she'll be back…"

Something was very wrong. Hollie had already known that, but now she was unable to push aside the feeling of doom. Calling the service provider for the new cell, she explained that she wanted ID blocking enabled on her account. When that was in place, she called Dalton.

"Hollie, where the hell are you? And why are you withholding your number?"

"I don't have much time." She used the excuse as a way of not answering his questions. "What's going on with McLain?"

"No one knows. She seems to have vanished. It's crazy here right now. But, Hols, there's something else… I don't know how to tell you this…"

She could hear the distress in his voice and it triggered answering prickles of dread along her spine. "Just say it, Dalton."

"Your apartment building burned down yesterday."

She sat down abruptly on the bed, closing her eyes as the room began to spin. "Was it the Incinerator?"

"It's too soon to say, but it's looking that way."

A wave of nausea washed over her. She wanted to run to Torque, to cling to him and be comforted. But she couldn't. Partly because he wasn't there, but also because to him she was Hollie Brown…and Hollie Brown didn't have an apartment. All those precious things the Incinerator had destroyed? The books, photographs and mementos? They belonged to Hollie Brennan, FBI agent, and Torque had never met *her*.

Her thoughts skittered around wildly. The attack on the Pleasant Bay Bar had been personal. That was bad enough. But this latest fire meant the Incinerator knew her real identity...

"Are you still there?" The sympathy in Dalton's voice made the lump in her throat swell until it felt like she was choking. "I'm sorry, Hols. Some things shouldn't be done over the phone."

"Can't be helped when I'm on the road." Her voice was gruff as she fought back the tears. *On the road. Careful, Hollie.* She didn't think Dalton could pick up on where she was and what she was doing from those words, but it showed how easy it was to slip up.

"I don't know what's going on with you, but you need to come in. Let us keep you safe."

She could hear the concern in his voice. It wasn't just because he was a colleague. He still cared and this had shaken him up.

He was talking sense. Dalton was what she *knew*. Okay, so she didn't love him, but he represented the real world. *Her* world. For some reason, the Incinerator had switched his attention to Hollie and she needed protection. She shouldn't hesitate on this. There was no way she should be considering staying with Torque. Ever since she had started this job, her head and her heart had been at war. Her head was trying to convince her to give it up, while her heart prompted her to stay with Torque. Now things had gotten a whole lot scarier.

She should do what Dalton was suggesting. Let the might and resources of the FBI protect her. She should go home...except the place she had called home no longer existed. And the nearest thing she had to it now was the man who had walked through flames for her.

She guessed her choices were that stark. Dalton and the FBI represented her head. They were security and reason. Torque? He was fire and magic. He was her heart.

Hollie had never believed in gut reactions. Her response to those who did was always with facts. Data, figures, science, proof…they were the things that mattered to her. Now her world had been tipped on its head. Her instincts were telling her, loud and clear, that she needed to stay with Torque. It was a primal warning, coming from somewhere deep within her. If she left his side, she was doomed.

"Got to go, Dalton. I'll call you soon." She heard his blustering protest as she ended the call.

Flopping back on the bed, she held the phone to her chest for a moment or two. The tears were fading. In their place, her determination to catch the Incinerator was growing stronger. So he had chosen to switch his attention to her? Well, he had been her enemy for the last four years. Now they would find out who was stronger.

If the arsonist was trying to scare her, he was succeeding. But, for some reason, alongside the fear there was a feeling of empowerment. The woman who had walked into that bar in Addison was not the same one who was here in New York. Fundamentally, she was still Hollie, but something inside her had shifted. It sounded foolish, but she had been living a half-life until now. Having experienced the difference, she wasn't going back and settling for less.

A knock on the door shook her out of her musing. "Hollie?" Torque's voice was muffled by the thick wood. "Rehearsal finished early. How do you feel about pizza?"

"Um, hold on a second." She padded barefoot across the thick rug. When she opened the door, he scanned her face. His gaze was like a caress. How did he do *that*?

It was almost as though he knew how she was feeling and he was using his presence to comfort her. "How do I feel about pizza? Pretty much the same way a drowning woman feels about a lifeboat."

He grinned. "After we've eaten, we'll get you some new clothes."

Hollie had been subdued since they arrived in New York. No, Torque could pinpoint exactly when her mood had changed. She'd been fine at first. Then, after he'd left her alone and gone to his first rehearsal, he'd returned and they'd gone for pizza. Although Hollie had done her best to maintain the pretense that nothing had changed, Torque could tell she was upset. Every now and then, she'd lapse into silence and he would catch a glimpse of real anguish in her expression.

It caused an answering tug of pain in his own chest. Something had happened while he was at his rehearsal. The most likely possibility was that she had called someone during that time and what she'd heard had caused this distress. More than ever, Torque wanted to put an end to this charade. To tell her once and for all that there was nothing she could do or say that would turn him against her. If he could find a way to do it that didn't involve explaining about shifters, fated mates and the reasons why he wasn't able to offer her a normal life, he would do so in a heartbeat. Instead, he tried to offer her a reassuring presence.

Torque sensed Hollie was grateful for his understanding, and the knowledge made him angry. Even though he could never have it, he wanted more than her gratitude. He didn't want to be viewed as the kindly friend with the broad shoulder on which she could lean. When he looked into her eyes, he saw everything he wanted. Love. Passion. Laughter. Warmth. All of those things and more. Forever.

"I'm still not sure this is a good idea."

Hollie's words drew Torque's attention back to another, more mundane problem.

Persuading her that meeting Beast prior to the tour would be fun had been hard work. They had been in New York for five days and the first concert was taking place in two days' time. Despite Torque's reassurances, she clearly viewed the approaching evening with dread. They were in a cab now on their way to meet the others, and her expression had been growing more apprehensive with each passing block.

Finding a place to eat that catered for the different tastes within the band was always difficult. Torque supposed that was true of any diverse group, but Beast was unique. Not that Ged was likely to share the precise details of their differences with a New York restaurateur. A booking for a dragon, two werewolves, three big cats and a bear? Oh, and Hollie would be joining them…so, yeah, they'd need the mortal menu, as well. Celebrities got away with a lot of weird stuff, but that wouldn't slip by unnoticed.

Being part of Beast was a curious balancing act. Living in the human world was all about one simple rule. Mortals must never know shifters walked among them. Anonymity was key, and all shape-shifters, no matter what animal form they took, went to great lengths to maintain it. Yet the members of the band were rock stars, constantly in the limelight.

Being a celebrity was high-energy, high-profile and high-stress. Torque had known how it would be when Ged rescued him from a life of servitude. This was the new beginning Ged had offered him, and Torque had embraced it with gratitude. He was good at what he did. He was an outstanding musician and a brilliant performer. But his inner dragon didn't want to be on display. Along with his bandmates, his life was a constant battle to meet the needs of both sides of his persona.

Things had improved over time. Fame had brought great wealth, which meant they could buy themselves some privacy. Since Khan's marriage and the birth of his daughter, Karina, everyone had reevaluated the pace and decided to slow down. But walking down the street without being recognized? That still wasn't an option. Going out in a group? They'd had to resort to some creative measures to make sure they didn't disrupt the entire restaurant.

The solution was Daria's, a small, family-run restaurant located in a Brooklyn side street. Since Ged knew the owner—Ged knew *everyone*—and Daria was prepared to close to other customers, privacy wasn't a problem.

"What will they think when you tell them I'm coming on the tour?" As they vacated the cab, Hollie tugged nervously at the new top she was wearing.

"They already know." Torque removed the shades he always wore when he went out. Along with the beanie he used to cover his hair, they constituted his standard disguise. "I told them."

"Oh." She chewed her lower lip for a moment. "What did they say?"

He draped an arm around her shoulders, propelling her toward the restaurant door. "Hollie, this is no big deal. Sometimes other people join us on tour."

He felt her indrawn breath. "But they must usually be…you know…"

"People we're having sex with?"

She turned her head to look at him and he enjoyed the sensation of her hair tickling his cheek. "Isn't that what they'll think? That this job you've given me is just an excuse?"

"Probably. Does it matter?"

She regarded him thoughtfully for a moment or two. "No. Because if it was up to me, we *would* be having sex."

Heat streaked through him, pooling deep in his abdomen, hardening his whole body. "Hollie." Her name was a groan on his lips, a brand on his heart.

"I'm being honest, Torque." She touched one finger to the corner of his mouth, a simple caress that almost brought him to his knees. "I wish you would."

"You want to talk about honesty?" He drew her closer, even though the action inflamed him further, spiking his arousal almost to the point of no return. "You want to go there?"

Fear flared in her eyes, but she tilted her chin defiantly. "If that's what it takes."

"Hey, guys, making out in the street? Way to get papped." It was Khan, the biggest, baddest tiger of them all.

"Later." Torque kept his eyes on Hollie for a moment longer and she nodded before they turned to greet the new arrivals.

Khan and Sarange were the ultimate celebrity couple. He was Beast's lead singer; she was a singer songwriter. He was a tiger; she was a wolf. At first glance, it wasn't a match made in shifter heaven, but it worked for them.

"This is Hollie," Torque said as he kissed Sarange and was lifted off the ground in one of Khan's overexuberant hugs.

He was aware of his friends regarding Hollie closely

and he could guess what they were thinking. Their dragon friend was with a mortal woman. A woman who didn't know who he was…didn't know any of them were shifters. It was going to be an interesting evening.

Torque had asked Ged to organize this meal so Hollie could get to know everyone before they embarked on the tour. He'd already explained to his bandmates that she was unaware of his true identity. He'd also told them the story of the fire and his obligation to protect her. Although he had been able to feel caution coming off them in waves, their loyalty to each other was absolute. For Torque's sake, they would accept Hollie and keep his secrets.

It wasn't the first time they had been in this position. A few years ago, their former bass guitarist, Nate Zilar, had helped a mystery woman called Violet when she lost her memory. Violet had joined Beast on tour and they had protected her from a pack of vicious werewolves. Nate left the band when he and Violet got married. Of course, Violet had turned out to be a werewolf herself, so the circumstances weren't quite the same. Hollie was human, which meant she needed special treatment.

Special treatment that does not include dragon sex. Given the steamy exchange between them and her enticing behavior just now, it was probably a good time for Torque to remind himself of that.

When they entered the restaurant, Diablo was already there. Beast's drummer exuded raw, brooding vitality, and suppressed menace. With his blue-black hair flopping forward to cover his face and bulging, tattooed biceps, he was even more stunning up close than onstage.

There was barely time for introductions before Dev

and Finglas arrived. Hollie could already identify
them, of course. Dev, with his white-blond hair and
pale skin, was the ice-man. Finglas, the replacement
for Nate Zilar, was the youngest and newest member
of the group.

Hollie picked up on the bond between Torque and
his friends instantly. Sarange was part of it, but it was
strongest between the men. They didn't need to speak.
Although they went through the ritual of back-slapping
and a few joking insults, there was an unusual warmth
linking them together. Perhaps it had been forged during all those years of working in such close harmony.
She wondered if they were even aware of it.

Then another man entered, and the feeling intensified. There was no mistaking him. Just from his size,
this had to be Ged Taverner. It was incredible the way
she could sense the affection the others felt for him.
Having been a Beast fan for a long time, she knew the
band members held him in high regard, but he must be
special to generate this sort of devotion.

"Hollie." He came straight to her. "Hi."

Her hand was wrapped in a warm clasp and she
found a pair of golden eyes assessing her. She understood what that gaze meant. He wanted to be sure she
wasn't going to hurt Torque. Clearly, this group of alpha
males looked out for each other.

What if I don't pass the test? Ged's gaze was scarily perceptive. What if he could somehow see through
her? If he could tell she wasn't who she pretended to be?

She risked a glance in Torque's direction and he
quirked a brow at her. The message was clear. *Stop
worrying.*

When they sat down to eat, she found she was at a
disadvantage. Daria already knew what everyone else

would be having. And the food choices were seriously weird. Ged was having fish. Dev, Diablo and Khan wanted lamb, cooked so it was still pink. Sarange and Finglas both had a liking for steak so rare it almost jumped up off the plate and ran away. Torque, on the other hand, wanted his own giant piece of beef well-cooked. Actually, when it arrived at the table, it was charred. She had shared many meals in his company recently, but she hadn't seen him eat anything like this.

Hollie, having ordered a pizza, was astonished at the sheer amount of meat her companions ate. "Are you guys on some sort of low-carb diet?" she asked Finglas as the Irishman started on his second steak. She couldn't help noticing that no one ordered sides. No fries, bread or vegetables. The only person who even touched his salad garnish was Ged.

"You could say that." Finglas choked back a laugh. "Touring uses up a lot of energy."

It had to be one of the unhealthiest diets she'd ever seen, yet they all appeared to be glowing with vitality. Maybe it was a celebrity thing. Possibly they had the same personal trainer who advocated this regime. Whatever it was, she wasn't going to be tempted to join them.

"Torque tells me you're going to help him make sense of his paperwork." Ged's deep voice suited his large frame.

"That's the plan. He has warned me it may not be an easy job."

"That's an understatement. Fan mail is only one part of it, of course, but it illustrates his disorganized approach. I'd be surprised if Torque has ever done anything other than look at it and put it to one side, both email and paper." Ged turned his head to look at Torque. "Has he mentioned he has some unusual followers?"

"Followers? That's a strange choice of word."

"Some of them are strange." Ged took a slug of his beer. "One of the downsides of fame is that some people feel they know you. They read about you in the press, or online, and they have no cut-off mechanism. They feel you owe them a part of yourself. It can be a fine line between fanatic and lunatic."

His words made Hollie shiver. "Is that what Torque has to deal with? People who are crazy?"

"Not face-to-face. That has never happened. But sadly, he does seem to attract more than any of the others. I've spent a lot of time trying to analyze why."

"Have you reached a conclusion?" Hollie looked at Torque, who was talking to Khan. It scared her that he might be in danger. It frightened her even more to acknowledge how much she cared.

"Fire," Ged said.

"Pardon?" That single word, so much a part of her life, rocked her back in her seat.

"I don't know how to explain it, but having read some of the letters and emails, I think that's the link. They see him playing around with it onstage. He gives off these fiery vibes. And these people see him as some sort of fire god who has a message for them. Someone they can worship."

Hollie regarded the rest of her pizza with a rising feeling of nausea. Ged's words were confirmation of one of her wildest suspicions. Was the Incinerator one of the people who viewed Torque as a deity? Had the fires she had spent so long investigating been started as a tribute? It made a horrible sort of sense. If the arsonist believed that Torque craved, or even controlled, fire, then his avid follower would be eager to give him what he wanted. Until she delved into Torque's chaotic paperwork, she wouldn't know if the fire starter had ever contacted Torque to tell him what he'd done in his honor. If he had, the reference must be obscure. She knew Torque well enough by now to be convinced he wouldn't ignore it.

There was a flaw in that line of thinking, and it related to Hollie herself. If the Incinerator was an avid fan who believed Torque was something more than a rock star, maybe something more than mortal, how had he, or she, switched his attention to her so fast?

There was an answer, and it was an obvious one, but she didn't like it.

"What has Ged been saying to make you look so worried?"

She hadn't noticed Torque swapping places with Finglas. "He confirmed that your filing system can only be described as chaotic." She did her best to keep her voice light. As always, she got the sense that he knew what she was feeling.

"Now the truth." Color shimmered in the depths of his eyes.

"This is too one-sided. I should be able to know what you're thinking and feeling." Although they were surrounded by other people, it felt like they were cocooned in their own little world. It had been that way since the first moment she met him.

"That's not how enigmatic works. Tell me what's troubling you, Hollie."

"It was something Ged said about your fans. About how some of them believe you have a connection to fire?" He nodded, and she sensed a new alertness in him. "I wondered if the person who set fire to the Pleasant Bay Bar might be one of them."

"It had crossed my mind."

"But if that's the case, that person had to know about me—about our first meeting—really fast." She bit her lip, not wanting to voice the next uncomfortable thought. Saying it out loud would make it real. "Don't you see what that means? One of your crazy fans must be watching you."

"I'd realized that, as well."

He clasped her hand, holding it between both of his, and she experienced that curious sense of her troubles slipping away.

"I can take care of myself, Hollie. I can take care of both of us."

"I hate to interrupt—" Daria came out of the kitchen in her chef's whites. "But there's news coming in of a fire in a luxury apartment building in Tribeca." She handed Torque her cell phone to show him the images. "Isn't that where you live?"

Chapter 6

Although the blaze hadn't reached Torque's apartment, the fire department was still at work when Torque and Hollie arrived at the building.

"Do you know what started it?" Even though Hollie asked the question, she was aware that she was wasting her time. She already knew the answer. It wasn't a "what" it was a "who." She looked around the darkened street. People had gathered to watch what was going on. She had profiled enough arsonists to know that the Incinerator was probably here somewhere, watching from the shadows. That would be even more likely if he believed he had a link to Torque.

Show me your face. After four years, she had built up an image of her opponent. In her mind he was half laughing, half snarling, barely human.

"It's too early to say." The chief fire officer at the scene spared a few minutes to talk to them, but he was busy directing operations. "Luckily, the concierge acted fast and the system is excellent. No one was injured, but there is some structural damage in the lobby. I'll have it made safe by morning."

"You can stay with us tonight." Sarange, who had driven them, linked her arm through Hollie's.

Khan and Sarange lived a short distance away in another luxury building. When they arrived at their home, the obvious difference between this apartment and Torque's was that it had been adapted to make it child-friendly. There was less glass and chrome, more rounded edges and a distinct lack of white.

Hollie was surprised when Sarange paid off the sitter. "I thought you'd have an army of nannies." She bit her lip. "I'm sorry. That sounded judgmental."

Sarange waved aside the apology. "We like our privacy. Let me show you to your room." She grinned. "And you have to admire our little tiger as we pass the nursery."

"Tiger?" Hollie followed her up the stairs.

She detected a hint of annoyance in Sarange's expression, as though she'd said too much. She shook the thought aside. *I must be tired.* Or the Incinerator was getting to her again, playing havoc with her imagination.

"Khan reminds me of a tiger, and Karina takes after him," Sarange explained.

The baby was sprawled on her back like a starfish in her crib, and Sarange rearranged the blankets over her.

"She's beautiful." Even in sleep, Hollie could see the little girl had inherited the good looks of both her parents.

Sarange smiled. "I already liked you. Now it's official." She checked the baby monitor was on before closing the door.

She led Hollie down the hall to a beautiful guest suite. The soothing creamy tones of the furnishings made Hollie feel instantly relaxed and she regarded the vast bed with pleasure. Although whether she would sleep with the Incinerator's latest attack on her mind was doubtful.

"Will this be okay for you and Torque?"

Ah. Now would be a good time to explain Sarange's mistake. Just a few simple words to clear up the confusion. *Torque and I are not in a relationship.* That should do it.

"This will be fine."

Because wasn't this what she wanted? And no matter how hard he tried to resist, it was also what Torque wanted. *So, let's see where sharing takes us.*

Aware that her thoughts of Torque had kept her silent for a long time, she shook her preoccupation aside. "Are you touring with the band?"

"I'm not performing with them, but I'll join them when I can. Although it's not easy with a baby, Khan and I made a decision when Karina was born that we would try not to spend more than two nights apart." Sarange glanced at her watch. "Do you mind if I leave you to settle in? Karina will wake up soon for her supper and I want to change out of these clothes before she does."

When she was alone, Hollie went to the window and stared out at the dramatic views. Three Incinerator fires were now linked directly to her. She couldn't ignore that. She also couldn't escape the reality that she was responsible for bringing the arsonist closer to other people and specifically to Torque. Prior to her arrival in his life, the Incinerator had been content to worship him from afar. Now he was pushing for a more meaningful relationship. And it looked like Hollie had been the catalyst.

With no way of contacting McLain or Vince King, she was running out of choices. Going back to Newark and letting the Incinerator team know what was going on seemed like the only option available to her. It felt like stepping back in time. Going back to the same routine. Picking up the pieces of a four-year investigation that hadn't caught the Incinerator yet. And it wasn't what she wanted. If only there was another way.

"So we're sharing a room?" She hadn't heard Torque approach until he was standing right behind her. Close enough to touch, but not touching. It didn't matter. His gaze was like a caress.

"Unless you don't want to?"

"You know I want to." His voice was gruff. "Like I said, we need to talk before we even consider anything else."

She nodded. Maybe there were other options after all. "I'm ready."

"So am I. But I came to tell you that the other band members have just arrived." His smile was rueful. "I decided Khan and Sarange needed some extra protection if you and I were going to be here tonight."

Hollie covered her mouth with her hand. "I should have thought of that."

His gaze remained fixed on hers. "We've both just given something away without even trying. You didn't ask how my bandmates can provide the protection we need… And I didn't ask why you should be the one who knows about the arsonist's next steps."

"I guess neither of us is very good at keeping secrets."

He ran a finger down her cheek, sending delicious heat shimmering along her nerve endings. "I wouldn't say that."

They had done this many times. When it mattered most, Beast was a formidable team. Onstage, they all came together as a unique entity, but their main strength was as a fighting force. This was what they did best. When one of their group was threatened, they closed ranks and worked together to protect that person.

They were shifters who lived in the human realm, and their responsibilities straddled two worlds. When they dealt with a problem that could draw the attention of mortals, particularly of law enforcement, they had to tread carefully, not only for their own sake. If their cover was blown, if the world became aware that the stories, movies and legends were more than hype, and that shifters lived among them, nothing would ever be the same again.

It was a fine line they always walked. On the whole, the supernatural world was a quiet one, but that could change in an instant. Passions ran deep and centuries-old conflicts could be reignited with a look or a word. Battle lines would be redrawn and shifters who believed they were living out their lives in peace might suddenly find themselves renewing ancient loyalties. With no immortal peacekeeping force, shifters had to find their own protection. For Beast, that meant relying on each other. And that suited Torque just fine.

Diablo, Dev and Finglas stayed at street level, taking turns to patrol the lobby and the sidewalk outside the building. Although their opponent was unknown to them, with their quick, shifter reflexes and heightened perceptiveness, they would notice anything unusual before the building's security guards did. Torque, Khan and Ged stayed in the apartment. Sarange was there, as well, but her focus was on the baby.

"What if this arsonist doesn't approach the building?" Ged asked. "What if he tries a different method this time? Some sort of remote control device, even a bomb?"

"He won't." Hollie's voice was calm, her expression resolute. "That's not his style. He gets up close."

Torque, who was seated next to her on the sofa, spoke quietly so only she could hear. "And the reason you can say that with such confidence is one of those things we need to talk about."

She turned her head, and he drank in the purity of her features. "No more secrets."

Could he do that? Tell a mortal woman everything? Would those clear green eyes still look at him with such trust once she knew it all? He would soon know.

A muffled cry over the baby monitor brought Sarange to her feet. "She's usually hungry at this time of night."

"Can I come with you?" Hollie asked. "I'd love to meet her."

"Of course, but be prepared to duck." When Hollie looked confused, Sarange explained. "Karina's eating habits are still hit and miss."

When the two women had left the room, Khan took Hollie's place. His expression was serious. "Do I want to hear this?" Torque asked.

"I'm your friend…"

Torque leaned back, looking up at the ceiling. "Whenever a conversation starts with those words it means I *don't* want to hear it."

"I just want to know you've thought this through. I mean, the whole dragon-mortal thing."

Torque knew Khan only had his interests at heart. He was saying exactly what Torque had just been thinking. But Torque didn't want to hear the words spoken out loud any more than he wanted them inside his head. He didn't want anything to come between him and Hollie, even if it made sense.

"You thought Sarange was mortal when you first met her," Torque said.

"That's not true. I always knew Sarange was a were-wolf. *She* was the one who didn't know it." Khan placed a hand on his shoulder. "Take my advice. Stay away from mortals." As Torque got to his feet, he raised his brows. "Where are you going?"

"See that?" Torque pointed to the glass door that led to the roof terrace. "I'm going to put myself on the other side. That way I don't have to hear your advice." He knew he was being unfair. He also knew it didn't matter how far away from Khan he got. He would still have to listen to the same doubts playing inside his own head.

Once he was outside, he sat on a bench that gave the sensation of soaring out over the rooftops. The height and the fresh air soothed him, but he craved a wilder setting. City living didn't appease his inner dragon. He ached for soaring mountains, swooping valleys, wild rivers and tumbling waterfalls.

"Care for some company?"

He looked up to see Sarange standing in the open doorway. One of the most famous and beautiful women in the world was dressed in baggy sweatpants and a faded, off-the-shoulder top. Torque decided against telling her that she had something that looked like oatmeal in her long, dark hair.

He scooted along the bench to make room for her. "Where's the baby?"

"With Ged." It afforded everyone in the band endless fascination that the giant were-bear and the tiny half wolf, half tiger got along so well.

"Did your husband send you to talk sense to me?"

"I thought we were friends. Does it matter why I'm here?"

He huffed out a breath. "I guess not."

They sat in silence for a few minutes. "Khan thinks I should forget her because she's mortal." Torque wanted to be strong and silent, but the temptation to talk about Hollie was overwhelming.

"Khan's a cat. They're not known for giving good advice. Too self-absorbed." They shared a smile. "But if you want her in your life, you have to tell her."

"How can I do that?" The anguish in his voice matched the misery that tore at his heart every time he contemplated telling Hollie the truth. Because he knew that, once he did, he faced the prospect of watching her walk away.

"It won't be easy, but you'll find the words. And maybe simple is best."

"You mean I should say 'I'm a dragon' rather than 'I'm a winged, fire-breathing, mythical beast of legend'?"

"You'll find a way. And if she loves you, she'll love all of you." She grinned. "Even the scales."

"My scales are my best feature, furry girl. And, by the way, you have baby food in your hair."

She patted his cheek. "Talk to her."

"That's the plan."

Hollie was drawn back again to the bedroom window with its view over the city. *He* was out there somewhere. She knew it. The Incinerator would not have left town.

Even if he wasn't planning an attack on this building, he would be drawn close by Torque's presence. Probably hers, too. She had been involved in the profile they had produced on him. Profiling wasn't her area of expertise, but she knew the classic traits of an arsonist by heart. Usually white male, unstable childhood, above average intelligence but poor academic performance, inability to form stable relationships, possible mental illness. And the biggest one of all…fascination with fire.

The profiler had been cautious about the Incinerator. "The information available suggests the arsonist is a man, but the deciding factor about gender will be motive." *Unhelpful.* "If the perpetrator is driven by excitement, vandalism or money, then it's a man. If the motive is revenge or extremism, the chances that you are looking for a woman will increase considerably."

In other words, until they could figure out the motive, the shadowy figure would remain unclear.

This time, when Torque opened the door, she heard him and turned her head. He remained where he was for a moment or two, just watching her face. Then he crossed the room until he was standing beside her. They looked out at the view together.

Although it was long past midnight, the tiredness that had gripped her when they first arrived here was gone. In its place was a tingling excitement.

"It's time to tell me your secret, Hollie Brown."

She took a deep breath. "My real name is Hollie Brennan. I'm an FBI fire investigator."

His lips quirked into a grin. "That's it?"

"I thought it was pretty explosive." The irony of the word wasn't lost on her and she returned the smile. "I'm guessing you have something better?"

His expression immediately became serious. "I'm not sure you're ready for this."

Hollie shook her head. "That's not how it works. We had an agreement. You don't get to back down just because you think your secret is too big for me to handle."

He was silent for a moment or two, staring down at her with a look she couldn't fathom. The opal depths of his eyes glowed brighter than she'd ever seen them before. When his lips parted, she was no longer sure she really did want to hear what he had to say. Wasn't sure she wanted to know the truth about the man the world called Torque.

"Very well. You want to know how I can walk through fire without getting burned?" His eyes darkened, their depths becoming haunted. "The answer is easy, but it's one you'll have to open your mind to understand."

Torque was an entertainer, but Hollie had the strangest feeling none of this was for show. It wasn't a big buildup. He was steadying his nerves as much as he was preparing her.

She placed her hand on his arm, feeling the heat of his flesh warming her fingertips. "Tell me, Torque."

"I'm a dragon."

That was unexpected. She frowned, trying to assess his meaning. "Is it a club? A society? I'm not sure I'm following you…"

He gripped her forearms, holding her steady and drawing her closer. "Hollie, I'm a shape-shifter. I'm part human, part dragon."

That was the moment her dream ended. It had been too good to be true. She had always feared that the man she had fallen in love with from afar couldn't really be everything she had believed him to be, and now she was finding out he wasn't.

Torque was crazy.

As she made a move to pull away from him, Torque slid his hands up her arms to her shoulders, and she shuddered. How could her body betray her this way? Thinking he was deranged as she did now, how could his touch still send that thrill through her?

"I can't do this." She said it with genuine regret. No matter what his problems were, she cared about him. And he had saved her life. Was that all part of this delusion? Had he been wearing some sort of protection so he could pretend he was a fireproof beast? She followed that thought a step further.

Oh, Torque. Are you the Incinerator, after all? Her heart was starting to race with fear now as she gazed up at him. Why had she never noticed the way his eyes could glow with inner fire?

"I can prove it."

"Torque, don't put yourself through this. Don't put *us* through it." All she wanted to do now was walk away, leave this situation while there was some dignity left. For both of them.

"You talked about the concert in Marseilles. The one where the wolves stormed the stage?"

She nodded, fascinated at the way he was staying so calm about this. As if he truly believed it.

"It wasn't special effects, Hollie. They weren't wolves. They were werewolves."

She broke free of his grasp and headed for the door.

"Watch that concert again with me now."

She paused with her fingertips touching the door handle. *It wasn't special effects.* She had never tired of watching the film footage of that concert. Like everyone else, she had pored over those incredible scenes, had devoured the comments from technology geeks about how it had been achieved. Just how had Khan changed into a tiger right in front of an audience of thousands? How had Diablo been playing his drums one second and become a prowling black panther the next? And Torque...what the hell kind of digital genius had come up with an effect that had him casting aside his guitar, pounding across the stage and taking flight, unfurling giant wings as he ran. Because...

She turned to face him, her back pressed against the door as the blood drained from her face. "You turned into a dragon."

"I *am* a dragon." This time, when he said those words, everything about him was different. His stance was proud, his voice was a low rumble originating deep in his powerful chest and the fire in his eyes became a blaze.

Despite every instinct screaming out to the contrary, she believed him. More than that, she wanted to bow before him, to honor him. It was clear that Torque wasn't just any dragon.

"I can't..." As her knees started to give way, he was at her side, scooping her up with one arm beneath her thighs and the other around her waist. Hollie raised a hand to touch his cheek. "It's true."

Torque placed her on the bed. "Let's watch that film."

"I don't need proof." Even though everything she knew about her world had just been thrown off course, his word was enough.

Torque's lips quirked upward into a smile and he lifted her hand to his lips. "Thank you. But I want you to see me."

His gaze ignited tiny fires along her flesh.

"To know me. I can't shift here in the city. Not without triggering a major incident. That film will show you the other half of who I am."

Even though he came and sat next to her, there was at least two feet of mattress between them. Torque reached into a drawer of the bedside table and withdrew an electronic tablet. When he'd connected to the internet and found the clip he wanted, he held the device out to Hollie.

She didn't take it. Instead, she closed the distance between them, colliding with his hard, warm body. "You said we'd do this together."

His indrawn breath reverberated through her. "Okay."

Hollie could feel his determination and something more. Tilting her head, she viewed his profile. The hard planes of his features were more obvious from this angle and she could see the tension in his jaw, the tightness around his eyes. Was he *scared*? Afraid of what she would think when she watched this film? Hollie had seen it before, of course, but she would be seeing now with a new awareness.

She couldn't make him any promises about her reaction. Sitting on a bed with a dragon...she hoped she would continue to see the man she knew. But this was so far outside anything she had ever experienced, her thoughts were in a whirl. All she knew was that no matter what happened next, her life had just changed completely. "Let's do this."

He nodded, swiping the screen to start playing the film. The concert had been filmed as part of a documentary about Beast, but the incident had also been captured on dozens of cell phones. It began with five figures plowing their way through the audience to the front of the arena and leaping onto the stage. The men landed in a crouch and simultaneously shifted into wolf form. Crouching low at the far edge of the stage, they bared their teeth at the band members.

Beast was playing up a storm. Behind the members, the LED screens were like a giant art installation showing their signature three-sixes logo, roaring flames and the snarling jaws of various wild beasts. Believing the invasion to be part of the show, the already excited crowd went into a renewed frenzy. The band's symbolic sign of the beast was being made throughout the stadium as howls of appreciation rent the air.

Onstage, everything went from stillness to action. Adding to the sense of theater, Beast turned as a group to face the werewolves who had invaded their performance space. Khan, leading the advance, had a bring-it-on snarl on his face as he moved forward with muscle-bound stealth.

In the blink of an eye the stage erupted. The werewolves sprang from their crouching position as a series of incredible transformations took place. Khan's clothing burst apart. Beneath it rippled brilliant orange fur slashed across with diagonal stripes, each as thick, black and straight as a hand-drawn charcoal line. In Khan's place a giant tiger covered the distance across the stage in one bound, his lips drawn back in a snarl that revealed huge white fangs.

At the same time, Diablo disappeared and, in his place, a muscular black panther was prowling the space before joining the tiger as an unlikely ally. Finally, Dev cast aside his guitar, shifting stealthily as a ghost into a huge snow leopard, sharp and white in contrast to the blur of color around him, before throwing himself into the fray. Landing on the back of one of the startled wolves, the mighty creature lowered his head and used its lethal fangs to tear a chunk of flesh from its victim's neck.

The crowd, still convinced they were watching a series of awesome special effects, continued to cheer and howl. At the side of the stage, Ged could be seen gesturing wildly to the security team at the side of the stage. He wasn't fast enough...

Striding across the stage, Torque raised his hands and unleashed a series of explosions in his path. As he walked, he grew in stature until he towered over everything around him. Even on the screen, Hollie could see his eyes were bright red, the color filling the entire surface. The pupils had become vertical black slits. As he blinked, both top and bottom lids moved in time to meet each other.

As Torque broke into a run, his clothes tore from his body. His arm and leg muscles thickened, and he dropped onto all fours, giant claws the size of a mechanical digger churning up the surface of the stage. His skin was replaced by shimmering scales that reflected the neon colors of the strobe lighting. Giant wings unfurled, and a spiked tail flicked out before he opened his mouth to shoot a stream of blue-white flame in the direction of the wolves. Transfixed, Hollie watched as Torque became a stunning, fearsome dragon. He rose and hovered, his wingspan covering the entire stage.

Then the stage lights went out, black screens came down and a film of Beast playing one of its biggest hits was projected onto it.

Hollie sat very still, unsure what to do with all the emotion coursing through her. Dragons were creatures of magic and mystery. They had captivated her when she was a child, but she had put aside that fascination as she grew older. Except in her dreams. Now she knew dragons were real…and there was one sitting right next to her.

She pressed her hand to Torque's chest, feeling his heart beating beneath her palm. "You're beautiful."

He pulled her close, pressing his face to her hair as though he was inhaling her. Placing a hand on each side of her face, he dropped a single kiss on her parted lips. At his touch, white-hot fire scorched through her. The need for more became a burning ache and she moved closer.

She was in control of what she was doing, but at the same time, she was lost in sensation. Her body had shifted to autopilot. Every muscle was tense, every nerve on high alert. Torque's eyes locked on to hers with an intensity that took her breath away. His mouth on hers was harder this time, demanding everything she needed to give. A soft sound escaped him as he parted her lips with his tongue. A groan that came from somewhere deep in his chest. It sounded like he'd found forever.

That noise was everything Hollie had ever wanted. Her whole body vibrated with pleasure as she slid a hand behind his head. Heat built in the pit of her stomach, radiating outward until the pressure became a sweet, unbearable pain. The air around them crackled with electricity as Torque's tongue caressed hers.

Hollie came alive in the storm that broke over her. Torque's touch sent a lightning bolt straight to her heart. She gave herself up to the tempest, allowing it to consume her, emerging on the other side of a moment that changed her life.

When she raised her head and looked into Torque's eyes, she saw confirmation of her own thoughts. "I haven't changed my mind, Torque. I still want you."

Chapter 7

Even though Hollie had accepted his true identity, there were still reasons why Torque needed to keep his distance. No matter how strong this attraction was, Khan was right. There were too many barriers between them. Hollie had a regular job, Torque was a celebrity. She was mortal, he was immortal. She was human, he was a dragon. So many lifestyle differences to overcome.

That was before he even started on the sorceress and seer who had sworn to destroy Torque and everything he touched. Happiness would never be for him, that was what Teine had told him all those centuries ago. If she couldn't have him, she would make sure no one else did.

Even as his head was reminding him of all the reasons why he should gently remove Hollie's hands from around his neck and leave the room to spend a sleepless night on a sofa, Torque's lips were returning to hers. Over and over.

It didn't matter what his rational self tried to tell him, she was in his blood. His mate was in his arms, and everything else faded away.

"Hollie…" He made one last attempt at doing the right thing.

"No more talking." She pressed a finger to his lips. "Unless it's to tell me what you like."

The sound that began deep in his chest was a groan of surrender. "You, Hollie. I like you."

Sliding a hand behind her, he eased them both down the bed until she was lying on her back and he was on top of her. Using his knee, he pushed her legs apart and settled between them as he returned to the heaven of kissing her. Tugging her lower lip between his teeth, he suckled the plump flesh before thrusting his tongue deep into her mouth. Hollie murmured with pleasure and arched up to him.

She took one of his hands in hers, sliding it under the crisp cotton of her blouse and sucking in a breath as his calloused fingers moved over the soft flesh of her stomach. When he reached the swell of her breast, Torque covered the plump mound and pushed aside the lace of her bra. Finding her nipple, he rolled it between his thumb and forefinger.

Her breathing was becoming erratic and Torque lifted his head to watch her face. A faint flush tinted her cheeks, and her eyelids were heavy. Pleasure jolted him. *Mine.*

Lifting her blouse higher, he bent his head and lightly flicked his tongue over the exposed rosy tip. Hollie shuddered with pleasure and Torque's erection jerked in response. She brought her legs up to cradle him, holding him pelvis to pelvis. When she rocked against him, Torque hissed out a warning.

"If you do that again, this won't last long."

Her laugh was shaky. "Good, because I don't think I can wait."

"Clothes." He seemed to have lost the ability to speak in sentences. "Off."

In a flurry of activity, their clothing was flung aside. When they were both naked, Torque ran his hands up from her hips to her breasts. She looked so pale and dainty in contrast to his muscular hands and arms. So why was he the one who felt helpless every time he looked at her?

He drew in a rasping breath as Hollie mirrored his movements, spreading her hands over his torso, raking her nails over his flesh. It was too much. Too much raw heat and sensation powering through his veins, flooding his whole system. He grabbed her hands, bearing her onto her back again as he moved over her. Skin on skin. Heat on heat. Pleasure spiked and demanded release.

Not yet.

He moved slowly down her body, kissing along her neck, down her collarbone, until he reached the soft flesh of her breasts. He sucked at her rock-hard nipples, biting them and flicking them with his tongue, first one, then the other. Hollie dug her nails into his shoulders, crying out in delight.

Torque slid lower, licking and nipping the curve of her waist, her jutting hip bones, and the flat plain of her belly. Gripping the inside of her knees, he tugged her legs apart, holding her open to his gaze as he kissed his way along her inner thighs. Hollie writhed wildly in his hold, lifting her hips and offering herself to him.

Torque paused, his heart expanding as he gazed at

her. She was perfection. Long-limbed, slender, pretty as a portrait. Elegance and light. Her emerald eyes glimmered at him from between half-closed lids, her lips were the color of rubies, her hair had the sheen of spun gold. The thought snagged a memory, then drifted away. There was no room for anything except his craving for her.

He wanted her so much it was an ache, but he was determined to make this moment last.

"So beautiful." Using his fingers to part her outer lips, he gazed down at her. "Pink and sweet..." He ran a finger through her center. "And so very wet."

Hollie's toes curled and her head thrashed from side to side. "Please, Torque." She buried her fingers in his hair. "No more teasing."

Obediently, he lowered his head and drew her clit into his mouth. As she began to tremble wildly, he sucked hard on the little nub. Panting, Hollie raised herself up on her elbows so she could watch what he was doing. Almost immediately, he felt her thigh muscles begin to tremble.

She threw her head back, her whole body bucking uncontrollably under the force of an instant climax. Torque didn't stop. He kept his mouth on her, circling her clit with his tongue, absorbing the ripples that crashed through her. He kept the waves coming and still continued to suck her.

"It's too much." Her voice was almost a sob. "No more, Torque, I can't..."

He eased up, slowing his movements and withdrawing gradually. His own breathing was coming harsh and fast as he moved back up the bed. Hollie gazed up at him with a dazed expression before wrapping her arms around him. Reaching a hand between them, she curved her fingers around his rock-hard shaft and stroked.

Luckily, a tiny part of Torque's brain was still clinging to a slither of reason. Leaning over the side of the bed, he snagged his discarded jeans with one hand. Hollie murmured a protest at the interruption.

"Condom."

"Are dragons always this well prepared?" Her voice was husky with a combination of laughter and residual breathlessness.

"This is my human side." He tore open the foil packet. "My dragon would choose to live dangerously."

Her hands traced molten lines of fire along the muscles of his back as he reached between them to get the protection in place. His erection felt like a steel girder, lying hot, hard and sheathed, pressing against her. Torque could feel Hollie's heart hammering a wild beat into his chest.

He couldn't wait any longer and Hollie's hands on his shoulders indicated she didn't want him to. Sliding his hands under her buttocks, he lifted her to him. She used a hand to guide him and he slammed all the way into her waiting warmth.

Hollie gave a little cry and he paused, looking down at her in concern.

She shook her head, her eyes tightly closed. "Don't stop."

He smoothed a finger over her furrowed brow. "I need to know you're okay."

"I'm okay." She opened her eyes. "It's perfect. New. Different, but perfect."

Different, but perfect. The ultimate high. If he hadn't known before that she was his mate, he knew it now. Adrenaline flooded his body, powering him into action.

He surged into her in heavy, powerful strokes. Hollie slammed up from the mattress in time with his movements. Every thrust increased the pressure, built the intensity, destroyed a little bit more of the control. Hollie went wild, writhing beneath him, clawing at his shoulders and upper arms. She called out his name, tensing as she came again.

Torque felt the tendons in his neck straining, his facial muscles pulling tight. Thrusting powerfully one last time, his body convulsed in time with Hollie's as his own climax hit. He pulsed deep inside her, and Hollie clenched around him, holding on tight. It was like lightning striking his spine and sending aftershocks along his nerve endings. The room started to spin as he rocked into her, gasping out her name. Everything faded except this. His heart was ready to burst. He couldn't believe he'd wasted so much of his life not experiencing this delicious joy.

Gradually, he came back down to earth. He could draw a breath, his heart was starting to beat normally. But he would never be the same again.

Returning from the bathroom, Torque lay on his side facing Hollie. Gently, he brushed long strands of hair back from her face. A glimmer of a smile touched her lips when he leaned over, kissing her lightly.

She turned into his embrace, her eyes widening as her gaze traveled down his body. "Um, is this a dragon thing?"

He was harder than ever. Huge and throbbing. "I'm a dragon, but this has never happened to me before."

She ran her tongue along her lower lip. "I'm human... but I feel the same. I still want more."

As Torque reached for another condom, her blood

felt like honey, running thick, slow and sweet through her veins. What she was feeling went beyond arousal. A thousand wonderful sensations blossomed from Torque's touch, warming from her toes to her fingertips. Her naked skin was fever-hot, and the cooler air in the room felt like ice in contrast.

Patience wasn't an option. They both needed fast and hard. Hollie didn't stop to question why. This was her new reality. Her new perfection.

She pulled Torque toward her and he pressed deep inside, muffling a groan as he began to pump his hips.

"Too good." His lips crushed hers as they rocked together.

Her own breath caught at the back of her throat. How could it be even better? She ground her pelvis against his, lifting to meet him, matching his demands.

When he pulled out, she called his name, trying to draw him back to her. Flipping her over onto her front, he drew her hips up so she was on her hands and knees. "Oh, yes."

She spread her knees wider, arching her back as he moved into position and drove into her from behind. He felt even bigger and thicker from this angle and she pushed herself up as he buried himself to the hilt. He held her steady as he pistoned into her in a series of frenzied thrusts. The pressure built, instantly taking her to the breaking point. Hollie clutched at the bedcovers, helpless to do anything other than hang on.

Barely recognizing the animal sounds that issued from her lips, she jerked, letting out a strangled gasp as every part of her body constricted and then slowly released in shuddering, luscious waves. Her eyelids fluttered shut as she shattered into a million pieces, writhing in place for a few seconds before going limp.

Torque gave a low growl of appreciation, his grip tightening just enough that his nails bit into her skin.

"Feels like heaven when you come around me," Torque murmured, grinding his pelvis against her.

Hollie gasped and shuddered through her climax as he thrust harder and faster. He drove in hard one last time and held himself taut. Then his whole body started to shake and he buried his head in her neck, nipping the skin lightly with his sharp teeth before collapsing on top of her.

As his hands slid away from her hips, Hollie sank forward. Torque slipped to one side of her, draping an arm over her back.

"I don't know what just happened." His fingertips were warm and slightly rough along her spine.

She turned her head to look at him. "Nor do I, but it was wonderful."

His expression lightened and he reached out a finger to touch her cheek. "It was, wasn't it?"

Her body was reeling and her head was spinning. This was Torque, the man she had worshiped from afar for years. He had also just confessed to being a dragon. She really needed to take some time to process what had become of the life she thought she knew. But she couldn't. Not while Torque was looking at her with a touch of anxiety in his expression. As if he was afraid he hadn't met her expectations.

She traced the perfect lines of his lips with her finger. "I want more of that."

He looked startled. "Now?"

She laughed. "Maybe not immediately, but sometime soon."

"I promise you there will be more and it will be soon." He drew her close and she wrapped her arms around his neck. "And dragons always keep their promises."

Lying in the semidarkness with him felt comfortable and right. And un-dragon-like. "Where are you from?"

"It's a long story."

She tilted her head to look at him. At the bladelike planes of his face and the grim set of his lips. "I'm not going anywhere."

A corner of his mouth lifted. "I'll tell you the abridged version. It began when the world was young and time was new, when elves and faeries walked the earth without hindrance. When humans understood the need for magic and sorcerers were all-powerful. In the land now known as Scotland, a sorceress reigned over the Highlands. One day, she entered a cave and spoke the words of a spell. The ground shook and split and flames roared up from the cracks. When the blaze died down, there were two huge eggs in its place, one white and one black. The following day, the eggs hatched into two dragons. The white one was the Cumhachdach, or the mighty, and the black was the Moiteil, or the proud. They were the founders of the first of the Scots dragon-shifter clans."

"Clans?" She tilted her head to look at him. "Like a family?"

"Exactly." He traced circles on her shoulder with the palm of his hand. "I am the only remaining member of the Cumhachdach."

Although his voice was neutral, she knew, from the tension in his body, that this was not a subject he wanted to discuss. Leaning on one elbow, she pressed her lips to his and felt him relax slightly.

"Maybe we should get some sleep? I have some plans for later that may need you to conserve your strength."

He smiled, drawing her back down to him. "I'm not good at sleeping, but I'll gladly watch while you get some rest."

When they were able to get back into Torque's apartment building, Hollie took time out to view the damage. It was minor and the concierge explained his theory that a bogus delivery driver had started the blaze.

"The guy gave me a stack of paperwork to fill out. When I'd finished it, he was gone. Soon after that, the fire alarm went off." The concierge showed them the point where the fire had started. "He didn't think it through. This lobby is mostly marble—it's not going to burn easily. And a building like this is going to have a sophisticated fire prevention system."

"It doesn't sound like the Incinerator," Torque said when they were alone again. "He's good at this. Surely, if he wanted to burn this place down, he wouldn't make any mistakes."

"It was him." Hollie sounded certain. "This was just to let us know he's in town."

When they reached the apartment, she took his hands in hers. Standing on the tips of her toes, she reached up and drew his head down until their lips were almost touching. Torque was enchanted by her, bound to her body and soul. He'd even managed to get a few hours of sleep with her in his arms. It seemed Hollie's presence was the antidote to Teine's centuries-old insomnia spell.

"I want you to do something for me." Her voice was a whisper.

"Anything."

"Show me this legendary paperwork of yours."

"I can think of other things we could be doing." He slid his hands down to her waist.

"I'm guessing that's the laid-back attitude that got you in this administrative mess." She took his hand and led him toward the room he used as a study. "I'll strike a deal with you. Let me see what I'm up against, and then I'm all yours."

He gave an exaggerated sigh. "You're strict."

She grinned mischievously. "Well, if *that's* what you want…"

This was what his life had been missing. This easy, comfortable warmth. When they'd woken up that morning, he wondered if things would be awkward. It wasn't exactly an everyday situation. How would they deal with the whole human-dragon thing? But they'd slipped into their own natural rhythm. Maybe it was pretense. They were living in the moment and ignoring the big stuff—the crazy guy lurking in the shadows, the imbalance in their DNA, the ridiculous age difference, that whole mortal-immortal, dragon-human thing—but they were having fun. And Torque had forgotten about fun. He was one of the most famous men in the world, and he was enjoying himself for the first time in… He tried to remember.

A thousand years? Two? It didn't matter. He was going to relish these precious moments, even though he knew they couldn't last.

Half an hour later, Hollie was seated on the rug with paper piled all around her and a look of intense concentration on her face. Torque, who had wandered away to the kitchen, returned with sandwiches and soda.

"Am I beyond salvation?" he asked as he joined her on the floor.

"Pardon?" Hollie looked up with a frown. "Oh, no. I didn't realize the sheer quantity of mail you get. No wonder you don't reply. Why haven't you employed someone to deal with it before now?" She took a bite of her sandwich before answering her own question. "Ah, I see. Privacy. I'll send a standard letter to most of these."

"It's more than I was going to do." Torque nodded at his laptop. "And there are the emails."

"As I go through it all, I'll search for anything that could be from the Incinerator." She stretched her arms above her head. "I may see clues you didn't. Did you never see the connection? That there had been fires in the towns you'd visited?"

"When we're on tour, it's a whirlwind. We visit a town, do a performance and move on. Never look back." He grimaced. "I hate to say it, but I'm not great at keeping up with the latest news. If it's not front and center in the headlines, I don't read it. If these fires really were a tribute to me, I haven't been very appreciative. I honestly didn't notice."

Hollie tapped a finger on one of the stacks of paper. "If I'm right and you are the connection, I think the Incinerator will have told you. Somehow he, or she, will have sent you a message. But it's unlikely to be straightforward. He's not going to confess up front. For one thing, he wouldn't be that stupid. And for another, it's more fun to keep us guessing."

Torque regarded her in fascination. "You talk as though you know him."

"In a way, I do. I've never seen his face, but I've been inside his head." The corners of her mouth pulled down. "It's not a nice place to be."

"You said you have no family. Is that true, or was it part of your undercover role?" Torque asked.

"No, it was true. Other than my last name and why I was in Addison, I didn't tell you any lies. My parents were killed in a car crash when I was a baby and I was raised by my grandmother. She died five years ago. I never knew any other members of my family."

"So neither of us has any clan?" Torque linked his fingers through hers, enjoying that immediate connection of her hand in his. "But you have your friend? The one you needed to check in with?"

"Ah." A faint blush stained her cheeks pink. "That's another thing I was less than truthful about. McLain is my boss. I was calling to let her know what was going on with my investigation." A frown pulled her brows together. "But she's disappeared."

"You mean you can't get in touch with her?"

"No, she's actually gone missing. I spoke to one of my colleagues and he told me McLain hasn't been seen since I went undercover." She lifted worried eyes to his face. "And my apartment building burned down at the same time."

Torque sat up straighter. "What? Why the hell didn't you tell me?"

"Um…I was undercover, remember?"

"But—" He ran a hand through his hair. "You lost your *home* and I didn't know about it? My God, Hollie."

His every instinct was on high alert, his emotions strained to the point of breaking. This was his mate, and she was being threatened. Her home had been destroyed and *he should have known*. Even if his human had no clue, he was half dragon and he should be doing more to take care of her.

"I can't help thinking the Incinerator is behind both those things," Hollie said.

"It certainly seems suspicious." Torque forced himself to remain calm, to keep the conversation going, even though he wanted to let his inner dragon loose, to snort smoke and belch fire and find the person who was responsible for the scared look in Hollie's eyes. "But it could be a coincidence. What does your colleague think?"

"Dalton? He wants me to go back, so the team can take care of me." A faint smile lit the depths of her eyes. "I didn't mention that I have you to do that for me."

"I can't imagine the FBI would approve of one of their agents consorting with a dragon-shifter."

"And Dalton definitely wouldn't." Torque raised inquiring brows, and she went on to explain further. "We dated a few years ago and although it was well and truly over at the time, I sometimes wonder if Dalton got that message." She shifted into professional mode. "Other than a crazed fan, can you think of anyone who could be the Incinerator?"

Torque hesitated. He'd come this far. Hollie knew who he was and she had accepted him. More than that, she still desired him. The thought made his whole body thrum. She had received the information that she would be traveling around the country with a group of shape-shifters with raised brows, but she had taken it well. Could he take that next step? Tell her all of it?

Aware Hollie was watching him in concern, he drew a breath, unsure of what he was about to say until the words came out. "No, can't think of a single one."

Was it his imagination, or did he see disappointment in those emerald eyes? He consoled himself that he was telling the truth. Teine was dead. He had seen her die. The sorceress who killed his family had felt the full force of Torque's own dragon fire before she plunged into a ravine.

"Torque?" Hollie's voice pulled him back from his recollections.

"Yes?"

"I said that once I'd seen what I was up against, I'd be all yours." She placed her sandwich down and crawled across the floor toward him.

With his lap full of Hollie, there was no room in his head for bad memories. His fingers moved to the top button of her blouse. "All mine." Right there, right then, it was the only thing that mattered.

Chapter 8

The stage was set on a huge island in the center of the stadium, bathed in brilliant white light. Hollie thought it had the appearance of something that had dropped there from outer space. She had been to many concerts, but this time it felt like there were too many people crammed into the vast arena. The crowd surged in a relentless wave like the ocean during a high tide. The band's iconic, sign-of-the-beast logo was everywhere.

The sound level was off the scale. Her eardrums were coping at a point just short of pain. She had arrived at the venue in the car Torque sent for her and she had been able to hear the pulse of the music through the surrounding streets as she approached. Now she could feel it in her blood. The ground beneath her feet moved in time with Diablo's drumbeats, each vibration passing up through her body. Even her teeth were chattering along with Beast's music.

Onstage, the band members were a constant burst of passion and energy, their gymnastics and pyrotechnics growing wilder with each number. Khan was as outrageous as ever, but it was Torque who drew Hollie's attention. His hyperactivity was more evident than ever. Never still, he wore a path across the stage as he ran back and forth, leaping, gyrating, scissor-kicking and diving. As he moved, explosions and fireballs followed him. He was electrifying, and Hollie, standing to one side of the stage with Ged and the security team, knew she wasn't the only one who thought so. The crowd was going wild throughout the whole performance, but it was Torque who drew the most applause.

The atmosphere was euphoric. Hollie looked out across the sea of bodies. The familiar fingers at the side of the head, the devil-horn gesture, were everywhere. She had no real expectation of noticing one person, or singling out anyone acting suspiciously in such a mass of people. There was no way of knowing if the Incinerator even attended Beast's concerts before moving on to set his fires.

The security team and police had been alerted about the danger. She wondered whether there were FBI agents here. How much had McLain shared before she went missing? Did the Incinerator team in Newark even know about the Torque connection? Maybe that was something she should ask Dalton. Except that would bring the whole investigation crashing down on them. She didn't want to do that to Torque and his friends. Putting them under that sort of scrutiny would be the worst kind of torture. She wasn't ready to do it. Not yet.

She was the person who knew the most about the Incinerator. For the last four years they'd been trying to catch him using conventional methods. Now that she knew there was a paranormal element to the case, perhaps that explained why they'd been unsuccessful. With Torque at her side, she might have a better chance of catching him by unconventional means. She at least wanted the chance to try.

Hollie knew Torque was holding out on her. When she asked him if he knew of anyone who could be the Incinerator, she had seen his hesitation. She had seen his pain, as well. He had lived for centuries and experienced many things about which she could only speculate. Maybe she shouldn't be shocked that his life story included deep troughs, but the depths of agony in his eyes had shocked her. It had also hurt her. She wanted to take it away, to soothe him. The only way she knew how to do that was with her presence.

She hid a smile. It seemed to work. Torque was *very* appreciative when she distracted him with her body. And who knew sex with a dragon could be so incredible? If it wasn't for the Incinerator lurking in the background, she'd be having the time of her life.

This concert was the start of the tour. Right after this, they'd be getting on the bus, the one the band called the Monster, and driving to a hotel in Philadelphia, ready for their performance there on the following night.

The Incinerator would follow them. She knew that with absolute certainty. And he would target her again. Ged had tightened security around all of them, and Hollie could barely move without a muscle-bound security guard at her side. The arsonist had been part of her life for a long time. Now it felt like she could almost reach out a hand and touch him. She was getting close, but he was still in the shadows.

Ged touched her arm and gestured to the exit, indicating that the band was about to start its final number. The crowd reached frenzy level as Hollie, flanked by two huge guards, followed Ged out of the stadium.

The Monster was unlike any bus Hollie had ever seen. More a traveling hotel than a vehicle, it had every luxury the band could cram into it. In addition to a comfortable living area and a smaller room that Ged used as an office, it had a well-stocked kitchen, a shower room, two restrooms and a long narrow hall lined with bunks. Torque had explained that they used hotels when they could, but the bus was their home away from home when they were on the road.

"Just be glad we're not on the Monster overnight." Ged held up the coffeepot, but Hollie shook her head. "The postconcert high is usually a killer. It can take hours for the band to come down."

"I'm not surprised." Hollie took a seat on one of the surprisingly comfortable sofas. "That sort of performance must use up some energy."

She was conscious of his penetrating gaze as he sat opposite her. "Torque told you who we are."

"Yes." There didn't seem to be much else to say.

"And you're okay with that? With us?"

She smiled. "I'd have been running in the opposite direction if I wasn't."

He laughed. "I guess you would. I'm glad you're here. For Torque. What happened to him was..." He seemed to be searching for the right word. "Devastating."

Hollie didn't know what to say. Should she explain that she didn't know what he meant? If she asked him for details, it would feel like a betrayal of Torque, who clearly didn't feel ready to tell her more. She was saved from any further embarrassment when the five band members burst onto the vehicle.

Ged was right about their postperformance energy levels. Although Torque came straight to Hollie, the other four were almost ricocheting off the sides of the bus with elation as they relived the atmosphere of the concert.

Dev pulled bottles of beer from the cooler and tossed them around. "Let's party."

"Let's not." Ged's voice was stern. "You have another concert tomorrow night, remember?"

"Ah." Dev sank back onto the sofa, chugging his beer. He quirked a brow at Hollie. "It's like high school around here, but without the long holidays."

"I think of it more as kindergarten," Ged said. "Tantrums, throwing up, eating and drinking the wrong things, taking each other's toys…"

Hollie laughed, snuggling closer to Torque as he placed an arm around her shoulders. "Is it always like this?"

"This is mild. Wait until Khan and Diablo try to kill each other."

"That's a joke, right?" She looked at the lead singer, who was almost horizontal on one of the sofas, and the drummer, who appeared lost in his own world.

Finglas, who had overheard, shook his head. "Happens at least once a day. It used to be more often before Khan got married and calmed down."

"Pass me one of those beers." Hollie gestured to Dev. "I don't usually drink much, but it looks like I might need to start."

As she spoke, the engines roared into life and the gigantic bus rolled out into the traffic. She was touring with Beast, a rock band of shape-shifters, and she had no idea where this adventure would take her.

* * *

Hollie couldn't sleep. The touring lifestyle didn't agree with her. After Philadelphia, Beast had performed in Pittsburgh, Cincinnati and Chicago. Now they were spending three nights in—her mind went blank. *Where am I?* Nashville. That was it. The home of country music was hosting a huge music festival, and Beast was one of the headline acts.

Leaving Torque, the self-styled insomniac, sprawled across the bed, she went into the sitting room of their suite and powered up the laptop. Torque had two email addresses. One was personal, the other belonged to his public persona. Hollie was simultaneously working her way through the stack of paper and his emails.

"I'm surprised Ged doesn't employ someone to take care of all this," she had said, referring to the fan mail. "You know, just have everything go through a management company."

"He does. Somehow people still manage to find me."

That had worried her. All these people had been able to contact him with ease. Once she had dealt with this backlog, she was going to tighten up his online security.

She started reading. Most of the emails were easy to answer. She was able to send the standard reply she'd composed—including an apology for the delay—before archiving the conversations. It had been the same with the letters. Most of the communications were genuine expressions of admiration.

Ged had been right about the extreme messages. Hollie thought she had seen everything when it came to fire, but some of these letters and emails opened her eyes to new extremes. From confessions of sexual arousal and sadism linked to fire, to occult and devil worship, they explored the darkest aspects of the human psyche. Some of them came close to threatening Torque, demanding he should share their fantasies.

She had started a database labeled *Possibilities*, listing the important information from each message and cross-referencing it to what she knew about the Incinerator. There was nothing that made her suspect the arsonist was among them. Maybe she was missing something.

She'd been working steadily for about an hour when she came across a message that made her pause.

Dark mists roll down the valley, blackened snow cloaks the peaks. Will ye no return again? The score remains unsettled, *mo dragon*, the fire unquenched.

Hollie frowned as she reread the words. There was no greeting and no signature. It was the date that made her pulse quicken. This email had been sent just over a year ago, but it was a forwarded message. The original had been sent three years earlier. Just before the first Incinerator attack.

The sender was Losgadh@ykl.com. A quick search revealed that ykl was an obscure internet provider with physical offices located in the United Kingdom. *Losgadh* was the Scots Gaelic word for "burning."

A prickle of awareness started at the base of her spine, working its way up until it lifted the hairs on her neck. For the first time ever, she felt like she had an insight into who the Incinerator might be. There was a motive here. The profiler had said the chances that the arsonist was a woman increased if revenge was the reason for the attacks. Did unrequited love count? Because that was what this message sounded like. She tapped a fingernail on the screen, following that thought. There was no clue that the writer was a woman; it could just as easily have been sent by a man.

She was still frowning over the message when Torque appeared in the doorway. He wore sweatpants and was bare-chested and bleary-eyed, his long red hair rumpled.

"Missed you." The words were uttered on a yawn and a stretch.

Hollie patted the seat next to her. "I need you to look at this. It may be nothing, but it intrigued me."

Torque flopped down next to her. She moved the laptop so it rested across both their knees and she pointed to the three-line message. The words had a remarkable effect on him. All trace of lethargy vanished and he sat upright as though electrified.

"No. That can't be. She's dead."

Hollie was alarmed at the look on his face. It was as if the hounds of hell had been unleashed and were pursuing him. "Who is dead, Torque?"

He raised a hand, raking his hair back from his face. "Teine, the fire sorceress. The woman who was present at my birth. The same one who imprisoned me for centuries in a cave beneath the Scottish mountains. She was also a seer and she told me I would one day find great riches. Gold, emeralds and rubies would be mine."

A dozen questions swirled around in her head at those words, but she started with the most obvious one. "What makes you think it's her?"

"*Mo dragon*. It's Gaelic for 'my dragon.' That's what she used to call me." He appeared calmer now as he re-read the message. "And the tone of that message makes it sound like it's come from her."

Hollie remained silent, waiting for him to explain. After a few minutes of silence, Torque got to his feet.

"I need to go for a walk. Some fresh air will help me clear my head."

"Can I come with you?"

He leaned down and kissed her. "I want you to."

They dressed quickly and slipped out of the hotel without being noticed. "Ged would go crazy if he knew we were out alone without protection," Hollie said as they wandered through the downtown streets.

"Hollie..." There was a distinct note of arrogance in Torque's voice. "You are with a dragon."

Even though the dawn light was just streaking the sky, there were still plenty of drinkers spilling out of bars and clubs. They walked in silence for a few blocks before Hollie spoke. "When you told me about the two dragon eggs that came out of the flames in the rock... one of them was you, wasn't it?"

"Yes. I was born from the fire that burned beneath the Highlands. I was the leader of the Cumhachdach." His lips twisted into a bitter smile. "I still am, for what it's worth."

"What do you mean?"

"Like I told you, I am the only one of my clan left alive." They had reached a low wall and Torque leaned against it. "Because Teine killed the rest of my family."

His voice was matter-of-fact, but Hollie could see the flash of pain in his eyes. Reaching out, she placed a hand on his arm. "I'm sorry."

He placed his hand over hers. "I've never been able to talk about it. Even to Ged, who was the person who rescued me from captivity. All he knew was that I was imprisoned by a sorceress. I never told him the story behind it."

"Can you tell me?" Hollie asked.

"I can try. We were the Highland dragon-shifters,

born in the fire that raged when the mighty mountains were forged. I was the first, along with Alban, the leader of the Moiteil. Our followers came later. Teine saw us as her playthings. At first there was peace between the clans. The Highlands are vast enough for two dragon clans to exist in harmony, but that didn't suit Teine. Calm and coexistence are not in her nature. Over time, she turned us against each other and we became bitter enemies, stealing each other's treasure and fighting over territory."

As he spoke, there was a faraway look in his eyes as though he was looking back into the past. "Teine would favor one of us, then the other. First Alban, then me. But over time, it became clear that I was her favorite." Torque's lips twisted into a bitter smile. "More than that, I became an obsession with her."

Hollie shivered slightly. *Obsession.* It was a word that summed up the Incinerator, and possibly the writer of that email.

"When she realized I was never going to return her love, she cast a spell on me. I was imprisoned in the very cave where I was born, destined to be Teine's pet dragon for all eternity. Once I was helpless, she wiped out the entire Cumhachdach. It gave her great pleasure to come to me each day and describe the killings. She tortured me with the details."

Hollie moved closer to him, wrapping her arms around his waist, and Torque rested his cheek against her hair. They remained that way for several silent minutes. "You said she was dead." She lifted her head to look at him.

"I saw it for myself. When Ged came to free me, I thought I was imagining things. Another person entering the cave seemed to be an impossibility, but it's what he does. Don't ask me how, but he discovers the where-abouts of shifters who are in danger, or distress, and he rescues them. I was one of the lucky ones. He got me out of the cave, but Teine appeared as we were leaving. There was no way I was going back into that prison. I breathed a stream of fire over her. She was engulfed in flames and staggered back, falling into a ravine." He pressed a fist into his open palm. "She couldn't have survived."

"But she was a sorceress. Didn't she have magic powers?"

He hunched a shoulder. "The sort that made her resistant to dragon fire and a fall from a mountain? She was good, Hollie, but she wasn't invincible."

Hollie tried out another theory. "Could the Incinerator be someone close to her? Someone who wants revenge for her death? If a family member, or someone close to her, knows you killed her, they could have sent that message."

Torque snorted. "I don't think Teine was the type to inspire loyalty. She has a twin sister, but they hated each other. Teine was fire and Deigh was ice—that's what their names mean in Gaelic—and they were opposites in every way. They stayed on their separate mountains and never met. It was a joke among the Highland paranormal community that no one had ever seen them together. I can imagine Deigh's main emotion at hearing about her sister's death would have been deep joy."

"But Deigh is still alive?"

Torque shrugged. "I assume so. The level of sorcery they had achieved made them immortal, but not invincible. Teine should have—must have—died when she was burned and fell from the mountain. As long as Deigh has avoided similar hazards, I guess, she still resides in her lonely ice palace on the mountain known as Càrn Eighe."

"What are we left with? A message that coincidentally sounds like it could be from Teine?" Hollie asked.

"That's how it looks." Torque didn't sound convinced, and his eyes, which were fixed on a point beyond her shoulder, had a hunted expression that made her uncomfortable.

"At least there haven't been any Incinerator attacks since we left New York," Hollie said.

Grasping her by the shoulders, Torque slowly turned her around. "I wouldn't be so sure about that."

Chapter 9

Torque gripped Hollie's hand tight as they walked toward the glow in the sky. He had known what it was as soon as he saw it. He was a dragon. Fire was in his blood; it pulled him the way a drug tempted an addict.

"It could be part of an organized display." Hollie shook her head. "I can't believe I just said that. We both know it's not."

She was right. There was already a large crowd gathered close to the burning building. It was an office block near the hotel where Beast was staying and just a few blocks from the concert hall where they had played on the previous night. Hollie pointed that information out to Torque as they stood behind the makeshift barrier the firefighters had erected. He nodded, pulling his beanie hat down as the group of people around them grew. The last thing he wanted was to be recognized.

The fire had taken hold fast, and every part of the

structure was blazing, with flames creeping along the roof and bursting out of the doors and windows. Even though he was watching a destructive force at work, Torque still felt the inevitable pull of attraction as he stared into the blaze. Swirling orange, red and amber, even purple. It drew him in. Called to him.

Beckoning fingers of fire licked up into the air and reached out toward the surrounding buildings, trying to catch hold and make more. More heat, more smoke, more devastation. Finding nothing to cling to, they fluttered away, rising again minutes later in another direction.

Smoke, the headiest of all scents to a dragon, tugged at his nostrils. It was diluted by burning rubber and electrical cables. Nevertheless, he inhaled it greedily. Guiltily. Getting his dragon fix, secure in knowledge that the building had been empty. The firefighters had answered that question when someone from the crowd called out. Closed for the holiday weekend.

Is this for me, Teine? A little gift for the pet dragon?

The thought brought all the humiliation and pain of the past crashing back down on him. Torque was part mortal, part dragon. Both halves of his psyche were equal, but his dragon traits had a strong influence on his human personality. He was hotheaded, energetic, arrogant and loyal. He could tick all those boxes. But he was defined by his pride. Honor was the watchword throughout the Highland shifter clans. Torque's society had rules that were built on dignity, chivalry and dragon supremacy. Teine had known that and had used it to bring him low. She had stripped him of his power as a dragon-shifter leader. That feeling of helplessness came back to him now, rising like bile in his throat.

He scanned the faces of the other onlookers, unsure

what he was looking for. If Teine had survived and she was doing this, she would be able to disguise herself in any way she chose. The sorceress he had once known could be anyone in this crowd. The middle-aged man standing slightly to one side? The youth taking tasteless selfies with the burning building behind him? The person who wasn't looking at the building at all, but who was staring at Torque and Hollie? He paused, looking again at the figure. He couldn't tell if it was a man or a woman. Most of the person's face was hidden by a hooded sweatshirt, but Torque caught a glimpse of the eyes. And a flash of venom in their depths.

As soon as Torque turned that way, the figure disappeared.

"What the...?"

Torque made a movement toward where he had seen the person. At that precise moment, there was a horrible groaning noise from the building as the roof started to collapse. The firefighters began moving everyone away from the scene. Torque, shoving his hands deep into his pockets and keeping his head down, went with the crowd, pulling Hollie along with him.

"What happened back there?" Hollie hauled on his arm. Becoming aware that she was having trouble keeping up, Torque slowed his strides to match her pace.

"I'm letting her get to me." He pressed the knuckles of one hand to his temple. "This is what Teine is good at. She gets inside your head and makes you doubt the evidence of your own eyes. Even after she's dead..." He took a breath. "It was nothing. I saw a person in the crowd. Whoever it was appeared to be watching us instead of the fire. When I looked their way, they disappeared."

"Disappeared, as in walked away? Or disappeared, as in vanished?"

"Back there, I'd have said vanished, but I'd been staring into a fire and inhaling smoke. Both of which used to be my favorite things." He was calming down now. Seeing a fire so soon after talking about Teine must have unnerved him. That was the explanation. Had to be. The person he'd seen had just blended into the crowd.

"Used to be?" Hollie hooked her arm through his. Looking at her upturned face helped him get some perspective. They were on a regular street; there was nothing sinister about the people walking past them. He could breathe normally again.

"Yeah. Then I met you and they dropped down to about a hundred on the list."

"Seriously, Torque." She looked back over her shoulder at the burning building. "Do you think it was Teine?"

"Seriously?" He didn't want to answer the question truthfully. He wanted to be able to brush it aside, to go back to their hotel room, close the door and pretend the rest of the world—including arsonists and sorceresses—didn't exist. "I think it could have been."

When they had returned to the hotel after the fire, it was almost dawn. Although they had attempted to snatch a few hours of sleep, it had proved impossible. The events of the previous day had chased away any possibility of slumber, and they had lain awake talking about Teine and the most recent fire. At least the day had been a busy one. Torque had spent most of it in rehearsals while Hollie had continued to plow through his old emails.

Now it was early evening, and to Hollie's intense relief, there was no performance that night. Some of the band were going out to a steak house, but others were catching up on sleep. Torque had gone with the early night option and they'd ordered room service. Having halfheartedly eaten some food, Hollie had decided she could no longer put off the task she'd been dreading. But she'd been standing in the bedroom, staring at her cell phone for at least ten minutes. Even though she'd rehearsed what she was going to say a dozen times, none of the words and phrases sounded reasonable. If she was truthful, all of them would sound crazy to her.

That's because all of this is *crazy.*

Blaming her reluctance on tiredness didn't work. She had been catapulted into a world that was wonderful, but that broke every rule of sanity.

Even without the inability to decide what to say, she was torn in two directions about calling Dalton. She desperately wanted to know if there was any news about McLain. And, of course, it would be good to find out how the Incinerator team was progressing with their inquiries. The ideal situation would be that they had arrested someone over this latest fire and the nightmare was over. She knew that wasn't going to happen, but it was nice to indulge in that brief moment of hope.

Hollie didn't want to call him because that other world was too far away. Her old life was another time and place. Since the last time she saw Dalton, she had fallen for a rock-star dragon-shifter. It was a pretty big lifestyle change and she felt like she no longer had anything to say to the people she'd once known. Although she still wanted to catch the Incinerator, she had no wish to go back to the things she'd once thought of as normality.

Anyone learning what had happened to her would have a reasonable cause to believe she'd undergone some sort of brainwashing. If Dalton got even a glimpse of her whereabouts and her companion, he was likely to suspect she'd parted company with her reason. But Hollie—sane, practical, *scientific* Hollie—had never been more sure of anything. She belonged with Torque.

Eventually, she decided the best way to do this was to just make the call and see where the conversation took them. Dalton was a friend as well as a colleague. They had once been close; he cared about her, and she knew he valued her professional opinion. He would listen to what she had to say. Probably.

"Hollie, my God. I've been out of my mind with worry."

He didn't have to say it, she could hear it in his voice. "Dalton, I'm fine."

"You need to tell me where you are right now, or go to the nearest field office." She could picture him pacing up and down as he was talking. "It doesn't matter where you are, I'll come and get you."

"Dalton, did you hear me? I said I'm fine." She didn't know whether to be touched, or irritated, at the depth of his concern.

"Hollie, we found a dead body in the burned-out ruin of your apartment."

It wasn't just the words that rocked her back on her heels; it was the change of pace from Dalton. Blunt, harsh, totally emotionless. If he was going for shock tactics, he was succeeding.

"Wh…what?"

"Specifically, she was in your bedroom." He waited a moment or two to let the information sink in. "And that's not all."

"No." Hollie didn't want to hear any more. Her mind was already filled with awful images and she had a horrible premonition about what was coming next. "Please, no."

"It was McLain."

The phone clattered out of her hand as she dropped to her knees. The edges of her vision went dark and she was only vaguely aware of Torque, alerted by the noise, coming into the room.

"She'll call you back." Torque ended the call to Dalton before lifting Hollie off the floor and carrying her to the bed.

As soon as he placed her on the mattress, the whole room began to spin wildly and Hollie bolted upright, covering her mouth with one hand. She just made it to the bathroom in time. With her whole body shaking violently, she leaned over the lavatory as her stomach emptied its contents. After a few minutes, she felt able to stand up, rinse her mouth and wipe her face. On legs that still felt wobbly, she returned to the bedroom.

Torque was sitting on the bed, an expression of concern on his face. "What happened?"

"My boss..." Her throat felt raw and she was still shaking like a leaf in a high wind. Her mind was playing a series of images of McLain. First there were the good pictures. McLain in the office, sipping her megastrength coffee while she jabbed a finger to make a point. McLain when they'd gone on an occasional night out, drinking and letting her hair down. McLain when they got a result, buying donuts and high-fiving her team. But other images kept intruding. McLain lying dead on Hollie's bedroom floor, her body blackened by fire...

"Slowly." Torque took her hands, and his touch acted

like a balm. Drawing her down next to him, he placed his arm around her shoulders and pressed his lips to her temple. "When you're ready."

"She's dead." The words came out on a gasp. "Burned. By the Incinerator. In my apartment."

His fingers tightened on her shoulder. The tears came then and she turned her face into his chest, unable to halt the storm of grief, shock and rage that took hold of her and flung her about like a rag doll. Vaguely conscious of Torque holding her and murmuring words of comfort, she clung to him. Guilt screamed inside her head.

Eventually, she straightened and took the wad of Kleenex Torque held out to her. Blowing her nose and wiping her streaming eyes, she tried to confront what she knew.

"This is because of me." She fought down a fresh wave of tears as she said the words. "I took the investigation in this direction. If I hadn't uncovered the link to you—if we hadn't met—McLain would still be alive."

"Hollie." Torque took both her hands in his. "You told your boss your findings because you are good at your job. And you were right. No matter how horrible this is, it proves that I *am* the link to these fires."

She nodded miserably. "By coming into your life, I've made things worse. The Incinerator doesn't like it."

"We can't live by the Incinerator's rules. This is probably not something you want to talk about right now, but I wonder why your boss had to die."

Hollie frowned, trying to follow what he was saying. "What do you mean?"

"From what you've told me of this case so far, the other deaths have been incidental to the fires. The people who died were tragically trapped in the place the

Incinerator chose. But this couldn't be more personal. You have no family, so he, or she, targeted someone who was close to you. It's a powerful message."

"I don't know." Hollie was having trouble following that train of thought. "I have a few friends, people I socialize with. McLain and I occasionally went out for a drink together, but our working relationship was clearly defined. She was in charge and we never became good friends because we didn't cross those boundaries. If the Incinerator wanted to send me a message, why would he pick her? Why not Dalton, the guy I called earlier? Of my work colleagues, I'm closer to him than to anyone, I guess."

"Who knows how it happened? I'm speculating now, but maybe he saw an opportunity and grabbed it?" Torque said. "I'm assuming she didn't die in the fire?"

"I don't know." Hollie cast a look of distaste in the direction of her cell. "I need to call Dalton back to find out the details. I grayed out right after he told me McLain was dead."

"Do you want me to stay with you?"

She nodded gratefully, wondering how she had ever gotten by without his strength. But she had never dealt with anything like this. Although her grandmother's death had been a sad time in her life, it had come at the end of a long illness. Sorrow had been combined with relief, and Hollie had dealt with the trauma in her usual, practical way. Nothing had ever derailed her like this. The sensation that someone else was in control and that person's venom was directed at her was terrifying.

Torque's presence sustained her as she called Dalton back.

"Who was that guy?" Dalton's voice was harsh, giving her no time to speak. "What's going on, Hollie?"

"I'm safe and I'm with friends. That's all you need to know."

"Are you kidding me?" He shouted the words so loudly she shifted the phone away from her ear. The action brought a frown to Torque's face and Hollie shook her head slightly to indicate everything was fine. She guessed she'd react the same way if she was in Dalton's place and he was the one who'd gone missing.

"Dalton, listen to me. I promise I will keep in touch so you know I'm not in any danger. Right now you can help me by telling me how McLain died."

"She was too badly burned."

Hollie could hear him battling to get his emotions under control.

"There was no way of knowing..." He took an audible breath. "The medical examiner identified her from dental records."

Hollie closed her eyes, letting the horror of that information sink in. "Have you any more information about the fire in which she was found?"

"Apart from McLain's body, it had all the signs of being a classic Incinerator attack." Thankfully, Dalton had calmed down and slipped into professional mode. "We need you here, Hollie. No one can analyze this the way you can."

"There are three other fires you may want to look at, if you aren't already considering them as part of the Incinerator investigation. Do you have a pen and paper?" She knew Dalton. He wouldn't have a pen and paper.

"Um...hold on."

Hollie rested her head on Torque's shoulder as she listened to the sound of long-distance rummaging.

"Go ahead."

"The first fire was at the Pleasant Bay Bar in Addison, Maine. A week later there was a small blaze in the lobby of the Tribeca Trinity apartment building. It only made the local news, but it was almost certainly set by the Incinerator. Then tonight, the head office of the Go Faster Cargo Company in Nashville was the target."

"You want to tell me how you know this? Or if there's a link between these three fires that I should be aware of?"

Hollie paused. The question instantly pulled her in two. She had told McLain about the Incinerator's link to Torque. Instead of sharing that suspicion with the rest of the team, her boss had come up with the plan to send Hollie undercover. It had been McLain's way of keeping the possibility that one of the most well-known men on the planet could be their suspect. Her decision on how to proceed would have depended on what Hollie discovered.

Right now it appeared that the only people who knew about the potential connection were Hollie and the members of Beast. Dalton was asking her to make a choice between her two worlds. If she told him the truth and admitted what she knew, she would be choosing her professional world. Keeping quiet would be about her own private motives, reasons that were entirely to do with the man at her side.

There was that feeling again. That deep-seated unease. It was the same additional sense that told her she could trust Torque. She had no idea where it was from. All she knew was she couldn't ignore it. She consoled herself that she wouldn't be lying to Dalton if she ignored his question. After all, nothing had been *proved*.

"I have to go now. Just one final thing...don't ignore the possibility that the Incinerator may be a woman."

Aware that she had left out the key piece of information, she ended the call. *The woman you are looking for may have magical powers.* She could predict Dalton's reaction. It would be exactly the same as her own would have been before she'd met Torque. To be fair, Dalton was likely to be more measured in his response. She'd have advised the person offering that information to seek medical help.

Sighing, she nestled closer in the circle of Torque's arms. "This is hard."

"Why don't we get out of here?" He gripped her chin lightly with his fingers, tilting her face up to his. "Your choice. What do you want to do, right here, right now?"

"Anything?" Would he go with it? She wouldn't know if she didn't ask him.

The iridescent lights in his eyes shone brighter. "Tell me your wildest fantasy."

"I want to see you as a dragon."

Chapter 10

Shifting in a built-up area was risky, but Torque had checked a map of the local area. There were a few islands on Percy Priest Lake, which was just outside the city. He made some calls, organizing a cab to take them there and a fishing boat so they could get out to one of the islands.

Hollie watched him with an expression that was somewhere between laughter and astonishment. "I wondered if you might be reluctant to do this."

"Hollie, I told you I need you to see the real me." He took her face between his hands. "If you're sure that's what you want?"

"I want all of you. The human you. The dragon you." She grinned mischievously as she led him to the door. "Let's go. I can't wait for you to breathe a little fire on me."

He groaned. "That's the sort of talk that would have

had a white knight on a charger seeking me out and trying to slay me back in medieval times."

They traveled down in the elevator to the hotel lobby. Torque donned his hat and shades, tucking his trademark fiery hair inside his denim jacket.

"Nobody would dare slay you these days. Dragons are cool," Hollie said. "They feature in books, movies, games, comics…" She ticked them off on her fingertips.

"There are worse things than being slain." Torque's face was serious. "Imagine what it would be like if my identity became known. You think I'd be left in peace? I'd end up in a research facility. Or a zoo."

The corners of Hollie's mouth turned down. "I never thought of that. No wonder you work so hard to protect your anonymity."

The traffic was light and the cab journey took less than half an hour. When they reached the lake, Torque told the driver he would call him when they wanted to be collected. He led Hollie to the water's edge, where a motorboat was waiting for them.

"There are advantages to the celebrity lifestyle," he said as he helped Hollie into the little craft. "One of them is that you can call up a local fishing charter company and hire a boat at short notice. Of course, I paid twice what the damn boat would cost to buy, just for a few hours' use."

He started the engine and the boat was soon skimming over the moonlit waters. Behind them the edge of the lake, with its rocky shoreline, began to fade. They passed a few small islands before they reached a larger one. It was roughly horseshoe in shape, covered in spiky pine trees, and with a jagged cove into which Torque steered the vessel.

When they stepped onto the land, it was fully dark

and a breeze was blowing off the lake. Torque pulled the boat up onto the pebbly shore. Before they set off, he had made sure that this was one of the islands that wasn't used by campers. He really didn't want to spark a major news story about a dragon sighting over the local tourist area.

There was a clearing in the center of the small land mass that was surrounded by trees, and Torque paused there. Casting a measuring eye over the ground, he nodded. There would be just about enough distance for him to spread his wings and take flight.

"Do you need to do anything?" Hollie asked. "Any rituals? Incantations to help you get in the zone?"

"I'm a human *and* a dragon," Torque explained. "Both beings are inside me all the time. I don't need to make an effort to find either of them. The word *shifting* perfectly describes what happens. It's a simple change from one to the other."

"And you don't mind that I'm here…watching you?" She gripped her lower lip between her teeth.

He took her hand and placed it on his chest, letting her feel his heart. The organ that powered his human and dragon selves. "I want you to see me. All of me." He grinned. "And now I have to remove my clothes."

The air chilled his skin as he stripped the layers of garments away. What he'd told Hollie was true. Shifting was in his DNA. Although it was magical, there was no skill or mystery to it. As he closed his eyes, Torque tried to remember the first time he had shifted. It was lost in the mists of dragon time, one of those memories of his Highland home he had put aside because it pained him to think of it.

You close your human eyes, now look inside your dragon. Shrug off your human instincts. Feel the for-

est around you. Mold your body. You no longer have a foot, instead you have dragon claws. Flesh becomes scales. Breath turns to fire.

His mind ran through the swift, subtle changes as his muscles relaxed into the familiar shape of his dragon self. He was ready. With a swish of his giant tail, he crouched low on all fours and opened his eyes.

With her back pressed tight against the trunk of a tree, Hollie was gazing up at him with an expression he couldn't define. It could have been fear. He believed it was wonder.

It was probably a good time to remind herself that she had asked Torque to do this. And Hollie wanted to see him shift, but that didn't mean she wasn't nervous as hell about it. Once it started, it all happened so fast.

One minute Torque was standing naked in the moonlight. Then he shimmered before her briefly. Next thing he was gone. In his place was the dragon from the Beast concert in Marseilles. He was the most magnificent creature she had ever seen, with wings that spanned the clearing. When he lifted them, they billowed and created an updraft that blew Hollie's hair back from her face. His claws were like giant scimitars, driving into the ground as he moved. Sleek, iridescent scales covered his muscular body, each one catching the glinting light and pulsing in time with his dragon breath. Wisps of smoke issued from his elegantly carved nostrils.

Moving slowly away from the tree trunk, Hollie approached him. Even though the dragon towered over her, as she looked up at his proud features, she could see a trace of Torque still remained. A slight smile softened her face and she relaxed. This was *her* dragon. The thought made her shiver.

Reaching out a hand, she placed it on his leg. Instead of the roughness she had expected, his flesh was soft, smooth and very warm. Torque lowered his head and Hollie leaned closer, resting her cheek against his face. She stayed that way for several minutes, listening to the sound of his slow, rhythmic breathing.

"My dragon." She ran her hand along his neck and felt a tremor run through his giant body in response. "I want to see you fly."

She stepped back as, rising upon all fours, he spread his wings. Breaking into a run, Torque lifted his head toward the sky and, with a flick of his tail, was airborne. Hollie watched in wonder as he gracefully soared above her, into the darkened clouds. Circling the bay several times, he swooped low as if checking on her before climbing higher, then disappearing from view.

Hollie sank down onto the grass, tucking her knees up and resting her chin on them. She tried to analyze what she was feeling, but her emotions were like splinters of glass. Too tiny, too painful, too delicate. She reached a hand up to her cheek and found it wet with tears.

Torque was the last of his clan, the only remaining member of a noble breed of dragon-shifters. And he had trusted her with his incredible secret. It was like tasting honey and acid at the same time. He was everything she had ever wanted, and she would never be able to hold on to him.

Too much emotion had been poured into her heart, filling it to a point where it was ready to burst. The wonder of watching him shift, the joy of knowing he belonged to her, however briefly, the recognition that this was *real*…each of those was counterbalanced by a matching darkness.

Their worlds had met right here, right now, but they were dancing to the tune of the deranged fire starter who had brought them together. And when this madness ended, they would have to face reality. Just as Torque's night flight must soon come to an end, so would the dream in which they were living. They had some serious talking to do about what the future could hold for a dragon and a mortal.

The sound of beating wings alerted her to Torque's return and she tilted her face back toward the heavens. It was hard to see him until he was immediately overhead. His body blended with the velvety darkness. Then he was there. So much power in one body. The man and the dragon were both perfection. Torque circled one last time before landing. His claws churned up the grass and he used the momentum to come to a halt. As he stopped, he shifted back. When he turned to face Hollie, there was a trace of uncertainty in his eyes.

She got to her feet, going to him and wrapping her arms around his waist. "You are beautiful."

She could feel the tension leave his body. "I should get dressed."

"Not yet." Hollie rose on the tips of her toes, fitting her body more intimately to his.

"Here?" Torque's lips quirked into a smile.

"Maybe somewhere less open?"

He picked Hollie up and carried her, and his clothes, toward the shelter of the trees. She twined her legs around his waist and hooked her arms about his neck, clinging to him and kissing along his jaw as he walked. Although her body pressed tight against him was the most delicious distraction, Torque clung to the remnants of his sanity long enough to find a secluded place among the trees. No one knew better than he did what the view was like from above. While he didn't anticipate any helicopters or drones would be flying over this area, he wasn't taking any chances.

"One of us is wearing way too many clothes." He placed Hollie on the grass.

"You should probably do something about that."

The moon filtered through the trees, giving just enough light for him to see her. It reminded Torque of bygone days. Of gloomy forests and beautiful maidens and treasure untold.

He kept his gaze on hers as he undid the buttons on her blouse and pushed it down her shoulders. Hollie helped him remove it by wriggling her arms free of the garment. Torque laid her back against the ground and trailed kisses down her neck to the point where her breasts swelled above the lace of her bra.

Behind her back, his hands worked on the fastening on her bra until he was able to toss it aside with her blouse. Leaning over, he brushed featherlight kisses across one nipple, then licked the delicate pink flesh. Taking the tender bud between his lips, he sucked it gently. Hollie's back arched, her breaths coming in bursts of sharp gasps. Pausing to smile down at her, Torque moved on to the other nipple.

While he pleasured her breasts, Torque undid her jeans. Hollie lifted her hips to help him as he sat back and removed her boots, jeans and underwear. Pressing her legs apart, he knelt between them. "Your scent—" he lapped once before circling her clit with his tongue "—your taste, everything about you, is perfect."

Moving over her, he reached between their bodies and slipped two fingers inside her, caressing her as he used his other hand to circle her nub before pausing to reach for a condom in the pocket of his jeans. Once the protection was in place, he positioned himself at her entrance. Gazing down at Hollie's features in the moonlight, he felt the greatest peace and passion of his life surge through him. A treasure more than emeralds, rubies and gold. That was what she was to him. She was what Teine had foreseen he would one day find. Hollie was his dragon hoard.

As he entered her, he pressed a kiss onto her mouth. His tongue swirled around hers and Hollie caressed him back. His beautiful mortal was showing him how much she loved all of him.

Hollie raised her hips to meet him, and Torque groaned at the near unbearable pleasure. He was fighting not to rush this, but his feelings threatened to overwhelm him. He lifted her so she was fully opened to him, and she bucked her hips, matching each long, powerful thrust. Reaching around his back, she dragged her nails along his muscles.

Torque's breath came faster and harder as his thrusts grew wilder. Primal instincts overtook them both. Her cries urged him on as her ankles locked around his hips. He pulled them up higher so he could drive even deeper.

"The feeling of you wrapped around me is the most perfect dream. I want it to last forever."

Pounding faster, he felt the first spasms hit her. Hollie threw back her head, crying his name to the treetops as her body shuddered in a series of unrelenting waves.

Feeling her explode around him, Torque held her closer, thrusting once more as deep as he could. Her inner muscles clenched hard around him, triggering his own release. Torque gasped, his cock spasming wildly. Hollie's hands locked on to his shoulders, pulling him tight to her as she jammed herself against him, every part of them in contact from groin to neck. He kissed her, and she cried out into his mouth.

Hollie's eyes were closed, her cheeks flushed and her lips slightly parted. *Forever.* If there was one moment Torque could choose to last that long, it would be this one. He gazed down at her, continuing to thrust slowly, even as the storm subsided and his body softened. Never wanting to break this connection.

Finally, his movements stilled as the shuddering stopped, his breathing slowed and his racing pulse ebbed. With their lips locked in a kiss, he withdrew and rolled onto his back.

Hollie rested her head on his chest. "Is it strange, when we have a luxury suite back at the hotel, to think this is the perfect way to spend a night?"

"Every night with you is perfect."

Torque gazed up at the stars, enjoying her warm, sweet weight against him. He had no need of anything except this. Even if he searched for another immortal lifetime, he wouldn't find the same joy he felt when he looked into her eyes.

Hollie was his treasure, his dragon hoard, and he would guard the enchantment she brought him the same way he had once guarded a looted treasure from a rival clan.

After the band left Nashville, the next few days seemed to be a blur of big arenas. Hollie felt like she spent the whole time getting on and off the tour bus with barely time to eat, sleep and shower in between.

"When we get to Dallas, you can take a break," Ged said, regarding her with sympathy. "We have two performances there, but we have three nights before the first one."

Hollie stretched her arms above her head in anticipation. "You mean I get to sleep in a real bed instead of a bunk?"

Khan flung himself down on the sofa next to her. "And you won't have to listen to Diablo snoring."

The drummer threw a plastic water bottle at him, narrowly missing his head. "Can it, tiger boy."

"Is Sarange bringing Karina when she meets us in Dallas?" Hollie asked. She had seen enough of the legendary clashes between Diablo and Khan to know it was best to deflect their attention from each other.

Khan's expression changed, becoming one of delight. "Yeah. Can't wait to see my girls."

Torque was asleep on one of the bunks and Hollie had the laptop open. The marathon task of making her way through Torque's emails still occupied much of her time and she hadn't found any more messages from Losgadh@ykl.com. Although she had come across a few more items for her *Possibilities* file, nothing else shouted out to her and made her think it could be from the Incinerator.

She was so deep in her task she barely noticed the downshifting of the Monster's engine and only looked up from the screen when the vehicle came to a complete standstill.

"Where are we?" She looked out the window, but could see only an empty parking lot, surrounded by trees.

"I asked Rick to find a quiet place to stop." Ged leaned forward to look out the window. "Somewhere we have a half-decent chance of not being recognized. I want to stretch my legs and grab a burger. There's a restroom here and a small convenience store."

He called out to Rick, the head of the band's security team who was driving the bus, to give them half an hour. As the others bounded from the bus, Hollie considered joining them and decided against it. She was wearing sweatpants and a Sign of the Beast extralarge tour sweatshirt. Her hair was half in and half out of a braid and she couldn't find one of her sneakers. Life on tour with a rock band wasn't as glamorous as she'd once imagined it might be.

Torque emerged from the bedroom area looking rumpled and confused. And adorable.

"What's going on?" Since he placed a hand over his mouth to muffle a yawn, she only just managed to decipher what he was saying.

"Your friends have made a bid for freedom." She jerked a thumb over her shoulder. "The last I saw of them, they were running for the hills."

He grinned. "Burgers and coffee, huh? You want anything?"

Hollie considered the question. "Cookies. And soda." He turned to go. "And ice cream." He looked slightly alarmed and she laughed. "Don't worry, I'm stir-crazy, not pregnant."

The words hung between them for a moment, filling the atmosphere with a new sentiment. Hollie couldn't identify it. Was it a simple acknowledgment that a family would never happen for them? It felt like more. For the first time, she experienced a tug of longing for children of her own. Children she would never have. Loving Torque meant she would never be with someone else in the future. Hard on the heels of longing came regret. A deep, profound sorrow that she would never have normality with the man she loved.

"So, sugar and plenty of it?" Torque broke the loaded silence. She could see her own pain reflected in his eyes.

How many ways could she fall in love with him, only to be reminded that it couldn't last? Seeking to lighten her thoughts, she indicated her bare feet. "If I could find my other sneaker, I'd come with you."

Torque knelt to retrieve something from under the sofa. "Is this yours?" He held up the shoe she had spent hours searching for.

Hollie slipped it on. "Lead me to my sugar rush." Reaching up a hand, she felt her braid and grimaced. "On second thought, let me find something to cover this."

Torque slipped his iconic guitar-in-flames hooded sweatshirt over his head. "Will this do?"

She pulled it on and placed a hand over her heart, batting her eyelashes at him. "Torque, you don't know what this means to me."

He flapped a hand at her. "Let's go before Ged eats everything in the store." Snagging another sweatshirt from his bunk as he passed, he tugged it over his head. "Can't be too careful. You never know who's watching."

They both drew their hoods up as they exited the bus. They had almost reached the store when Torque muttered an exclamation. "Left my cash on the bus. There's a handful of notes and coins on the table."

"I'll go back for it while you order what we want." Hollie was already running back toward the bus as she spoke.

She clambered quickly up the steps, dashing into the living area. As she snatched up the money Torque had mentioned, the laptop pinged with an incoming email. Her attention was instantly caught by the address… Losgadh@ykl.com.

Holding her breath, she read the message.

Look close into the shadows, *mo dragon*. Your maiden of gold and emeralds will be the sacrifice.

She was moving fast, on her way back to Torque, when the vehicle was rocked from side to side by an explosion. Staggering from the impact, Hollie emerged from the central living area to see flames engulfing the driver's cab and licking their way along toward the kitchen.

Her fire investigator instincts kicked in. It looked like a firebomb had been thrown in through the driver's window. Turning back, she headed along the bunk-lined corridor toward the emergency exit in the rear of the bus. Before she reached it, there was a sound of glass smashing. An orange ball of flame filled the area that Ged used as his office.

Hollie was trapped in the middle of the bus and all the exits were blocked.

Chapter 11

Torque was at the counter of the convenience store when he heard the noise. He knew all the sounds fire could make, and this was the unmistakable *whumphing* of a firebomb being thrown. Instantly, the hair on the back of his neck prickled and he ran outside.

Rick had been Beast's head of security since the band became famous. Torque often wondered if he knew they were shifters. He figured the big, long-suffering guy at least knew there was something very unusual about the rock stars he guarded. Since Ged paid Rick well for his discretion, there were no questions asked on either side.

Rick's specialty was protecting the band's privacy. Instinctively, he had parked the bus under a clump of trees, as far as possible from any prying eyes inside the store. Now Torque watched in horror as flames began to pour from both the front and rear windows.

"Hollie!" He raised a hand, signaling to the others to follow him.

Breaking into a run, Torque shifted, his feet pounding the tarmac. He could hear his friends behind him. As his dragon muscles burst through, his clothing tore from his body. By the time he reached the bus, he was already in dragon form, his giant wings unfurling.

Hovering a few feet above the burning vehicle, he hooked his claws into one end of the metal roof, rolling it back like the lid of a tin can. Throwing the torn metal aside, he lowered his head to get a better view of the interior of the bus. The driver's cab was fully alight and the rear appeared to have recently started to burn.

Hollie was in the living area, in the center section. Crouching low to avoid the smoke, she appeared unharmed and was crawling toward the fire extinguisher. Conscious of the need to move fast before the fire reached the bus's gas tanks, Torque landed beside the vehicle. Raising one mighty claw, he ripped a hole in the side of the bus. Shifting back, he stepped through the jagged gap.

"Torque." Hollie leaped up and closed the space between them. "We don't have long."

He could tell his beloved scientist had already analyzed the situation. "Let's get out of here." He lifted her through the opening, handing her to Ged, who was waiting on the asphalt.

Getting away from the bus fast was Torque's first priority. He would worry about his nakedness and any possible witnesses later. They headed for the cover of the trees with the rest of the band following, making it just as the bus blew up. Flames spiked and black smoke billowed. Glass and metal rained down onto the parking lot.

"I didn't get your ice cream," Torque said as he pulled Hollie down onto the grass with him.

She stared at him for a moment, her eyes huge and round; then she started to laugh. At first he thought she must be in shock, but her amusement was genuine. He raised questioning brows at her. Shaking her head, she pointed at the bus. "It's just as well it blew up. I can't imagine what my fire investigation colleagues would make of the way you casually ripped that bus apart to get me out." She became serious. "But I'm very glad you did."

"Did you see who did it?"

"No, I didn't see anything."

Torque turned to look at his friends. "You guys?"

"Nothing." Khan looked disgusted. "Whoever did it got away fast."

That was one of the many things racing around in Torque's head, but he decided to deal with the practicalities first. "This is one of those times when it will be impossible to avoid the human forces of law and order. I'm guessing the cashier has already called them. First, we need to discover if there is security camera footage of the parking lot." He grimaced. "It would be useful to see who did this, but I don't want anyone to get hold of film of me shifting."

"I'll go check that out before the cops get here." Khan left the trees and headed toward the store.

"Meanwhile, maybe Rick could find me something to wear?" Torque asked Ged. "It isn't the first time one of us has unexpectedly lost all our clothing, but the circumstances have often been different."

Ged laughed. Beast's hell-raising exploits were legendary and Rick had often been called upon to extricate one, or more, of them from a difficult situation. "Rick can do that while he arranges alternative transport for the rest of the tour. Dev, Finglas, come with me. You can keep a lookout for the cops."

When they'd gone, Hollie turned to Torque. "This is not quite the same atmosphere as last time you were naked in the woods."

Although she made an attempt at humor, he could see the panic in her eyes. It mirrored his own alarm. Twice the Incinerator had come close to killing her. If Torque hadn't been a dragon-shifter, Hollie would have died in that blazing bus.

"There was another message. It came through just before the bus caught fire. It said you should look into the shadows and your maiden of gold and emerald would be the sacrifice." Hollie shivered as she spoke. "He, or *she*, must have been following us. That blaze wasn't started remotely."

Torque forced himself to concentrate. He had been so focused on his concern at what had just happened to Hollie, so wrapped up in the terror of losing her, that he was barely able to think straight. He had convinced himself that this attack was about her, but what if it wasn't?

"What if he thought it was me on the bus?" He was thinking out loud, the words racing ahead of his thoughts.

"What do you mean?" Hollie asked.

"You were wearing my sweatshirt with the hood pulled up. Okay, you are a lot shorter than me. But if he wasn't close, he'd have seen a figure who looked like me getting back on the bus. Alone."

Comprehension dawned on Hollie's face. "So we don't know if the target of the attack was me or you."

It didn't matter to Torque. An attack on Hollie was

an attack on him. She meant more to him than his own life. He had to stop this monster from taking control and paralyzing him with terror. Torque knew what fear could do. It could be a knife in his gut slowly twisting deeper, or a hammer pounding inside his head. Fear could shackle him...or it could drive him forward.

He drew Hollie into his arms, feeling her begin to relax as she rested her head on his shoulder. Drawing strength from her at the same time as he comforted her, he knew what he had to do. If Teine was out there, he had to find her. And he knew where to start his search.

Hollie was growing accustomed to her own capacity for dealing with the highs and lows of this new life. Her body amazed her with its capacity for absorbing shock and moving on. She suspected Torque's presence had something to do with that. He was her comfort blanket. After he had rescued her from the bus, her insides felt icy, her stomach muscles tightly contracted. Inside her chest, her heart had been an explosion waiting to happen, while her skin had been clammy, her breathing fast and hard.

Torque only had to place an arm around her and those physical symptoms receded. Within minutes, the horror had receded. It wasn't gone, but she was able to dig into her own reserves of strength and deal with it.

The practical aftermath of the bus fire was surprisingly calm. Hollie quickly learned that the members of Beast had the experience and the resources to deal with anything that came their way. Khan had discovered that there were no security cameras on the secluded area of the parking lot where Torque had shifted. That was fortunate because it meant they weren't facing a situation where the police might stumble across the biggest scandal of the century. Scrap that. A man shifting to become a dragon in rural Texas would be the biggest story *of all time*. Add in the fact that the man concerned was John "Torque" Jones, legendary guitarist with mega rock band Beast, and the world would go wild. Luckily, the cashier hadn't witnessed the incident because he had been calling 911 at the time Torque shifted.

At the same time, it was unfortunate that there was no CCTV. If they had been able to get their hands on any film before the police arrived, they might have been able to see who was responsible for the attack. The cashier confirmed that no one had been into the rest stop convenience store in the half hour prior to Beast's arrival. Rick was adamant that, even though he had chosen a secluded location, there were no other vehicles in the parking lot when he arrived.

"If someone was following us, how did they approach the bus within minutes of us stopping if they didn't pull into the parking lot?" Torque asked. That was the puzzle to which they needed to find a solution.

Rick explained to the cashier that one of the band had been sleeping naked when the bus caught fire. The guy was a Beast fan and he had been overawed by the whole situation. The sweatpants and T-shirt he had donated were stretched taut over Torque's muscles, but at least he was covered up. As he and Hollie explored the trees behind where the bus had been parked, there was no longer a risk of him stumbling naked upon a hiker or dog-walker.

It didn't take them long to find a dirt track that ran parallel to the road leading into the parking lot.

"There." Hollie pointed to evidence of recent tire tracks. "If the Incinerator was following the bus and saw us pull off the highway into the rest stop, he could have driven down here."

There was a line of trees and shrubs between the track and the parking lot. As they pushed through knee-high, scrubby grass, Torque gestured to a flattened section. "Looks like he stopped right over there."

From the place he indicated, the whole rest stop area, including the location where the bus had been parked, could be observed.

They stood in silence for a few minutes, surveying the wreckage of the Monster. It was no longer recognizable as a vehicle. Chunks of smoldering metal lay strewn across the asphalt, and the air was thick with the smell of burning gas, oil and plastic. Some of the debris was still on fire, while acrid smoke rose in black plumes from other parts.

"He was just waiting for a chance, wasn't he?" Hollie said.

"Looks that way."

She looked back at the fresh tire tracks in the dirt. "If Teine did this, would she need to follow us in a car?"

Torque's expression was grim. "She has magic powers, but they are limited. Teine can't transport herself from one place to another. In that sense, she is as restricted in her means of travel as a human. But this?" He indicated the destruction on the parking lot. "This is the action of a human. I don't know what to think anymore, but maybe that's what she wants. Teine is good at screwing with people's minds."

Two police cruisers pulled into the parking lot, ending the opportunity for further conversation. Torque turned to look at Hollie. "This is your call. If you talk to the police about what just happened, your colleagues in the FBI will find out where you are. I can make sure the police get all the information they need without telling them you were involved. No one needs to know you were on that bus."

How far had she come? Mere weeks ago law-abiding Hollie Brennan would have been shocked at the suggestion that she would conceal information that could help with any inquiry, let alone the Incinerator case. Now she clutched at Torque's suggestion like she was drowning and he had thrown her a life preserver.

She couldn't analyze why it was so important for her to remain hidden. It wasn't as if she was doing a good job of hiding from the Incinerator. He had found her at the Pleasant Bay Bar and now, if she was the intended target, it looked like he had found her here. All she knew for sure—and it was not a sixth sense or a hunch—was that she needed to be with Torque. Whether that was for her security or her well-being, she didn't know. There was a strong possibility it could be both.

"I want to stay out of it," she said.

"Leave it to me."

Those words summed up everything about what had happened to her since she'd met Torque. No matter what else life was throwing her way, no matter how bizarre the situation, she knew she could place her life in his hands.

Hollie thought she'd coped well with everything life had thrown at her over the last few weeks. Rock stars who were really shifters, a dragon lover, attempts on her life…she'd taken them all in her stride, emerging, if not unscathed, at least quietly restrained.

But *this*? This was taking irrational to a whole new level.

"Let me get this straight. You are going to fly from

here to Scotland—*crossing the Atlantic Ocean*—and you want me to ride on your back?" Her voice was getting higher and higher as she spoke, ending in something that was close to a screech.

"It's perfect timing." Torque appeared not to notice her near stratospheric levels of incredulity. "We have a few rest days in Dallas, so we can be there and back before the next performance."

When she tried to discuss the logistics, including important things like her survival at altitude, he waved them aside. "Och, you'll be with a dragon. Trust me."

"Did you just say 'och'?" She regarded him in bemusement.

"It must be the prospect of a return to Scotland." Although he smiled, she heard a touch of apprehension in the words. Going home after all this time would be hard on him. Going home in search of answers about the woman who had destroyed his family? That had to hurt his soul. And Torque was doing this because Hollie was in danger.

She placed a hand on his arm. "I do trust you, but I can't help thinking of all the things that could go wrong. What if I fall off?"

A smile glinted in the opal depths of his eyes. "Then I'll catch you."

She believed him. He had saved her from death twice, and both times he had done it in a way that no human could have achieved. "Okay. Let's do it." She gave a squeal as Torque seized her and spun her around.

Having made this decision, Torque seemed invigorated by it. His energy levels, always high, were off the scale as he paced the hotel room, throwing items into a backpack that Hollie would carry. When they were ready to leave, they stopped by Ged's hotel room.

When Torque explained his plans, Ged regarded him with a thoughtful expression. "And you finally feel ready for this?"

"At long last, I believe so."

"Then be careful." Ged turned to Hollie. "Since Torque has no sense of time, I'm relying on you to get him back here for the next performance."

She smiled. "I'll do my best, but he's in charge of the travel arrangements."

Torque had checked a map of the area and chosen the nearby Cedar Ridge Nature Preserve as the best place to shift. They took a cab to the scenic area. As they left the vehicle and followed an isolated trail, the moon was full and round.

"Perfect for a dragon ride." Hollie's voice quivered with nerves. She still couldn't quite believe she'd agreed to this. "Sorry, bad joke."

Torque grinned. "Every night is perfect for a dragon ride."

When they found a sheltered clearing that suited his needs, Torque slipped off his clothes and handed them to her. Hollie placed them in the backpack, ready for when they reached their destination. Even though she was prepared for him to shift, Hollie still found she was holding her breath. If she lived to be a hundred, she would never tire of this moment. If only she could live to be *more* than a hundred...

Torque shifted quickly, almost impatiently. Neck stretched out and wings held high, he crouched low, waiting for Hollie.

So, we're really doing this. I'm really going to fly halfway across the world on the back of a dragon. Or die trying...

Hoisting the backpack in place on her shoulders, she

caught hold of one of Torque's wings and levered herself up onto his back. Settling into position, she straddled the base of his powerful neck, just in front of his wings.

Once she was in position, Torque spread those incredible wings to their full extent. Hollie could feel his muscles tensing in preparation. His mighty feet pounded across the ground as he broke into a run, gaining speed before launching into flight. Flattening herself tight to him, Hollie felt her face stinging as the air rushed past. When she risked a look down, her stomach swooped alarmingly. The ground dropped away as they soared above the trees, quickly reaching altitude.

It was like riding a horse bareback, with the same rocking and bucking motion, but on a larger scale. They flew up into cloud and down into clear skies. Time became meaningless, and in the darkness below her, Hollie caught glimpses of oceans and land masses, of vast cities and of mountains and rivers. Although the air around her was cool, she could stand its bite. Pressing close against Torque's scales, she let the heat of his body warm her. No, she shouldn't have been able to survive at this height. But she was riding on the back of a dragon. Nothing about this made sense. It was magic. Reason didn't come into it.

When Torque swooped and soared, it was as exhilarating as the most white-knuckle fairground ride. The wind brought tears to Hollie's eyes and the wind whipped her hair straight out behind her like a flag on a pole. The best part of the flight was when Torque stilled his wings to glide, letting the air currents carry him for long distances. Without the heaving *whumphing* sound of his beating wings, there was only silence. Except when she pressed her cheek to his scales, then she could hear the strong, rhythmic beat of his dragon heart. Impossible as it seemed, she might have slept.

Or maybe it was an illusion, the sense of time passing too quickly. Because long before it should have been, the night was over. Daylight was streaking the sky, and Torque was dipping low over snow-covered summits.

When they landed, Hollie looked around in amazement. The low ground was dark, with patches of purple heather and green gorse. The mountain peaks glowed white against a sky that was endlessly gray. It was beautiful, majestic and forbidding. She knew this place. She had been here many times in her dreams.

Torque shifted back and slipped on the clothing she handed him.

"Welcome to Scotland." There was a fierce pride in Torque's voice. "The weather is unpredictable. It could hail, snow, rain or shine. And it could do all of those things within the next hour. These Highlands will show you their moods with no room for misunderstanding."

"You love this place." It was evident in everything about him. Even the way he held himself had changed. There was a new pride in his bearing.

"Aye."

She'd never heard him use that word before.

"It's my home."

"But this is the first time you've been back here since Ged rescued you from Teine?"

He tilted his head up toward the mountains as though drawing strength from their beauty. "There was too much pain for me here. And too many memories. But now we've an arsonist to hunt down." He took her hand. "And I have you. The memories are still here, but they don't hurt as much with you by my side."

She leaned in close, nestling her cheek into the curve of his neck. "I'll be by your side as long as you want me."

"How about forever?"

Neither of them took the thought further, even though the reality was always with them. There was no happily-ever-after for them. A human and a dragon? That whole mortal-immortal thing was a real barrier. They could do long-term, but it would last for Hollie's lifetime. Which meant Torque was left staring down the barrel of a long, lonely forever. The Fates had gotten it wrong this time. When they decided to interfere and make them mates, it was like a magic trick that had gone wrong.

"Let's get going." Torque pulled on his beanie and shades, apparently feeling the need for his disguise even in this remote location. "If we walk to the nearest road, we can catch a bus into Inverness."

Hollie started to laugh. "Maybe you can make the switch that quickly, but I'm having trouble adjusting. One minute I'm flying on a dragon's back, the next I'm a regular tourist taking the bus into town?"

"Welcome to my world. Straddling the human and the paranormal is all in a day's work."

Chapter 12

Hollie soon learned that Torque hadn't been joking about the weather. They waited at the roadside for the regular bus from Fort William in drizzling rain, but by the time they arrived in the city of Inverness, the sun was shining.

"Who are we here to see?" she asked as Torque led her down a narrow street. "Tell me it's not a sorceress."

"No." He grinned as they halted outside a quaint bookstore. "It's a dragon."

He pointed to the sign above the door. *The Book Hoard.* It was accompanied by an image of a dragon guarding a pile of leather-bound books.

Before she could respond, he was ushering her inside. The interior was gloomy and it had that old-book smell that was instantly recognizable but couldn't be categorized. Hollie thought of it as aging paper, with a dollop of dust, and a hint of incense. It always made her feel slightly giddy, as though she was in a place of magic and mystery. The difference was that, on this occasion, her instinct told her that was exactly where she was.

The store was long and narrow and the walls were covered from floor to ceiling with book-filled shelves. Oddly matched easy chairs were dotted about the place, and a large ginger cat dozed in the middle of a sagging red velvet sofa.

"It's like something out of a fantasy story," Hollie whispered.

"It may have featured in one or two," he whispered back.

The shop was quiet, with only a few people browsing the shelves. Torque walked confidently through to the rear, until they reached an office with glass windows that overlooked the whole shop. As they approached, a man who was seated at a desk inside the tiny room, looked up. He went very still, his hand hovering in the act of pushing his half-moon glasses up his nose.

Hollie had heard the expression "cut the atmosphere with a knife," but she'd never felt it until now. As Torque and the other man stared at each other, the air seemed to heat up and thicken. She could feel the relationship between these two. Although she couldn't understand how, the memories and emotions of centuries were right there in that curious old bookstore. It was as if she could reach out a hand and pluck them from the motes of dust that floated around them.

"Hollie, I'd like you to meet Alban."

The man who rose from the desk was stick-thin and very tall. He had the slightly stooped air of someone who has spent his life trying to compensate for his height. His shoulder-length hair, pointed beard and neatly trimmed mustache all shimmered silver. Everything about him, including his long, hooked nose and piercing blue eyes, seemed to enhance the impression of a wizard who had accidentally wandered out of his own time period.

"Alban?" Hollie muttered the word out of the corner of her mouth. "Isn't he...?"

"The enemy?" Alban came out of the office. Hollie's first impression had been that he was old. Now that he was up close, it was impossible to judge his age. "Have you been telling tales about me, Cumhachdach?"

"Only the truth, Moiteil."

As they gazed at each other for a moment, the outcome appeared in doubt. Hollie wondered if they were about to fight or embrace. Then Torque moved forward and grasped Alban's forearm. "Too long."

The other man clamped a hand on Torque's shoulder. "It was your choice to stay away."

"You know why." Torque's voice was rusty with pain.

"Aye." Alban shook his head. "She did for you. Just as she promised she would. What brings you back now?"

"Her. Always her." Torque's jaw muscles were tight. "Can we go somewhere to talk?"

Alban looked around the store. "Give me a few minutes."

He walked away and Hollie watched in amazement as he started hustling his few customers out the door. "Closing time, folks." He pointed to the scarred grandfather clock in the corner of the room. "Och, I know the sign on the door says we're open until five, but you cannae always trust those things."

"Isn't that bad for business?" Hollie asked when Alban had locked the door.

"Possibly." He beckoned for them to follow him up

a flight of stairs that was tucked away behind the office. "But I do this more as a hobby than for profit. I've a pretty hoard tucked away." He lowered his voice and cast a look in Torque's direction. "But don't tell yon thieving Cumhachdach."

"I've a tidy sum of my own. I've no need to raid the Moiteil cave," Torque said. "Not this time."

"The stories about dragons and their hoards are all true, then?" Hollie asked. She was in Scotland, in the company of two dragons, sharing a joke with them. Life didn't get more surreal than this.

"Aye, we like our gelt. But you'll be pleased to know we know longer demand the sacrifice of a pretty maiden." Alban led them into an apartment above the store...and took them back in time.

Everything about the place, from the heavy wooden beams that meant Alban and Torque had to stoop low, to the wood-burning stove, seemed to be from another era. Hollie looked around her with surprise and pleasure. This was the home of a fearsome dragon leader? These cozy, floral cushions, woven rugs and fringed lamps were straight out of a 1950s English detective movie.

"I like my home comforts." Alban seemed to follow the direction of her thoughts. "If you've a long life ahead of you, why not enjoy it?"

As he spoke, another cat, this one a huge black-and-white ball of fluff, wandered into the room. Favoring them with a look of disgust, it jumped onto the window ledge and proceeded to ignore them.

"Tea? Or will you take a wee dram?"

Since Alban was already reaching for the whiskey bottle that sat on a table beside a winged chair, there seemed to be only one answer to that question. Alban's idea of a "wee dram" was a hefty slug of fifty-year-old Scotch, and Hollie sipped the heady liquid cautiously.

"She's dead, Torque." Alban didn't mince his words. "We both saw her die."

Hollie looked from one to the other in surprise. "Alban was with you when Ged freed you from captivity?"

Torque nodded. "I told you Teine delighted in playing us off one against the other. When she imprisoned me, she thought Alban would be pleased. His enemy was destroyed. The Moiteil would reign supreme."

"It doesn't work like that." Alban swirled the whiskey around in his glass. "We dragons are honorable. What Teine did to the Cumhachdach was murder most foul. My clan was not going to tolerate that."

"Alban and the Moiteil tried to rescue me," Torque said. "It didn't go well."

"No." The look in Alban's eyes reminded Hollie of Torque's expression when he talked of Teine. "It couldn't have gone any worse."

Torque raised his whiskey glass in a half-mocking salute. "You are looking at the last of the two Highland dragon-shifter clans."

"She killed the Moiteil, as well?" Although Hollie had already heard the horror story of what Teine had done to Torque and his family, it was hard to believe that she had repeated her atrocities.

"Like I said, she considered us her playthings. But Teine was like a child having a tantrum, and when things didn't go her way, she stomped on her toys. The dragon-shifters who lived in these Highlands were the casualties."

"She threw me into the cave with Torque. Told me if I had become so fond of him, we could spend eternity together." Alban's laughter had a hollow ring to it. "I thought we would. Which reminds me, how is Gerald?"

"Ged," Torque explained when Hollie raised questioning brows. "He's fine. Still saving the world, one endangered shifter at a time."

"We saw her die, Torque." Alban returned to the subject of Teine. "There is no more to be said."

"We saw her fall." There was a challenge in Torque's eyes. "Can we be sure she died?"

Alban sighed. "I suppose you have a reason for asking this?"

"Someone is lighting fires that appeared to be a tribute, but have now become a warning, to me."

Torque drew a piece of paper from his pocket. On it was the message from Losgadh@ykl.com. When Alban read it, his already pale complexion lightened by several shades. "It certainly appears to be from her."

"I came to find out if you'd seen, or heard, anything that might make you think she could still be alive," Torque said.

"Hell, no. If I thought that, I'd seek her out and kill her all over again myself," Alban said. "And enjoy every minute." He tapped the piece of paper. "But if Teine is behind this, she wouldn't have returned to her old, secluded life here in the Highlands, would she? She's a sorceress, but her powers are not unlimited. She would need to be able to travel around and start these fires."

"What can she do?" Hollie decided it was time to find out more about the enemy. "And why do you call her a sorceress and not a witch?"

"There is a hierarchy of magic, and at each stage the practitioners can be male or female," Torque explained. "Witches can learn their magic, or they can inherit it. The most powerful are those who use a combination of both. Their spells are low-level. Love potions, healing, finding lost pets…that sort of thing. Although they can also turn their hand to darker spells like relationship breakups and spoiling crops. The next step up is to wizardry. Wizards combine alchemy with witchcraft, exploiting science and mathematics to create magical potions. The final stage, having mastered wizardry, is sorcery."

"Let me guess." Figuring she wasn't going to like what she was about to hear, Hollie took a slug of her drink. "They are the rock stars of the magic world?"

"Oh, yes. They make Beast look like amateurs. Sorcerers must progress through the ranks, but they must also have magical parentage. Once they reach that level they are more or less all-powerful, within certain limits. They can act as a force for good or evil, but their magic must have a target."

"So, when Teine decided she wanted to kill your families, she had to come up with a spell that was aimed specifically at them?"

"Yes. She can't fly, or make herself invisible, and she doesn't have superhuman strength. So Alban is right. If Teine is the Incinerator, she would have to physically be in the place where the fires took place. She would have to get close to the building to focus her magic on it. If she traveled back and forth each time she started a fire, she would do it as a mortal, on an airplane, in a car or by whatever means necessary. Which means she must have a human identity."

Hollie's two worlds were colliding and nothing was making any sense. She could understand why Torque and Alban would believe Teine, if she was still alive, was behind the fires. They had been raised in a sphere where magic was the ruling force. The supernatural was normal to them and the evil sorceress had ruled over their whole existence. When anything bad happened, it must be natural for them to suspect she was behind it.

But Hollie came from a different place. Her world was one of logic. She had studied for years to gain an understanding of science and technology. She needed facts, data and hard, cold evidence. And after hunting the Incinerator for four years, she knew what she was looking for.

"What you are saying doesn't fit with the way the Incinerator operates. He—" Hollie still couldn't think of the arsonist as a woman "—sets the fires himself. He's what we call a professional. By that we mean he keeps it simple and he prefers to use fuels he finds at the scene. That way, he minimizes the risk of being caught. So, he takes trash he finds at the scene and piles it up. Then he uses copier toner to light it. If he can't find any toner, he raids the janitor's store and searches for another accelerant. He knows what will work. Paint, glue, mop cleaner, uncured polyester resin, brush cleaner... He's used all of those things." She frowned. "If Teine could stand within sight of a building and cast a spell on it to set it alight, why would she go to all that trouble?"

"Hollie has a point." Alban tilted his glass toward Torque.

"But that message is from Teine." Torque's tone was insistent. "Has to be."

They lapsed into silence as they finished their drinks. "You know what we need?" Alban asked.

"A crystal ball?" It was hard to tell if Torque was joking.

"The next best thing."

"Dinner at Kirsty McDougall's?"

"Och, that's mighty nice of you." Alban's eyes twinkled appreciatively. "I'll fetch my coat."

Kirsty McDougall's was an unashamedly traditional Scots restaurant located in the heart of Inverness. Serving dishes such as clootie dumplings, rumbledethumps, Arbroath smokies and cranachan, it was popular with locals and tourists alike. It was one of the places Torque had missed most while he was away. As soon as he walked through the door, the smell that met him made him feel at home.

Alban was greeted with a hug from a short, plump woman with a broad accent. "It's about time. I've no seen you for at least a month." She looked beyond him to Torque, and her hand went up to cover her mouth. "Is it yourself indeed?"

"It really is, Kirsty." As he stooped to kiss her cheek, she punched him so hard in the shoulder he went staggering back.

"Aye, you may well look shocked." She placed her hands on her hips. "Think you can forget me for all these years, then stroll back in and expect a warm welcome?" After glaring at him for a moment or two, she burst out laughing and embraced him. "Och, I cannae stay mad at you for long. It's a sight for sore eyes you are."

She ushered them to a table, talking constantly and eyeing Hollie with interest. When Kirsty bustled away to fetch drinks, Hollie leaned close to Torque. "Is she...?"

"Witch." He nodded. "Harmless." He rubbed his shoulder. "Mostly."

Kirsty returned with the inevitable bottle of whiskey and four glasses. She took a seat next to Alban.

"I've told them in the kitchen you'll be having haggis, neeps and tatties."

Hollie looked slightly alarmed. "Haggis with turnips and potatoes," Torque said. She didn't appear even slightly reassured by his explanation. "It's a national dish."

"Tell me why you're here," Kirsty said. They were seated in a booth, slightly apart from the other diners, where they were able to talk without being overheard.

"We wondered if you'd heard anything about the fiery one," Torque said.

Kirsty's pleasant face instantly twisted into an expression of distaste. "We're about to eat."

"Is there any chance she's still alive?" Torque persisted.

"I'll tell you what this is." Kirsty spoke directly to Hollie. "This is a dragon plot to spoil my peaceful existence. You didn't know what it was like when *she* was alive. None of us knew what she'd be about next. It was all about Teine. All that mattered was what she wanted…and if she didn't get it? Hoo! Stand by for fireworks. I've a touch of the third eye myself. It's a mere fraction of Teine's skill for seeing the future. And I try to use it for good, whereas she used her mighty gift for personal gain." She pointed a finger at Torque. "Do I think she's still alive? No. And I'll tell you for why. Because my teeth dinnae ache when I say her name."

"Seems pretty conclusive to me. Kirsty knows everything that goes on in the Highlands." Alban raised his glass in a toast. "I suggest we eat."

Torque reluctantly agreed. He still wasn't convinced. Ever since he'd seen that email, he'd been sure Teine had somehow survived the fall and was determined to get back at him. It made a strange kind of sense. Although

Teine had believed she loved him, Torque didn't think the sorceress was capable of love. What she felt for him was more like ownership. When her toy dragon hadn't done what she wanted and returned her feelings, she'd been incensed. Her revenge had been all-consuming.

Even so, watching him from afar, burning buildings in towns he'd visited…it wasn't quite Teine's style. If she was going to turn into an evil stalker, she would be more hands-on. But who knew what might be going on in her twisted mind? She could have decided on a change in approach just to be infuriating. She could take her time. Like him, Teine was immortal.

The dramatic change in pace and approach when Torque met Hollie definitely suggested Teine was the arsonist. Seeing him with another woman would have sent her into a frenzy. There was no way she'd tolerate that. He almost laughed out loud. *Tolerate?* He was surprised they weren't both a pile of ashes already, consumed in the fire of her jealous rage.

And maybe that was another reason to believe Teine *wasn't* the Incinerator. Could she have learned restraint since he'd watched her plummet off a mountain in a ball of flame? He didn't think Teine was capable of learning. She just *was*…or had once been. The frown between his eyes as he tried to think it all through was making his head ache.

Instead of trying to unravel the mystery that might not even exist, he turned his attention to the more enjoyable task of watching Hollie. He was instantly soothed. No matter what else was happening, he would always rather be watching Hollie. The food had arrived and she was viewing the haggis on her plate with suspicion. A corner of his mouth quirked up.

"It's a traditional sausage made from lamb's liver,

lungs and heart mixed with oatmeal, onion, suet and seasoning." His grin widened. "All stuffed into a casing made from a sheep's stomach."

"Yum." She gave him a challenging look. "I flew here on the back of a dragon, Torque. You think you can scare me with a sausage?"

"Is that the whiskey talking?"

"Possibly." She started eating. "It's actually really good. Where are we sleeping tonight? Tell me it's not in a cave."

"Och, lassie. Dinnae fatch." Kirsty waved her fork at her. "You'll stay in my spare room, of course."

As they ate, Torque was content to listen while Alban and Kirsty talked of people and places he knew. It seemed the thriving paranormal community that lived alongside the humans was having some problems. He hadn't realized until now how much he'd missed his Highland home, hadn't understood what that ache in his heart was all about. He'd believed he had to stay away because the memories were too painful. After Ged had freed him from his captivity, he hadn't wanted to see the familiar faces and places. At that time, all he'd wanted to do was get as far away as he could and stay away forever.

Guilt and sorrow had been twin demons gnawing on his heart. He had blamed himself for the annihilation of his clan. If he'd handled Teine differently, been able to predict her reaction, even pretended to love her... No matter how hard he tried, he had never been able to shake off the feeling that he could have—*should* have— done more. Burying himself in his new life, reinventing himself as a rock star, had helped, but it had never driven away the anguish.

Now that he was here, he could acknowledge the

truth. He had been desperately homesick all that time. Although he had tried to suppress the cravings, they had never gone away. This was his land. These Highlands owned him and they would never let him go. Torque didn't want them to. He was stronger when he was here.

His attention was drawn back to Kirsty, who was tapping on the table with her fingertip to make a point. "It's become an epidemic."

"What has?" Clearly, whatever they were discussing was serious.

"Och, it's the strangest thing," Kirsty said. "When it first started, it was barely noticeable, so no one talked about it to their friends because they thought it was just *them*. Then, gradually, it got worse. People started sharing their stories and we realized it was affecting more and more people. Now it seems the whole paranormal community is afflicted by insomnia."

Torque sat up straighter. "What?"

"Aye." Alban nodded. "Every single one of us. No matter what we try, we cannae sleep. What do you think it is?"

"I think it's the final proof we need that Teine *is* alive." Torque dashed off the last of his whiskey. "She's cast her trademark insomnia spell on all of you."

Chapter 13

Kirsty's spare room was small and cozy, but the only things that interested Hollie were the wood-burning stove and the double bed.

"So tired," she said as she kicked off her boots and held out her hands toward the warmth.

"Really?" Torque came close, running his hands through her hair. "How tired?"

When he kissed her, the world fell away. It was soft and slow, soothing her in a way she hadn't known she needed. More than words could ever have done, the touch of his lips drove away the strangeness of everything that had happened. His hand rested below her ear, his thumb tracing her jawline as their breaths mingled. She slid her hands beneath his sweater and around his back, pulling him closer, wanting no space between them, needing to feel his heart beating against hers.

"Maybe not *that* tired."

His mouth moved to her neck, his stubble rasping deliciously over her skin. Soft kisses, sighing breaths, tiny nibbles…each one had her squirming with delight. Then he kissed her lips again, demanding more this time. Like he couldn't get enough. *She* couldn't get enough.

"Clothes off," she murmured. "At least it's warmer in here than the rest of your homeland."

When they were naked, Torque's mouth was on her flesh again, tracing a line from her collarbone to her breasts. His hands slid down her spine as he pulled her close, letting her feel his erection. Lost in sensation, she writhed against him. Swinging her into his arms, he carried her the short distance to the bed.

"It's been a long day, we'll go slow."

"Slow sounds like heaven."

Placing her down gently, he turned her onto her side, spooning his body tight against hers. His chest hair was warm and rough on her bare back, his lips igniting fires over her neck and shoulders. Hollie held his arm and tucked it across her waist, twisting her head to reach his lips.

He stroked his hand down her side, idly circling his fingers on the sensitive skin of her hip as he kissed her bare shoulder. Soft sighs left her lips as his touch soothed away thoughts of everything except here and now. Torque kissed along her back, his hand cupping her right breast and circling the nipple with his finger, making the flesh harden into a peak. "Lift your leg."

As she raised her thigh to her chest, opening herself to his touch, Torque cupped her buttock, kneading the firm flesh. Lowering his hand, he ran a finger down her cleft, and her muscles twitched in anticipation. Circling her wetness with his finger, he applied more pressure each time he pushed against her entrance. Not entering, just teasing.

"Please…" Her breath hitched as she writhed against him, impatiently pressing into his hand.

Torque obliged by slipping a finger inside her, stroking softly. He pulled out slowly, then pushed forward again. Taking his time, he caressed her tenderly and her body welcomed him with a rush of overwhelming pleasure.

As he added another finger, she felt his erection pressing hard into her spine. Gripping the edge of the mattress, she surrendered to sensation, loving how her walls stretched to accommodate the width of his fingers and her muscles clenched.

Finding her clit with his thumb, he gently flicked the swollen bundle of nerves as he hooked his fingers inside her. Hollie gasped as she spasmed around him and Torque muffled a groan into her shoulder as he continued to stroke and rub.

"Need you now." Hollie managed to gasp out the words on a wave of approaching orgasm.

The bed dipped as he moved away and her body adjusted to the sudden cold. She heard him rummage in his clothing and the sound of foil ripping. Then he returned and his warmth was tight up against her again.

Tilting her hips to meet him, he slid into her from behind. Hollie bit her lip at the feeling of raw power filling her slowly, inch by inch. Torque's teeth were sharp on her shoulder; then they both remained still for a few moments, relishing the perfect connection. His hands reached down, stroking her thighs, making her skin tingle in the wake of his touch.

"You're so…" She gasped as he pulled out and slid in again. "Torque!"

"Ah, Hollie. Nothing sounds as good as hearing you say my name when I'm inside you."

She felt his teeth against her earlobe. Then he groaned as he started to pump.

Each time, when he slid in, it felt like he was impossibly deep. Hollie thrust back against him, and he groaned with every thrust.

Torque kept his movements slow and luxurious, his hands kneading her breasts and teasing her nipples. Even though she begged him to hurry, he continued to move with deep, lazy strokes. Every now and then, he pressed his lips to her ear and whispered dark, carnal words that stoked her passion to a fever pitch. Hollie's whole body was quivering as he kept her poised on the edge of climax, her senses filled with Torque and this magical, erotic moment.

She reached a hand behind her, raking her fingernails over his sensitive flesh and cupping him in the palm of her hand.

"Oh." His head dropped onto her shoulder. "Oh, Hollie. Just like that..."

He held her hips harder, pulling her tighter to him and thrusting faster now. Hollie arched into him, crying out and squeezing her eyes shut. He was so big, strong and virile. Every stroke pushed her to limits she'd never known existed. She felt her release building like a gathering storm. Her cries were coming in time with his groans, the slick sounds of their bodies moving together filling the room. She clung to the mattress, matching his movements.

"So close." He hissed out the words. His hips jerked wildly as his whole body shuddered and one hand tightened in her hair.

Her breathing hitched as she felt it begin. A moan

started somewhere in the region of her curling toes and then she was crying out, her whole body juddering. Torque was still thrusting, but she could tell from the tensing of his muscles that he was close, too. She bit her knuckles, riding the waves of pleasure washing over her as she felt Torque stiffen and heard him groan. His fingers dug into her hip while he rode it out, his grunts matching her panting breaths. He wrapped his arms around her, pulling her up to his body as she trembled in his embrace.

After several long minutes, when the room was quiet except for the sounds of their sighs, Torque rolled over, taking Hollie with him.

"At first I thought the Fates were mad to throw us together. I thought they must have got it wrong, that nothing good could ever come of this. How could a dragon and a human be together?" His voice was quiet and reflective as he ran a hand down the length of her hair. "Now I'm starting to wonder if the Fates knew what they were doing, after all."

"What do you mean?"

"There's a fight ahead, and before I met you, I didn't have the strength or the heart for it. We don't know who the enemy is yet. But whether it's Teine, or some other faceless evildoer, there's one thing I do know…" He smiled down at her, the glow in his eyes warmer than the heat from the stove. "With you at my side, they don't stand a chance against the last of the Cumhachdach."

Torque woke early. Easing carefully away from Hollie's sleeping form, he pulled on his clothes and slipped quietly from the room. When he stepped outside the building into the chilly morning air, he wasn't surprised to see Alban waiting for him. They walked in silence along a road that led them out of the town.

Alban spoke first. "There is no getting away from it."

"No." Torque gazed up at the mountain peaks.

"She is the only one who will know for sure if Teine is alive."

"Yes." The snow-covered mountains stood out against the gray skies. Càrn Eighe couldn't be seen from where they were, but he could feel its presence. "She doesn't welcome visitors."

Alban snorted. "That's an understatement."

Torque sighed, digging his hands deep into the pockets of his jeans. "I suppose there's no other way?" Even as he asked the question, he knew the answer.

For thousands of years, Teine and her twin sister, Deigh, had ruled over the Highlands. Teine was the Scots Gaelic word for *fire* and Deigh meant *ice*. The two sisters lived up to their names. Teine ruled over a kingdom of heat and fury. Deigh was icy and unmoving. Unlike most twins, they had no love for each other. Even so, Alban was right. Deigh might be able to tell them what was going on with Teine. Most important of all, she would be able to discover where her sister was. If she chose to cooperate. Where Deigh was concerned, *if* was a very big word.

"You made this journey," Alban said. "Do you want to leave wondering, or knowing?"

Torque nodded. Alban was right. He and Hollie had to leave that night. He wouldn't get another chance like this until after the tour was over. If they didn't approach Deigh now, he would be left in a constant state of speculation about what she knew. Even worse than that, if there were more fires—and more deaths—he would question whether he could have prevented them by speaking to her.

"Okay. Food first, crazy ice woman later. There's only so much insanity a man can take before breakfast."

They retraced their steps, pausing on an incline to watch the city as it came to life.

"So… Hollie?" Alban's face was turned away, his voice expressing mild interest. Torque wasn't fooled. They had been born from the same fire. Teine might have turned them against each other once, but the bonds that existed between them had been reestablished when she imprisoned them both and destroyed their families. Even though they were from different clans, they were as close as brothers.

Alban didn't have to tell Torque what it would mean if he fell in love with a human. A human life span was the blink of an eye to an immortal dragon-shifter. If he was foolish enough to fall for a mortal…well, he would be storing up a pain-filled future for himself.

"Yes?" There was no fire in the word. Alban could see through him. He would have been aware of Torque's feelings as soon as he first saw him with Hollie.

"We are the last of our kind. I wish with all my heart that wasn't so." When Alban turned to look at him, his expression was anguished. "We will never find one of our own kind, you and I. Teine saw to that. I can see you love Hollie, and I wish I could shake your hand and wish you well. But I have to say this."

"No." Torque's throat tightened painfully, so the word came out as a croak. "No, you don't. I already know."

Alban's hand on his shoulder felt like the heaviest weight in the world. "The Fates are supposed to guard against a dragon and a mortal falling in love. When it happens for other shifters, they can choose the difficult step of converting their mate with a bite. We don't even have that."

"Yeah. The Fates don't let that sort of screwed-up madness happen. Do they?" Torque asked. "Except it has happened. And I can't undo it. I can't make these feelings go away." They had reached Kirsty's place and he looked up at the window of the room where he had left Hollie sleeping. "I don't want to."

"Then, when this madness is over, you, my friend, must find another way," Alban said.

"You think there is one?" Torque was aware that he was clutching at possibilities...or maybe impossibilities.

"I don't know." Keeping his hand on Torque's shoulder, Alban guided him inside the restaurant, where the aroma of bacon and coffee greeted them. "But there is someone who will have the answers you seek."

Torque frowned, trying to follow what he meant. After a few moments, realization hit him. Of course. There was one person who was a walking reference book about shifters.

"Ged." Torque said his friend's name like it was a revelation. "What he doesn't know about our history and legends isn't worth knowing."

"Will you tell Hollie about you and Deigh?" Alban's voice acted like a bucket of cold water extinguishing the tiny flicker of hope he had just glimpsed.

Torque thought about it. Would he explain to Hollie that he had once been stupid enough to get involved with the frosty sorceress? It had lasted about as long as it took him to realize that, although she wasn't as demented as her fiery sister, Deigh had a block of ice in place of a heart. He had no reason not to tell Hollie;

it was just where to start. *Of all the stupid things I've done in my life...*

With perfect, or perhaps imperfect, timing, Hollie appeared in the doorway, cutting short any further conversation on the subject. Torque's heart flipped over at the sight of her. There had to be a way for them to make this work. He couldn't feel this way only to let her go. As she took a seat next to him, he turned that thought into a vow. He would find a way.

Càrn Eighe wasn't a difficult climb, but Torque and Hollie didn't have much time. They had to get back to Dallas in time to rejoin Beast for the next concert.

"One last flight?" he asked Alban.

"No." Alban shook his head. "One *more* flight."

"You're right." Torque nodded. "I haven't come back only to stay away for good. We will fly together again. Many times."

He and Alban had engaged in a lengthy discussion about whether Hollie should go with them. Torque explained to her that the mountain was popular with walkers and climbers, but they weren't taking any of the traditional routes. Once they reached the summit, they would be stepping into a mystical realm, one known only to those who were not mortal. Beyond the physical peak, the temperatures plummeted and the world became a hostile, icy kingdom ruled over by a ruthless sorceress. Torque hadn't been sure he wanted to expose Hollie to either the weather conditions...or to Deigh.

Hollie was not about to be sidelined by a pair of alpha-male dragons who thought they knew best. She had listened to their arguments, then faced Torque with a stubborn expression. "I'm coming with you."

"Deigh isn't Teine, but she can be vicious."

"You've seen me before I've had my morning coffee. I can match any evil sorceress." Hollie slid her arms around his waist. "This is my investigation, Torque. Okay, it's taking some unexpected turns, but you can't shut me out of it."

"Okay. But you do as I say."

She opened her mouth to protest and he silenced her with a finger on her lips. "This is not about me being an arrogant dragon-shifter, Hollie. This is about facing a devious magician who will target you because you don't have the same powers she does. Together, Alban and I can protect you from Deigh. We were defeated by Teine because she caught us unawares. I will never let that happen again. But you have to trust me to know how to handle this."

"I do. I trust you completely." She grinned at him. "I was going to ask if we have time to buy some warmer clothes before we set off."

He laughed. "We're in Scotland. The stores are full of warmer clothes."

They went to one of the larger chains that catered to hikers and walkers. When they set off toward Càrn Eighe, Hollie wore thermal undergarments beneath her jeans and a sweater with waterproof outerwear over the top. Sturdy boots and thick gloves completed the look. Her movements felt slightly clumsy, but at least she was warm.

Once they reached the lower slopes of the mountain, the two men found an isolated place and prepared to shift.

"Shifting and flying in daylight is always risky, but at least we are in a remote part of the world and our camouflage hides us once we take to the skies," Torque explained.

When they had removed their clothing, Hollie placed it in her backpack, since they would need it again once they shifted back on the mountaintop. She took a moment to consider how her day was going. She was halfway across the world from her home. No one from her former life knew where she was. The two naked men standing before her were about to transform themselves into dragons. She had been in some unusual situations as a fire investigator, but no one could call this an average working day.

When Torque and Alban had shifted, they unfurled their giant wings. Both dragons were a similar size, but Torque was more muscular. Alban's scales were darker and more silvery than Torque's and his eyes retained some of their blue sheen.

Torque crouched low so Hollie could climb onto his back, and once she was in place, he broke into a run and immediately took flight. Alban was right behind him. It was easier for Hollie to see how the dragons blended into their environment now that she could watch Alban. As he soared high, his scales changed to match the murky gray of the low cloud, but when he swooped lower, he became part of the brown and black of the mountainside.

The mountaintop was a horseshoe ridge, and the dragons followed its edge, dipping low into a snowy basin. Hollie gasped in surprise as they almost immediately left the bleak Highland scene behind and entered a whole new world. This was a land blanketed in ice and snow, a wonderland of white where even the air glistened and the icy gale cut through Hollie's warm clothing as if it wasn't there.

Torque and Alban landed on a snowy plateau and

Hollie was shivering by the time they had shifted and quickly dressed.

"There." Torque placed an arm around her shoulders and indicated a point just above them. Although it was difficult to see through the swirling snow, she could just make out the outline of a building.

As they moved forward, ice cracked beneath her feet and her breath frosted the air. The snow began falling more heavily and the wind howled out in fury.

"Is the weather getting worse because of *us*?" Hollie had to shout to be heard.

"Yes," Torque yelled back at her.

It was almost impossible to keep going. The world had become a swirling mass of screaming white. Hollie raised a gloved hand to shield her eyes, but it had no effect against the onslaught. The wind was razor-sharp on her face, and the snow blinded her. All she could do was to bow her head until her chin was touching her chest and try to stay upright. Her feet were starting to freeze as they sank into the drifts with each stride, slowing her almost to a standstill.

Torque placed an arm around her waist, keeping her tight against his side and using his own strength to propel her forward with him. It helped, but it still felt like the weather was going to win the fight.

A high-pitched screech, like ice scraping over rock, claimed her attention. Without warning, the gusts died away and every snowflake hung in the air in perfect, frozen stillness. As her vision cleared, Hollie saw they were only a few feet from the building. With gleaming towers and turrets, it looked like a palace carved from ice.

The sound she had heard was a giant door opening. Pressing closer to Torque, she watched as it was pushed wider, shards of ice cracking and shattering all around it as it moved. When the opening was wide enough, a woman stepped into view.

"I do not wish for visitors." Everything about her was white. From her ivory skin, to her silver hair, and her flowing, misty robes. The only hint of color was in her light blue eyes.

"We dinnae come expecting a dram and a tattie scone," Alban said. "Although, if you're offering..."

Ignoring him, the woman turned her attention to Torque. Her expression didn't change, but the ice in the air glimmered brighter. "Cumhachdach."

"Deigh." He bowed his head. "We come in peace."

"Mine is a land of ice." She swept a hand around her, and fresh snow fell in a shimmering arc. "There is no place here for fire-breathers. You mistake me for my sister." She turned to go back inside.

"Wait." Torque spoke urgently and Deigh paused. "How can we mistake you for Teine? She is dead."

A slight smile touched her colorless lips. "Of course. How foolish of me to forget."

Torque took a step forward. "Deigh, you have no more love for Teine than we do. If she is alive, you can help us by sharing what you know."

Hollie watched the sorceress in fascination. She was like a china doll, beautiful, but unblinking. It was almost as if her thought processes had been slowed down by the cold.

After a few minutes, Deigh sighed. "You should come inside." For the first time, her eyes flitted over to Hollie. "Humans don't last long in the cold."

"It doesn't look much warmer inside," Hollie whispered as they approached the building.

"Stay close to me. I'll give off enough heat for both of us." Torque kept his own voice low.

The interior of the palace was jaw-dropping. Everything about it was elegant and fit for a fairy princess... except it was all carved from ice. Hollie was reminded of movies she had watched and fairy tales she had read as a child. This was the enchanted castle that existed in the frozen wastelands. This was the place the characters sang about.

Except the reality was she couldn't feel her feet and she didn't like the way Deigh was looking at Torque. It was like she had been waiting her whole life for a dragon-shifter to adorn her home. Hollie cast a sidelong glance in Torque's direction. Could he feel it? Did he know Teine wasn't the only sorceress who had a massive crush on him? It was a reminder of the chasm that existed between them. All those centuries of his life about which Hollie knew nothing.

"Is that why you came here after all this time? To ask me if Teine is still alive?" There was no escaping the look in Deigh's eyes as she fixed her gaze on Torque's face. It was raw longing. "No other reason?"

Hollie felt almost embarrassed for her. For an instant, she was gripped by an insane desire to tell Deigh to have a little dignity. *Don't make it so obvious. Try for a little subtlety.* It was probably a bad idea to offer relationship advice to a magical being on account of that whole possibility of violent death thing. *Plus, he's my dragon-shifter.*

"Deigh, I have to leave Scotland soon. People are dying. I need to know if there is a chance Teine survived." Torque's manner reminded Hollie of an adult talking to a child. Patient, but firm.

Deigh laughed and the sound made Hollie think of ice tinkling in a glass. "Anything is possible."

"There is a problem within the Highland paranormal community," Alban said. "We seem to be under a spell that leaves us unable to sleep. Do you know anything about that?"

With an obvious effort, Deigh dragged her gaze away from Torque and turned to Alban. "The spell is Teine's."

"That was what I thought," Torque said. "But if she cast it, where is she? Teine enjoys watching her victims suffer."

For the first time, Deigh really smiled and Hollie glimpsed how stunning she could be if she let the icy persona drop. "Don't we all?"

"Is she alive, Deigh?" Torque seemed to be losing patience.

Her eyes rested on Hollie's face. For an instant, something flickered in their depths, rocking Hollie backward. Despite the subzero temperatures, the ice sorceress had scorched her. Before they settled back into a neutral expression, pure venom was overlaid on the porcelain features.

"She may be."

"How do you know?" Torque asked.

"You came onto my mountain uninvited. You asked me a question. I answered it. You don't get to demand proof."

Hollie could sense Torque battling to maintain control of his temper. "It would help us if we knew how she survived and where she is now," she explained.

There it was again. That flash of otherness as Deigh looked her way. But she was at the top of the sorcery hierarchy. It was hardly surprising that she gave off unexpected vibes. "I don't deal with mortals."

"Just tell us, Deigh." Torque spoke through gritted teeth.

"It's a twin thing." The sorceress lifted one slender shoulder. "As for where she is..." The pause went on a little too long. There was the hint of a sly smile. *You know, but you're not telling.* "We were never that close."

"Well, that was helpful," Alban said. "I don't suppose you know a way to counteract the insomnia spell?"

She cast a look of dislike in his direction. "Tell your witch friend to make an infusion from the leaves of lavender and chamomile. It must be used when the moon is full and the songbirds are silent. Do not drink the liquid. Inhale the steam through the fronds of a fresh young fern. Once you remember how to sleep, the spell will be broken." The air around Deigh glittered brighter as her mood changed and she took a half step toward Torque. "Are you back for good? As you know, there are circumstances that can tempt me down from my mountain."

There are? Hollie cast a sidelong glance in Torque's direction, but his expression was closed.

"No." He took Hollie's hand. "We have to leave." If looks could kill, Hollie would be dead on the spot with a shard of ice through her heart. "Thank you for your help."

Hollie was inclined to agree with Alban. Apart from a grudging suggestion of how to break the insomnia spell, she couldn't see that Deigh had been of any use. A vague hint that Teine might be alive? It didn't move their investigation on a single step.

When they stepped outside, the storm had died down. The air was still and crisp, and thick snow lay like cake frosting over the ground. Instead of the disap-

pointment Hollie had expected, Torque and Alban ex-
changed a smile.

"She's alive." They spoke the words together.

Chapter 14

"I don't understand." Hollie looked from Torque to Alban in bewilderment. "Deigh didn't tell you anything. How can you possibly walk away from that conversation and say with certainty that Teine is alive?"

"Because Deigh told Alban how to undo the insomnia charm. It's not her spell. Only the person who cast it knows how to reverse it. Teine must have told Deigh what to do."

"Why would she do that?" Hollie asked. "I thought you said they had nothing to do with each other."

"Think about it." Torque took her arm, propelling her through the deep drifts. "Imagine you are an evil sorceress, you've just been burned by dragon fire and fallen into a ravine. Against all the odds, you survived. Everyone in these Highlands hates you and is celebrating the news of your demise. You need help and a place to recover. Where do you go?"

"To the only other evil sorceress in the vicinity," Alban said. "Your icy twin."

"But why didn't Deigh turn her away? They didn't love each other, but they were both in love with you." So Hollie had noticed that. To be fair, it was hard to miss. Deigh wasn't exactly subtle. "If Teine was her rival for your affections, why not let her die?"

"They don't understand love. Either of them. Who knows why she chose to help her? Maybe it was, as she said, a twin thing."

Alban snorted. "You mean foul blood is thicker than water? It's a pity you don't have time to take her up on her offer."

"What do you mean?" Torque asked.

"You know. Tempt her down from her mountaintop. Sweeten her up with that Cumhachdach charm of yours. Find out what really happened." Alban appeared oblivious of the glare Torque was giving him.

"Alban has a point," Hollie said.

"Is this a conspiracy?" Torque growled. Why would Hollie want him to spend time with his crazy ex? Not that she knew the details about the depths of how unhinged Deigh could be.

"It's obvious she'll talk to you." She stopped and looked back at the ice palace. "You should set something up."

He tapped his watch. "We don't have time. I have to get back for this little matter of a concert in front of thousands of people."

"Invite her." He blinked at her. "Not to the one we are rushing back for, but to the next one in Denver. Ask her to be your guest at that."

"Hollie, we probably need to have a serious talk

about some things. Set a few relationship boundaries, but not right now—"

She caught hold of his arm. "Torque, listen to me. I don't want you to spend time with a mad ice witch who looks at you like she wants to lick every inch of you. But I do want to catch the Incinerator. And if you giving Deigh a VIP pass to a Beast concert and taking her out to dinner is what it takes, I can live with that." She paused. "I'll hate every second, but I can do it. I think."

"I could offer to be Deigh's traveling companion," Alban said. "It won't be much fun of a trip, but at least we'll know what she is doing."

"Do you have a passport?" Torque asked. "I doubt Deigh does."

"I'm sure she can conjure one up for herself, but I actually keep mine up to date." Alban grinned at Hollie. "While yon Cumhachdach deals with the icy one, you could take me out for a decent, well-done steak."

"So you two get to go out and have fun, and I get to go on a date with Deigh? Build her hopes up and spend the night fighting her off?" Torque groaned in frustration. "Thanks, guys."

"Isn't it worth it to find out, once and for all, if Teine is the Incinerator?" Hollie asked.

"If there was any other way…" He gave a sigh of surrender. "Wait here."

As he walked back toward the ice palace, Alban's sympathetic tones followed him. "Och, you cannae blame him. Deigh is as mad as a box of frogs in a thunderstorm."

Torque knew a moment of longing for the days when Alban was the enemy. A good dragon fight, with claws and fire-breathing…that was just what he needed right now to release his tension. He was supposed to be in charge around here, so how the hell had he ended up in this position? More time than was necessary with the very woman he had spent the best part of several centuries avoiding was not an option he liked. And tricking a sorceress? Never a good move.

At least Deigh didn't have Teine's legendary fortune-telling talents. If she had been able to see into the future and know what was coming, they'd be storing up a world of trouble. He frowned. He didn't *think* Deigh had the same skill. She'd never mentioned them, whereas Teine boasted of her ability to predict the future.

But Hollie was right. This was about finding the Incinerator. Nothing they'd tried so far had brought them any answers. Maybe it was time for an unconventional approach. He just hoped he could keep it low-key. He bit back a laugh. This was *Deigh*. Back when the first King Kenneth had been on the throne, Torque had glanced her way once and she'd been ordering her bride clothes. Unfortunately, he hadn't known about that and had worked on the assumption that she was sane when he got involved with her. It hadn't taken long for him to discover his mistake. "You came back." Deigh turned to him with shining eyes as he walked back through the frozen portal.

Even though he knew iced water ran in her veins and she had a cruel streak a mile wide, he pitied her in that instant. If there had been another way to get this information, he'd have taken it. Recalling some of her deeds helped stiffen his spine. This was the woman who had caused a landslide and buried a whole village. The reason? She overheard someone say that one of the maidens was prettier than her. And that time when the crops failed for three consecutive summers? Deigh had been harboring a grudge because a visiting sorceress had been welcomed into the home of a Highland witch. Both the witch and her guest had been found incarcerated in a block of ice—even though it was high summer—and hundreds of people in the surrounding area had starved.

Yeah, he could harden his heart against Deigh's hopeful smile. Particularly if she was covering for her even more sinister sister.

"I wondered if you might like to take a trip."

Hollie hadn't timed Torque's last trans-Atlantic dragon flight, but she knew they were cutting it dangerously fine if they were going to make it back to Dallas for the concert. Even factoring in magic, dragon speed and time differences, Ged would be tearing his hair out and cursing Torque's legendary unpunctuality. Leaving a dozen questions unspoken, they said goodbye to Alban on the summit of Càrn Eighe.

"Och, won't I be seeing you again in just a few days?" Alban winked at Hollie. "Remember what I said. Steak. Well done. No sides."

She stood on the tips of her toes to kiss his cheek. "I'll take you to the best steak house in Denver."

Alban grinned at Torque over her head. "I think I did better than you out of this deal. At least my date is sane."

"I knew there was a reason why we fought the Moiteil for all those years." Torque scowled. "Just get Deigh to America in three days' time. I'll have someone contact you when the travel and accommodation arrangements are made."

"Separate rooms, right?" Alban's flippant air was replaced by a hint of nervousness.

Torque's smile was pure mischief. "I'll have to see what I can do. Hotels get so busy at this time of year."

"Stop tormenting Alban." Hollie lightly punched his upper arm. "We have to get going. *Right now.*"

Flying back felt different. Perhaps it was because the exhilaration was there but the fear was gone. And a whole new side of Torque's life had been opened up to her. He was a dragon, but he had spent most of his life living among humans. Those humans were also shifters, or, like Kirsty, they had additional powers. But they lived otherwise normal lives. Their hopes, fears and dreams looked a lot like Hollie's own. Except for the wicked sorceress who had lurked in the background, of course. Even so, Hollie's own world wasn't very different. Instead of enchanted spells, the villains carried guns and knives.

It was still right against wrong, still ordinary people trying to get on with their lives, sometimes in the face of monumental evil. That brought her thoughts back to the Incinerator. Her world and Torque's had collided because of the arsonist. But which of those worlds did the fire-starter come from? Had he stepped from her world of science and logic into Torque's magical sphere? Or was it the other way around? Would they catch him with conventional weapons, or could he only be defeated with supernatural powers?

Tired of thinking, she rested her head against Torque's neck, letting his warmth and strength soothe her. It seemed like only minutes later that he was swooping low over the dark outline of the Cedar Ridge Nature Preserve.

"How much time do we have?" he asked as soon as he had shifted back.

"The concert starts in an hour." Hollie drew his clothes from the backpack and handed them to him.

"Plenty of time."

She managed to stop her mouth from dropping open. "Dear Lord. You're serious."

He pulled her close, kissing her quickly on the lips. "Let's go."

Taking his cell phone from the back pocket of his jeans, he called a cab as they walked along the moonlit trail. They reached the highway and waited only a few minutes before the driver drew up at the edge of the sidewalk. When Torque gave him directions to the stadium where the concert was being held, he shook his head.

"I dropped two guys off there an hour ago and the streets were already blocked. No way we'll get near that place now."

"Get us as close as you can." When the driver started to protest, Torque withdrew a wad of cash from the back pocket of his jeans. "And fast."

"I'll see what I can do." He turned the cab around.

Hollie could see the arena as they approached. The huge building was located on a hill just outside the city, and searchlights positioned on the edge of the open roof lit up the night sky. As they got closer, the traffic slowed to a crawl and then came to a standstill. Police cruisers blocked the exit roads. Although there were people on the sidewalk, the lack of crowds was an indication that the concert was about to start.

"We'll walk from here." Torque shoved another handful of money into the driver's hand and gestured for Hollie to follow him out of the cab.

"Torque." She was torn between laughter and dismay. "We are still at least ten minutes from the venue."

"Then we need to move faster." Grabbing her hand, he broke into a run. Powering past people who were walking toward the stadium, he kept going, only pausing occasionally to check that she was okay.

Laughing, Hollie nodded. "Just get there. I promised Ged," she panted.

By the time they reached the entrance, her lungs were about to collapse and her leg muscles had given everything they had. Luckily, the security guard on the door recognized Torque and waved him through.

"Ged?" Torque asked.

"He's backstage. Along this corridor and turn right."

The opening bars of the first number were playing as they dashed toward the stage. Hollie could see a stand-in guitarist in Torque's usual position. At the same time that Khan erupted onto the stage from the rear, Torque vaulted on from the front. Grabbing his guitar from the stand-in, he high-fived the startled guy, grinned at Dev and gave one of his trademark leaps into the air. The audience, clearly believing it to be part of the performance, went wild.

Hollie sidled around to the rear of the stage to where Ged was standing with his arms folded across his huge chest. His expression was unreadable as he glanced down at her.

"Thanks for getting him back on time." Even though he had to yell to be heard, she picked up on the sarcasm in his voice.

After a minute or two, Ged nodded toward the stage, where Torque was on his knees. He was bent backward so his head touched the floor and his flame-colored hair fanned out around him. As they watched, he jumped to his feet and powered across to the other side of the stage. Explosions followed in his wake. Even from a distance, Hollie could feel raw power coming off him in waves.

"I didn't think it was possible for Torque to have even more energy," Ged said. "But something has invigorated him."

Hollie nodded. She had seen the love he had for his Highland home. Now that he had been back there and accepted that it was part of him, could he continue to stay away?

The following morning, over breakfast, Ged brought them up to speed with the police inquiry into the bus fire.

"There is very little to tell. What was left of the vehicle was in such a poor state the fire investigation team didn't have much to work on." Ged turned to Hollie. "You'll probably already know what I'm about to say next. There was no trace of an additional accelerant, so it was likely he used gasoline. Since there was gas in the tanks, however, that can't be taken as conclusive. They are working on the theory that a container, probably a bottle, of some sort was thrown through the front window and then the same thing through the rear window."

"A Molotov cocktail," Hollie said. "The simplest and most effective way of making a firebomb. You fill a bottle with gasoline, or another accelerant, stuff a rag in the neck, light the rag and throw the bottle through the window of the building or vehicle you want to set fire to. As the bottle breaks, the accelerant spills out and catches alight."

"There was a lot of glass and fabric remnants at the scene, as you'd expect from a bus that was a home on the road, but it hasn't been possible for the investigators to get anything useful from them."

"What about the person who did this?" Torque asked. "Have the police come up with any ideas, even any suspects?"

He had told Ged about Teine and the plan to bring Deigh to Denver in an attempt to get more information from her. It was always helpful to have Ged on his side and Beast as backup, particularly now that Hollie's safety was at risk.

"Nothing so far. Obviously, they don't think it was a random attack. Their advice was to increase security, which I've already done. From now on, Rick's security team will be following the new bus. When we stop, they'll patrol the exterior."

Hollie slumped back in her seat. "So we are no closer to knowing who is responsible?"

Torque leaned across the table and took her hand. "All we know for sure is that this is escalating."

Although he couldn't say why, he felt like the end was approaching. A final confrontation was looming and he had to put himself and Hollie on the right side of it. It was just so hard to achieve that goal when their opponent remained faceless.

The encounter with Deigh had brought him an answer…of sorts. It seemed his conviction that Teine was alive had been proved correct. There was still a long way to go before he could confirm the connection between Teine and these fires. And then he had to do the hardest thing of all. He had to stop her…

Even if Teine wasn't the Incinerator, if she was alive, she was trouble. One day, Torque would have to face her again. Since he was never going back into captivity, that meant he had to defeat her. Or die trying.

When Ged left, Hollie regarded him over the top of her coffee cup. "We never did talk about you and Deigh."

"Does that bother you? It shouldn't."

She tilted her head to one side as she considered the question. "No, it doesn't bother me in *that* way. How could I be jealous of something that happened in your past? I suppose I'm curious. You and her?" She shook her head. "I can't see that."

"I'm not going to pretend to be a victim, but the Deigh I became involved with wasn't the woman you saw on that mountaintop. We met in the valley—yes, she left her ice palace—and she appeared normal. Did I think she was the love of my life? No. Was I attracted to her? Yes. I was stupid, or horny. I guess the two things can often be the same. I got into a relationship with her without knowing anything about her. It didn't take me long to realize she was insane. And, of course, I discovered she was a sorceress, who just happened to be Teine's sister. While I was backing off, Deigh thought she was in the middle of the greatest love affair of all time. Our breakup wasn't pretty."

"Did she leave her ice palace specifically to seek you out?" Hollie asked.

"I never thought of it that way." Torque considered the question. It was so long ago, and some memories were better left in the past. "Why do you ask?"

"I'm not sure. It just seems strange that both sisters had this intense thing for you." She gave him a teasing smile. "Not that I don't get it, of course. But I wondered if Deigh came looking for you as a way of getting at Teine. You said they hated each other, and it would be the ultimate way to hurt her sister. Steal the guy she's crazy about. How did Teine react when she knew you and Deigh were together?"

"I don't know. I can't imagine she took it well, but I never saw the two of them interact. Like I said, it was well known in the Highlands that they kept well away from each other." He scrubbed a hand over his face. "God, this is hard."

Hollie returned the clasp of his hand, anxiety in the depths of her eyes. "What is?"

"All of it." He raised her hand to his lips. "I'm a dragon. I should be able to control this. Whatever the hell *this* is."

"If we hadn't met, none of this would have come your way…"

He was out of his seat and at her side in one explosive movement. "Don't ever say that." Dropping to his knees, he wrapped his arms around her waist. "Don't even think it. When you came into my life, you changed everything. You made the world right. If only there was a way—"

She rested her cheek against the top of his head. "A way we could have forever?"

"If there was, would you take it?"

When she lifted her head to look at him, her eyes had filled with tears. "I would do anything."

At that moment, there was a knock on the door. Muttering a curse about bad timing, Torque went to answer it. Since the security team wouldn't allow just anyone to approach his room, he knew it had to be one of his friends. Sure enough, it was Sarange and Karina.

"Khan asked me to remind you about the sound check," Sarange said as she kissed Torque on the cheek.

"Was he as polite as that?" Torque asked.

She laughed. "He may have used the words 'sorry,

unpunctual, dragon ass' somewhere in the original message."

She placed Karina on the floor. The baby had just learned to walk, but faced with a new environment, she reverted to a devastatingly fast crawl. As Sarange darted after her, removing objects from her grasp, Torque turned to Hollie.

"Let's continue our conversation at another time."

She nodded. "I meant it. Anything."

What he saw in her eyes was the future he wanted. There was no more pain and darkness, only love and light. He wanted to see that every day, to have the assurance that it would never go away. He wanted Hollie in his heart and in his arms. He didn't want to watch her grow old while he stayed young, or to wake one day and find that she was a dear, sweet memory. *Forever.* It had to be within their grasp.

"I'll find a way."

Chapter 15

One of the consequences of the bus fire had been that everything the band had with them was lost. Clothing, cell phones, electronic devices, bank cards…everything had to be replaced. Rick had gotten organized and most things had been speedily replaced, but it meant Hollie only had a few outfits. And she didn't like any of them.

"I'm really not a combat gear sort of girl," she explained to Sarange as they drank mint tea in her hotel suite and took turns to extricate Karina from trouble. Although the baby had a pile of toys, she was ignoring them. The silken fastenings from the drapes had been chewed and cast aside, elegant cushions had been flung to the four corners of the room and a glossy magazine had been carefully shredded.

"Ew." Sarange wrinkled her dainty nose. "Rick is great, but would I trust him to buy my clothes? I'd rather send Khan, and that's saying something. Why don't we go shopping now?"

Hollie was torn. The prospect of buying some new clothes was appealing, but the shadowy image of the Incinerator rose before her eyes. "I don't know."

"I always have security with me when I go out," Sarange said. "And I wear a disguise. This won't be any different. It just means you need to do the same."

Hollie succumbed. "Let's do it."

Organizing security and getting Karina ready took some time. Just as they were about to leave, Sarange covered her mouth with one hand. "Give me a minute." She dashed toward the bathroom.

Hollie squatted next to Karina's stroller. "I guess Mommy isn't feeling too great."

Karina grinned and punched the toys that hung in front of her. Clearly, she hadn't noticed her mother's distress. When Sarange returned, she looked pale, but composed.

"Are you okay?" Hollie asked. "Could it have been something you ate?"

"Morning sickness." Sarange grinned. "I was the same with Karina."

"Oh, my goodness." Hollie jumped up and hugged her. "Congratulations."

"You are the only one who knows," Sarange warned. "Apart from Khan, of course. We're going to tell the other guys at a special meal after the final concert."

"I won't say a word," Hollie promised. "Do you want to stay here and rest instead of going shopping?"

"Are you kidding? I'll be fine now. Let's hit those stores."

Three hours later, Hollie was starting to wonder if pregnancy hormones had given Sarange a burst of energy. Her own head was spinning and her feet were aching after they had dashed in and out of a dozen stores in the high-class mall. The upside was that she had managed to purchase some new clothes during the whirlwind tour. Now, as they flopped into a booth in a coffee shop, she let out a long sigh of relief. "Do you always shop like it's a competition to reach the finish line?"

Sarange, who had her long, dark hair tucked up inside a hat, lifted her shades to give Hollie a pitying look and kept her voice low. "I'm a werewolf. Everything I do is a competition to reach the finish line." She grinned. "Plus, I don't get out much."

After they ordered drinks, Sarange took Karina, who had just woken up, to the restroom for a diaper change. While she was gone, Hollie glanced around, her eyes seeking out the security guards who had remained at a discreet distance from them during the retail expedition. She was reassured to see the two burly figures standing close to the door.

Her attention was caught by another man. He was close to the serving counter, talking on his cell, with his back to Hollie. Dressed in a dark suit, he was tall and slim with light brown hair. There was nothing unusual about his appearance. Except she knew him. She'd have recognized him anywhere. As he turned and she got a clearer view of his profile, her heart gave a curious, uncomfortable thud. What was Dalton Hilger doing in this coffee shop?

Abandoning her packages, Hollie was on her feet and moving toward him without thinking. This couldn't be a coincidence. The only reason for Dalton to be in Dallas was as part of the Incinerator inquiry. The coffee shop was crowded and her progress was hindered as she made her way around busy tables. By the time she got close, Dalton had slipped his cell into the inside pocket of his jacket and was on the move.

She called out his name, but he was out the door and mingling with the crowds in the mall before she could reach him.

"You want me to go after him?" One of Rick's security guys was at her side in an instant.

Hollie shook her head. Feeling dejected and confused, she returned to the table, where Sarange was waiting with a look of surprise. She could call Dalton, but if she told him she'd seen him, she'd be giving away her location. If she questioned him about the Incinerator case and any connection to Dallas, would he even talk to her about what was going on? She no longer knew what her status was regarding the investigation. The truth was that she had cut all ties to Dalton and the FBI. They were no longer a part of her life, but she hadn't told anyone about it yet. On balance, it was probably just as well he'd gone before she could speak to him. Having a big, life-changing conversation thrust upon her unexpectedly wasn't the way to go.

"Someone you know?" Sarange asked as Hollie slid back into her seat.

"Just a mistake." She smiled. "Now, where are those drinks we ordered?"

When Torque returned to the hotel and found Hollie was still out with Sarange, he decided now was as good a time as any to talk to Ged. They headed for the bar.

"Is this a conversation that requires the good cognac?" It was a tradition within the band. The more serious the subject, the better the brandy needed to be.

"Yeah. Go for it."

The room was almost empty, but they took their

drinks to a quiet corner where there was no chance of being overheard.

"This is about Hollie." Ged opened the brandy bottle and sloshed the aromatic liquid into their glasses.

"Of course it is." Torque sipped his drink. "How can this have happened to us? How could a dragon-shifter and a human have been fated to become mates?"

"It's an unusual, but not an unknown, situation in the shifter world. Over time werewolves, were-bears, were-tigers and others have all taken humans as their life partners. Of course, the mortal must become a convert. He, or she, must be willing to take the bite of their partner and transform into a shifter themselves." Ged studied Torque over the top of his glass. "It's never an easy decision."

"I can't imagine how anyone asks that question of their partner," Torque said. "Where do you start when it comes to giving up being human?"

"Once the step has been taken, there's no going back. But I guess it's a lot like proposing marriage. You both give up your old lives and begin a new one. In the case of a human taking the bite of a shifter, it's just more dramatic." Ged's gaze was searching. "Is this leading somewhere?"

Torque shrugged. "Can it? I suppose that's my question. You know what my problem is. Dragon blood must remain pure. I've never heard of a human taking a dragon bite."

Ged tented his fingers beneath his chin, his expression thoughtful. Torque wanted to hold his breath. What if the answer was a simple negative?

No, you can never claim Hollie as your permanent mate. Prepare to spend the rest of forever in hell.

His heart had soared when Hollie said she would

do anything to be with him. But what if there wasn't anything she *could* do? Dragons were unique among shifters. He had been raised to believe in the proud purity of the dragon bloodline. The simplicity with which other shifters could convert a mortal was not for them. Now he longed for that ease. Asking Hollie to become a shifter wouldn't be something he took lightly, but he would love to have that choice.

Just when he thought Ged was never going to speak again, his friend nodded slowly. "Have you heard of the dragon mark?"

Torque was about to shake his head, when he paused. There *was* something, way down deep in the mists of his memory. "Forged in fire?" His hand shook as he dashed off the rest of his drink and reached for the bottle. "That's it? That's the best you can do?"

Ged held out his hands, palms upward. "That's all I've got."

"The dragon mark was a way of ensuring fealty to a clan leader." Torque frowned as he dredged up the ancient ritual from the recesses of his mind. "It was never about mating."

"That's true, but I heard a story, many centuries ago, in China. It was the tale of a dragon prince who fell in love with a human. His father, the king, refused to hear of his marriage to a mortal unless she *could* be converted. The only way was to use the ancient rite of fealty. She took the dragon mark and became his dragon bride."

Torque sat up a little straighter. "You saw it for yourself?"

Ged shook his head. "No. I only heard about the story."

"So if I want to be with Hollie forever, I have to ask

her to step into a pit of fire with me while I sink my dragon fangs into her neck? All based on a story you heard a few hundred years ago?"

"That sounds like an accurate summary." Ged tilted his glass toward him.

"Damn it all to hell, Ged. How do I introduce *this* into a conversation?"

"That is a question that will require a second bottle."

Torque was in a mildly alcoholic haze when his cell buzzed with a message from Hollie letting him know she was back in their room. The brandy hadn't numbed the shock of what Ged had told him, but their conversation had given him some thinking time.

The dragon mark had always been more the stuff of legend than reality. He'd never known anyone who wore it, never heard of a human who had taken that step. To blindly walk into a fire for love? All based on a story that Ged had once been told? He couldn't ask that of Hollie. She had said she would do anything, but she hadn't known the reality of what "anything" might mean.

When he reached their suite, he found her unpacking a number of bags. Although she smiled when she saw him, he could tell there was something on her mind. As he drew her into his arms, she sniffed the air.

"My goodness. I'm surprised your dragon fire didn't set light to all that alcohol," she teased.

"Ms. Fire Safety." He kissed the tip of her nose. "What's troubling you?"

"I saw Dalton Hilger today."

"Your ex? The FBI guy?"

She nodded. "He was in the coffee shop Sarange and I went to. He didn't see me, but I know it was him." Her eyes grew more troubled. "He must be in town because of the Incinerator."

"That's not necessarily a bad thing. It could mean they're getting close."

"I tried telling myself that." Her expression became even more gloomy. "But what if it turns out Teine is the Incinerator? Human cops won't be able to arrest her. That means Dalton is in danger."

"But you can't call him and warn him because you'll give away your location," Torque said, following her thought processes.

"Exactly, although I could live with telling him everything if I thought it would end this nightmare. It's more about not wanting to draw the FBI's attention to you and your friends." She sighed, resting her cheek against his chest. "Anyway, Dalton would think I was crazy if I tried to tell him all of this mayhem was caused by a woman with supernatural powers."

Sensing her need for reassurance, Torque held her close. It was always this way when her two worlds were in conflict. He knew she had made a commitment to him and this new life, but sometimes she was torn. The scientist in her was strong. Hollie hadn't been raised in the ways of magic and legend. and even after a dragon flight, it was hard for her to accept them.

After a few minutes, she raised her head. Lifting a hand to stroke his cheek, she smiled. "You know how to make me feel better. I love you so much, Torque."

Emotions stormed through him, setting his blood alight. Even though he had always known Hollie loved him, it was the first time she'd said those words out loud. Hearing them from her lips made his world feel right. No matter what else happened, he would always treasure this moment. Before he could push past the lump in his throat to respond, Hollie was speaking again.

"When we talked earlier about finding a way to have forever...that would mean everything to me." Her eyes were shining with unshed tears.

He loved Hollie more than life. She was his mate. She loved him in return. Ged had told him of a way they could be together... Torque almost lost it and told her about the dragon mark. Almost.

"I love you, too. More than words can say." He kissed her forehead. "And I'll keep on searching for a way to find forever."

"I miss the Monster." Dev was lying stretched out on a sofa in the bus, eating potato chips and drinking soda.

Hollie looked up from her new laptop. "This bus is almost identical."

He gave a theatrical sigh. "It doesn't have the ambience."

"You mean it doesn't have the same memories and beer stains," Torque said.

They had left Dallas immediately after the performance, traveling overnight. The mood was curiously subdued, but Hollie wondered if that could have something to do with Khan's absence. The larger-than-life lead singer was driving Sarange and Karina in their own car.

"Rock 'n' roll and baby sick? I don't think so." That had been Sarange's official explanation. Privately, she'd told Hollie that her morning sickness was getting worse. "All-day sickness, more like."

The closer they got to Denver, the more restless Torque was becoming. Hollie knew the reason, of course. Beast had one sell-out performance on the following night, but that wasn't the explanation for his nerves. No, his roller-coaster mood was all about the approaching reunion with Alban and Deigh. Ged had arranged VIP passes for Torque's guests and they would be staying in the same luxury hotel as the band. Hollie had emailed Alban with the arrangements and they would be arriving in Denver on the following day. All Torque had to do was charm Deigh into revealing more about her sister without raising any false hopes that he was in love with her. No pressure.

Hollie was worried, as well. The high drama of the encounter on the snowy mountaintop was fresh in her mind. While she trusted Torque to protect her from Deigh, she didn't want to feel all that malevolence up close once again. She had enough to think about without Deigh's ice-dagger stares and swooning glances in Torque's direction.

She had left Dallas on a sigh of relief, feeling she could breathe again when she saw the city's bright lights receding in the distance. There had been no Incinerator attacks there. Could that be because the arsonist knew the FBI were on his tail? Or, if Teine was the arsonist, had Deigh told her sister about their visit to her chilly lair? Whatever the reason, Hollie was glad there had been no fire-related drama recently.

In addition to his unease about meeting Deigh again, Hollie sensed a deeper trouble going on inside Torque. She knew it was linked to her. It was evident in the way he watched her. As though she was a dear memory that would soon be gone. It scared her, but when she tried to talk to him about it, he became evasive. Now, unable to focus on the screen in front of her, she wandered into the kitchen in search of coffee.

Ged was there and he poured her a cup, pointing to

cream and sugar. Hollie shook her head. "Strong and black is what I need."

He was watching her face with something that looked a lot like sympathy. "He told you about the dragon mark, then?"

She paused in the act of blowing on her coffee. She had always known this man was not what he appeared to be. The hold he had over the members of the band was stronger than just that of their manager. Once she knew they were shifters, Torque had talked about the part Ged played in rescuing them. Now it seemed he might also have another role. That of confidant.

"Hmm." It was as noncommittal as she could get. She wanted to encourage Ged to keep speaking without admitting she had no idea what he was talking about.

"It's a huge step. Walking into a pit of fire and allowing your mate to sink his fangs into your neck? All so you can become a dragon convert? It's not quite the same as the whole dress, flowers and cake scenario most mortal women dream of. I expect you need some time to think about it."

"Yeah." Hollie cast a glance along the corridor toward the living area. She could just see Torque's profile as he leaned against the window, gazing moodily out at the view. "I guess I do."

When she returned to her seat next to Torque, she tucked her feet up under her and rested her chin on his shoulder. They watched the scenery flash past in silence for a minute or two. "What were you and Ged talking about in there?"

She turned her face into his neck, hiding a smile. "How to play with fire."

"I guess you're already an expert on that." There was a hint of surprise in his voice.

"It's a subject about which I aim to become even more knowledgeable."

Chapter 16

Alban called Torque to confirm that he and Deigh had arrived and they arranged to meet prior to the concert. Apart from the fact that his old friend was in town, Torque could find nothing positive in the situation. The truth was he hated subterfuge. He hated bringing Deigh into his new life. He hated that Hollie was being pushed to the sidelines while she was here. He hated every god-damn thing about it.

"If the Incinerator would step out of the shadows and face me, none of this would be necessary." He slouched moodily around the hotel suite as the time to leave drew closer.

"I don't like this any more than you do, but if Deigh gives you some more details about Teine, then it will be worth it." Hollie linked her fingers behind his neck, pulling him down for a kiss. "Just as long as she keeps her icy hands to herself."

"Hollie, I am going to take her to dinner, ask her some questions and leave. You can't possibly be worried there will be anything more to it."

She laughed. "I'm not. And I'll be with Alban."

"You'll have more fun." He frowned. "And you should be with me now when I'm going to meet them."

Hollie shook her head. "The idea is to get on Deigh's good side. There's no point in antagonizing her by turning up with me holding your hand. If I stay in the background, it may keep her sweet."

Torque ran a hand through his hair. "Deigh is mad. Did I mention that? I can't believe we're having a conversation about keeping her sweet. It's like discussing the best way to feed a rabid dog."

Hollie stepped back, studying him with her head on one side. "If looks have anything to do with it, she won't be able to resist you."

He growled. "I am not a sacrifice to the ice sorceress. What will you do while I'm gone? The concert doesn't start for hours."

"I told Sarange I'd take Karina off her hands. I'll take her out for a walk."

"Won't Sarange go with you?" Torque asked.

"I don't think she's feeling too great."

Torque spared a moment to feel surprised. Sarange was a werewolf and a superfit human. He'd never known her have a minute's illness. "I hope she's okay."

"I'm sure she'll be fine." Hollie placed a hand in the small of his back, pointing him toward the door. "I don't want to send you off to meet another woman, but this has to be done."

"Kiss me again to make it bearable."

When her lips met his and her taste flowed through him, everything else faded away. His inner dragon surged, demanding release, urging him to possess her. Forcing himself to retain control, Torque still couldn't keep his hands from her. Gripping her hips in a rough, possessive hold, he pulled her tight against him, letting her feel his arousal. Hollie gasped at the pressure and pushed back. Shaking at the effort to maintain control, Torque covered her mouth with his, dominating her, forcing her to open for his possession. Her enthusiastic response stoked the fire higher and higher until they broke apart trembling.

"Ah, Hollie." He rested his forehead against hers. "What you do to me."

"Maybe you could be a few minutes late..."

Torque sucked in a harsh breath, leaning back against the door as she sank to her knees. A tremor of pleasure ran through Hollie's body as she grasped his thighs and leaned into him. She paused for a moment, pressing her face to the bulge in his jeans as she inhaled his scent.

When she reached for his zipper and button and freed his straining erection from the confines of his jeans, Torque's heart rate skyrocketed. Tangling his hands in her hair, he gave himself up to a firestorm of emotion.

A soft whimper came from Hollie as she moistened her lips and pursed them to form a heart shape. When she leaned forward and softly kissed the head of his cock, Torque almost went into orbit. Hollie's eyelids fluttered closed as she sighed. Slowly, she kissed down his shaft and back up again.

Opening her eyes, she kept her gaze fixed on Torque's face as she licked all the way around his sensitive tip. Her pink tongue was warm and slightly rough and his flesh twitched at the delicious sensation.

His erection hardened and tightened as she moved her mouth along it, kissing and licking, judging to perfection where the most sensitive nerve endings were concentrated. Now and then, she applied a slight sucking pressure that spiked his pleasure even higher.

"Hollie..." He couldn't take much more of this.

Shifting position, she brought her open mouth to him and closed her lips over the crown. Bobbing her head in a slow up and down motion, she relaxed her mouth on the downstroke, sucking and tonguing him as she glided back up. Watching his throbbing flesh slide in and out of her mouth was the most erotic thing he had ever seen.

The pressure began to build deep inside him, the veins at his base pulsing and burning, aching for release. Holding the sides of her head, he moved his hips in time with her mouth, feeling her moans vibrate all the way along his length. "So close."

With Hollie's hot, sweet mouth surrounding him and her tongue lapping him, he was lost in her. Throwing his head back, he closed his eyes, and braced his leg muscles, letting it hit. An orgasm close to explosion pounded his hypersensitive nerve endings at full force. Rapture was like liquid fire being poured into him, triggering a series of stunning aftershocks. Slowly, he came down from the searing high.

Feeling Hollie gently withdrawing her lips, he opened his eyes and looked down at her upturned face. Her eyes were bright with tears. His hands were still on either side of her head, but his grip was light. Even during the storm of his emotions, he was sure he hadn't tightened it.

"Tell me I didn't hurt you." His voice was shaky.

"Of course you didn't hurt me." She smiled and he was reassured that her tears were an expression of how intensely she had felt their physical connection. "You're my dragon."

Leaning down, he placed his hands under her arms and lifted her to him. Time. Since they'd met, it was the one thing they had never had enough of. Even if they managed forever, would he be able to find the words to tell her how she made him feel?

"And you're mine, Hollie. All mine."

Hollie had researched places to go with a one-year-old and decided on the aquarium. It proved to be a hit with Karina, who was fascinated by the sea creatures. Cooing and babbling, she waved her arms delightedly as Hollie, with two bodyguards following at a discreet distance, pushed the stroller around the exhibits.

Hollie herself was even more entertained by Karina's delight than she was by the creatures around her, but nothing could keep her thoughts from straying to Torque. She knew how emotionally draining the meeting with Deigh would be and wished she was there at his side to support him. Anything that took him back to his past was hard for him. Knowing the story of what Teine had done to him, she could understand why.

Alongside the grief he felt for his family and the life he had lost, his pride and self-esteem had been destroyed. Torque was an alpha-male, a leader among dragons. Teine had taken that from him, leaving him with no one to lead and shackling him to her. Hollie's heart cried out at the thought of her proud dragon-shifter chained and imprisoned, unable to soar.

As well as her concerns for Torque's well-being, she was still buzzing with erotic memories from the recent scene in their hotel room. Although her body had been overheated, it was the emotional connection that burned deepest. Torque was in her soul, and that was what made sex between them so good. She bit back a smile. *Good? I meant rapturous.*

Although Karina couldn't talk, she was good at making her needs known. When she lost interest in her surroundings and started lifting her arms up to come out of the stroller, Hollie figured it was time to stop for refreshments. Finding a seat in an area away from the crowds that thronged the main walkways, she took Karina's bottle out of its thermos and lifted the little girl onto her knee. The baby gave a sigh of contentment as she started to drink.

Sarange's instructions had been clear. Karina would have formula and then some solid food. Next would come a nap in the stroller, followed by a diaper change.

"You're going to be gentle with me on that one, aren't you, sweetheart? I'm new to all this." She murmured the words into Karina's hair, and the little girl gently patted Hollie's cheek as she drank.

Hollie became vaguely aware of someone approaching her, only looking up when that person paused right in front of her. Her gaze traveled upward from a pair of hand-stitched tan shoes—*I know those shoes!*—following the suit pants, white shirt and navy tie upward until she was looking into Dalton's frowning gray eyes.

Among the dozens of thoughts swirling through her mind in that instant, there was only one that mattered. Once again it fixed itself in her mind.

This is not a coincidence.

"Did you follow me here?" Of course he had followed her. The chances of seeing him in the coffee shop in Dallas were remote. Seeing him a second time in Denver? Hollie's mathematical brain tried and failed to calculate those odds.

"It's nice to see you, as well, Hols." He took a seat next to her, nodding at Karina. "Whose baby?"

"A friend's. Answer the question, Dalton. Did you follow me?"

Conscious of one of the bodyguards signaling to her, she caught his eye and shook her head, the gesture so slight that it went unseen by Dalton. Hollie and Karina were in no danger and she needed answers.

"Kind of." He grinned and she relaxed a little. This was *Dalton*. He was her friend and her colleague. Or ex-colleague. She still didn't know what was going on with her FBI status. Right now it was about the least important thing about this whole situation. "Would you believe me if I said I saw you coming out of your hotel? I mean, once that happened, I had to go after you, didn't I?"

"Why didn't you approach me as soon as you saw me? Why wait until now?"

"Jeez, Hollie. Why all these questions? This is *me*." He looked slightly bemused as he echoed her own thoughts. "If you must know, I was making sure you weren't being followed by anyone else."

"Oh." She subsided, chewing her lip. His reply sounded reasonable. Scary, but reasonable. "This is about the Incinerator."

"Of course it is. What the hell else did you think it was about?" He gave her a sidelong look. "So you finally did something about it."

Hollie could guess what was coming, but she was going to look him in the eye and force him to say it. "About what?"

"Come on, Hols. *Him*. Torque. You're obsessed with him. Always have been. It's what split us up. Now you're with him."

Dalton used to laugh about her "*Torque-thing.*" It had been a joke between them. *It's what split us up?* It was like he was trying to rewrite history. It was also *not* like Dalton.

She drew in a breath. "I wouldn't have this sort of conversation back when we were dating, Dalton, so I'm sure as hell not doing it now. You know better than to think I would give you a say in how I live my life."

"The difference this time is it matters to an investigation." There was a hint of triumph in his voice.

"I know that," she snapped back at him. "*I* told McLain the Incinerator was targeting places Torque had been. Now instead of trying to score points because you don't like him, tell me if you are any closer to finding the person who killed her."

Hollie forced herself to get a grip on her anger, partly because it wasn't helpful, but mostly for Karina's sake. Cuddling the little girl's warm, plump body close, she reviewed the situation. Dalton had shown no sign of surprise when she let slip that she had told McLain about the connection to Torque. That must mean the FBI had been investigating the link all along. She wasn't sure whether that was good, or bad. On the one hand, no one had come pointing any fingers at Torque or interrogating him and his friends. On the other, they hadn't caught the Incinerator, either.

"I'll be honest with you, this case is as puzzling as ever." Dalton dug his hands into his jacket pocket and stretched his long legs in front of him.

"But you're here," Hollie persisted. "There must be a reason for that."

"You've been right so far. Wherever Torque goes, the Incinerator follows. It made sense for the investigation to be there, as well."

"But no one from the FBI has spoken to Torque." Hollie was confused. She had assumed that, when the investigators kept their distance, it must mean that McLain hadn't told the team of Hollie's suspicions. If they knew Torque was the link, keeping their distance made no sense.

"We haven't needed to do an interview, Hollie. Not when you've been right up close to him."

The note in Dalton's voice surprised her and she turned her head to look at him more closely. She could see hurt in his eyes, and it shocked her. After all this time, he still cared that much?

The pained look deepened. "Even sharing a room. When McLain sent you undercover, she couldn't have expected that sort of dedication from you."

"McLain told you I was working undercover?" Hollie frowned. "You never mentioned that when I called you."

His smile was lopsided. "I guess you're not the only one who's good at keeping secrets."

"This isn't about scoring points, Dalton." A little flare of anger made her speak more harshly than she'd intended. "We're on the same side here. We both want to catch a dangerous arsonist before he does any more harm."

As she finished talking, Karina drank the last of her milk and sat up straighter. The baby regarded Dalton with wide golden eyes for a moment or two. Apparently deciding she didn't like this stranger, she nestled closer to Hollie, burying her face in the front of her blouse and starting to cry.

"Look, you're busy and I have to go." Dalton got to his feet.

Hollie wanted to cry out in annoyance. All Dalton had given her was a series of nonanswers. "I'll call you."

Her priority was trying to soothe Karina, but the whole situation was intensely frustrating. If anything, Dalton's presence in Denver had deepened the mystery. As she watched him walk away, the questions she wanted to ask rose to her lips. She couldn't pursue them now, but she was determined to get the answers from him. He had spoken as if her undercover role was still being treated as part of the investigation. Well, if that was the case, he could step up and brief her fully.

"Hey, sweetheart." She reached into Karina's bag and produced a tub of pasta. "Want some of this?"

Karina did a quick check to make sure Dalton had really gone before clapping her hands to express approval of the plan. As she fed the baby her lunch, Hollie's thoughts returned to Torque. She really wanted to see him, or call him, to tell him about the encounter with Dalton. Bumping into her former boyfriend at the same time Torque was meeting his evil ex was the worst kind of timing.

"These days, there doesn't seem to be any other kind," she said to Karina. In response, the baby cheerfully smeared pasta sauce onto the front of Hollie's blouse.

Torque met Alban and Deigh in the hotel lobby. Alban greeted him with a look of relief that told Torque everything he needed to know. Not that he had ever imagined a trans-Atlantic journey with Deigh would be easy.

He had seen Deigh away from her mountaintop often enough to know that the key to her behavior lay in the decisions she made. When she chose, she could be charming. It never lasted long, but she could sustain the appearance of normality for short periods. It was, after all, how she had tricked Torque into their brief relationship.

With relief, he observed that, on this occasion, she appeared inclined to be pleasant. The only oddity was her clothing. Although she had disposed of her ice princess robes, she hadn't taken account of the hot and humid weather. Deigh wore white jeans and a pale blue sweater with a long white coat over the top.

"Did you mention that, even at night, it's over seventy degrees?" Torque murmured to Alban as they headed out to a waiting cab.

"No, because I've given up on trying to make conversation of any kind," Alban said. "If it's not about you, my friend, she doesn't want to know."

Torque winced. Those words didn't inspire him with confidence that he was going to be able to keep this light and walk away. His mood lowered even further when, once they were in the cab, Deigh pressed up close to him, her eyes shining as she gazed at his face.

Ice sorceress unleashed. Was this really such a good plan?

That night's performance was at Denver's iconic Red Rocks Amphitheater. The naturally formed, outdoor venue was world-famous for its acoustics and ambience. Torque had been looking forward to this concert more than any other on the tour. Now he was wishing himself a thousand miles away. Just him and Hollie on a deserted island somewhere...maybe recreating the scene from the hotel room earlier.

Aware that Deigh was talking, he pulled himself back from the edge of a delicious fantasy.

"Where is your little pet?"

Torque's inner dragon fired up at those derogatory words used in connection with Hollie. With an effort, he forced himself to remain calm. This was what Deigh did best. By prodding and pushing, she would get him to reveal his feelings. If he let her. "I don't know what you mean."

Even away from her natural environment, her laugh sounded like breaking ice. "Come, now. Your golden girl with the emerald eyes."

He stared at her for a moment. The words were uncomfortably close to Teine's prediction about his future and to the words of the latest email. But he was on edge, unnerved by Deigh's presence, uncomfortable with this whole situation and missing Hollie. Jumping at shadows. Or seeing coincidences where they didn't exist.

"We're here." Relieved to have a distraction from Deigh's probing, Torque pointed out of the window at the majestic jutting rocks. The cab took them around to the rear of the stage, where they exited the vehicle.

The other band members were already there and Torque experienced a profound sense of relief when he saw them. As always, the team came together in times of difficulty and he could feel the hostility toward Deigh coming off his friends in waves. The problem was, he was fairly sure she could feel it, too. A slight smile tugged at the corners of her lips as she looked around her. Torque wanted to warn his bandmates. *She thrives on conflict. Hating her will only make her stronger.* He consoled himself that the members of Beast could look after themselves.

Alban provided a contrasting ray of light in the tense atmosphere. Abandoning his naturally serious demeanor, he appeared genuinely stagestruck and interested in the workings of the special effects. As Ged gave him a guided tour, Torque was left alone with Deigh. He sent a help-me glance in Khan's direction.

To his relief, the tiger-shifter sauntered over. It was a classic case of antagonism at first sight.

"I don't wish for company." Deigh tried her usual icy tones.

"I have a daughter who has that same attitude." Khan's grin was more of a snarl. "She gets away with it because she's only twelve months old. And she's pretty."

The drop in temperature had nothing to do with Deigh's powers. She turned to Torque. "When do we leave here?"

He indicated the stage and, beyond that, the audience of thousands. "There's the little matter of a concert for all these people who have paid good money and traveled to see us."

She hunched a shoulder. "I hope you will make sure it is over fast."

It was with relief that Torque handed her and Alban over to Rick so he could escort them to the VIP area. Once they'd gone, he tried to focus on the performance. Those fans had come to see Beast, and he wasn't going to sell them short.

A tap on his shoulder made him turn abruptly and he encountered Hollie's mischievous smile. Instantly, his restless spirit was soothed. "I'll be with Ged." She jerked her thumb in his manager's direction. "When I saw Alban and Deigh leaving I wanted to say hi."

Casting a quick glance around, he backed her up against a bank of speakers, kissing her until she murmured a protest. "I think the others are ready to go on-stage."

He groaned. "I hate it when real life gets in the way."

She patted his cheek. "We can finish this later."

"Oh, we will." He watched with pleasure as the blush

stained her cheeks pink. "I owe you from earlier, re-member?"

With one final kiss on her parted lips, he bounded toward the stage. A heavy, thumping beat filled the air, and Torque caught a glimpse of the almost ten-thousand-strong audience. Excitement, anticipation and exultation showed on the waiting faces. Thick, theatrical smoke rolled like fog from the stage and out into the waiting crowd and, within it, colored strobe lights danced in time with the music.

Giant LED screens were positioned at the rear of the stage. On them, alternating images of fire, close-ups of snarling animals and a stylized symbol that looked like three entwined number sixes flashed up. At the side of the stage, random explosions went off, shooting orange flames into the air.

A glance at the VIP area showed him Alban was getting into the mood of the concert. Torque could see him joining in with people around him and putting his fingers on either side of his head to make devil horns as he moved in time with the beat. Next to him, Deigh stood as still as an ice statue.

The tension built further as the crowd sensed something changing. The lighting shifted, becoming focused on a podium at the rear of the stage that supported Diablo's vast, gleaming circular wall of drums. Even above the music, the roar of the crowd filled the air as the drummer ran on from the side of the stage and vaulted into his seat behind the drums. His chest was bare and his tattooed biceps bulged as he pounded out a furious beat, his blue-black hair flopping forward to cover his face.

Torque nodded to Dev on the opposite side of the stage and, synchronizing their movements to perfection, the two of them dived into place. For this time, while he had his guitar in his hands and those devoted fans in front of him, he could lose himself in the moment. The band was more than the sum of its parts and the members reenergized each other through their music.

Torque let the power of Beast wash over him, secure that Hollie was close by. He needed this, needed the contrasting raw power of the performance and the healing balm of his mate. Both would help him conserve his strength for the coming battle of wits.

Chapter 17

After the concert, Hollie took Alban to the Mountainview Steak House. Having eyed the menu thoughtfully, he cast it aside.

"You know what I'd like?"

She regarded him with a smile. "A large steak, burned to a crisp, and no sides? Better yet, two large steaks."

"How did you guess?"

"I may have dined with a dragon once or twice before tonight."

She gave their order to the waiter, opting for a slightly more conservative choice of burger and fries for herself.

"Ah, yes." Alban gazed out the window at the nighttime view of the city with its mountain backdrop. "I wonder how Torque is getting along with his quest to learn more about Deigh's evil twin."

"Is there an evil twin in that partnership?" Hollie

asked. "From what I've seen of Deigh, she's not exactly one of the good guys."

"But you have never encountered Teine," Alban pointed out. "She makes Deigh look like a Girl Scout."

"Were they born evil? Or did something happen to make them that way?" Hollie asked.

"Now, there you have me." Alban frowned over the question. "As you know, to become sorcerers, they had to rise through the witching ranks and must also have had magical parentage. Their father was one of the greats. Known throughout the Highlands and beyond, he was Draoidh. The name itself means 'magic.' His time was before my birth, you understand, but the legends have been passed down."

Alban was a natural storyteller and Hollie found that listening to him, sipping her beer and enjoying the mood all took her mind off her worries about what Torque must be enduring.

"Although Draoidh was powerful, he was benevolent. Until a rival came along. Her name was Eile. She was a sorceress who wanted to steal Draoidh's place as the dominant force in the Highlands. The only way she could do that was to take Draoidh's magic from him. The two fought constantly, with no true outcome. Gradually, Draoidh changed. He was no longer the benign presence the Highlands had come to trust. Driven by his desire to defeat Eile, he became bitter and vengeful. One day, the two met in a mighty confrontation. Storms raged over the mountains for days. The outcome was unexpected."

His story was interrupted by the arrival of their food. Once they were alone again, Hollie, who had become engrossed in the ancient tale, leaned forward. "What happened?"

"Somehow Eile had managed to overpower and kill her stronger rival. A glimpse into her method became clear when it was seen a few months later that she was pregnant. Once or twice, she boasted that she had seduced Draoidh and murdered him while he was…um, distracted."

"Nice lady. I'm guessing she didn't find herself another partner?"

Alban laughed. "I don't think she was looking. Eile also claimed that she had absorbed all of Draoidh's power. She was now twice as strong. When her child was born, it would have enough magic for two. It was later seen as a prophecy."

"Because she had twins?"

"Yes, although their separateness started right from birth. Eile kept them hidden up on her mountaintop and didn't show them off among the villages. All anyone ever knew was that they were fire and ice."

"What happened to Eile?" Hollie asked.

"The rumor is that Teine killed her. Some argument over her mother trying to stop her throwing rocks at the mountain goats. No one knows for sure, but Eile disappeared about six years after the twins were born."

"Whoa." Hollie spluttered on a mouthful of beer. "You're saying Teine could have killed her mother when she was *six*?"

Alban tilted his head to one side. "She may have been seven," he conceded.

Hollie held her hands up. "Maybe Deigh is the good twin, after all. Have you ever seen them together to make a comparison?"

Alban shook his head. "I don't know anyone who has."

"Weird."

"Look at the parents," Alban said.

Hollie started to giggle. When he raised his brows in a question, she tried to explain. "I can't believe I'm sitting here with a dragon, talking about two evil sorceresses."

He wagged a finger at her. "That's because you are used to the company of a rough-and-ready sort of dragon. I'm an intellectual. I prefer the slow and steady approach. Some things cannot be rushed. Time finds a way to heal all wounds and settle all scores."

"What do you mean? Are you talking about Teine setting these fires as revenge?"

He took a sip of his drink. "Strangely enough, I'd forgotten about Teine."

Torque had no idea what sort of cuisine would impress Deigh, but he knew she liked snow and mountains. The Rooftop Restaurant had views across the whole city toward the distant peaks. The care he had taken in choosing somewhere that would appeal to her appeared to have been wasted, however. Deigh barely spared a glance at her surroundings, preferring to fix her gaze on Torque's face.

There was an awkward moment when they were shown to their table and the server approached her. If looks could kill—and Torque reminded himself that, in Deigh's case, looks actually *could* kill if she chose to let them—the poor guy would have dropped dead on the floor the instant he raised his hands in her direction.

"He's offering to take your coat."

"Oh." She appeared to weigh the situation. Surely she wasn't going to keep it on? After a moment or two, she shrugged the garment off and handed it to the server.

Her thick high-necked, long-sleeved sweater still kept her well covered.

They took their seats and Torque ordered a beer. "What do you want to drink?" he asked Deigh.

"Iced water." She waved an impatient hand.

Figures. Her veins probably needed a top-up.

"Tell me why I'm here."

Torque was pinned in the light blue beam of her gaze. "Pardon?"

"I could continue to torture you while we pretend you brought me all this way because you want my company, but we both know that's not true." Deigh smiled and Torque's skin went cold all over. "I will regret bringing this little charade to an end. You know how much I enjoy causing pain."

Torque leaned back in his chair, relieved that the pretense was over. Of course, Deigh would not allow this deception to go unpunished. She would demand a retribution and he knew from experience she would do her best to make it hurt. His task now was to keep her focused on him. Deflect her attention from Alban. And, most of all, keep that icy glare away from Hollie.

"If you knew there was an ulterior motive, why come here?"

Her laugh would shatter an iceberg. "The temptation to torment you was irresistible." Her gaze softened. "*You* are irresistible."

Torque squirmed slightly. "This is about Teine."

Their drinks arrived and she sipped her iced water slowly. "It always is. Do you know how it feels to have spent my life fighting my way out from beneath her shadow?"

Of the two sisters, Teine, with her fiery personality, was the one who naturally drew the most attention.

Had he given the question any thought, Torque would have said that was the way Deigh preferred it. Now it seemed he'd have been wrong.

"She's alive." He didn't need to phrase it as a question. He knew it was true.

Deigh sighed as she gazed out at the mountains. "I wish she wasn't."

"Where is she, Deigh?"

Something flickered in the depths of her eyes. Something dark and malignant. It rocked Torque back in his seat and planted a seed of doubt in his mind. Then it was gone and he was left questioning his own sanity.

"For once, look beyond your dragon arrogance." Deigh's voice was almost sad. "The answer is staring you in the face, but you refuse to accept it."

Torque wasn't in the mood for her games. "Is Teine the person who is setting fire to these buildings?"

"Can't you see it yet?" She got to her feet, leaning across the table until her face was inches from his. Gold sparks brightened the blue depths of her eyes. "Are you still so blind?"

Whirling away from him, she ran toward the exit. Muttering a curse, Torque threw some cash down on the table and followed her. Part of him wanted to let her go, but the consequence of leaving an angry sorceress loose in a built-up area wasn't one he wanted on his conscience. He found Deigh giving the elevator doors an icy glare. Clearly, she thought she could make them open by force of will.

He pressed the button. "Wait here while I get your coat."

Her eyes narrowed as she considered the situation, and then she nodded. Torque returned with her coat just as the elevator doors closed with her inside. Racing down the stairs, he reached street level in time to see Deigh exiting the building. Luckily, her silvery hair made her hard to miss even in the darkness. He chased after her, catching hold of her arm as she reached a quiet side street.

"Explain it to me, Deigh. Tell me what I'm missing."

She started to laugh, and the sound chilled him... because it didn't *chill* him. It wasn't Deigh's laugh. As he stared at her, she jerked her arm away from him. Because he still had a tight grip on her sweater, the fabric tore, revealing the skin of her arm. Torque started to apologize; then his attention was caught by the scars on her flesh. They were the marks of someone who had survived a terrible fire. The sort of blaze caused by the breath of a dragon...

He raised his eyes to her face. "Teine?"

She made a sound that was somewhere between a sob and a laugh. "You see it at last."

Torque watched in horrified fascination as a battle for control seemed to take place within her. One minute, Deigh's cool features were visible; the next they were replaced with Teine's stormy visage.

"I don't understand."

"Of course you don't. No one does." She dropped to her knees on the deserted sidewalk, wrapping her arms around her waist. "There never was a Teine *and* a Deigh. We are one, not two. Our mother told the story that she gave birth to twins because the enormous power we inherited was enough for two. We are fire and ice, but we both reside within one body and the fight for dominance is constant."

Torque ran a hand through his hair, trying to process what she was saying. Essentially, he was looking at a case of a magical split personality. Two people—two sorceresses—living in one body.

"What name do you prefer?" he asked.

Her lips drew back in a snarl. "I am Teine. Fire is always stronger than ice."

He stared down at her in fascination. Two beings who hated each other sharing a body? It must be the ultimate torture. No matter how much he hated Teine for what she had done to him, he pitied her for the torment he could see on her face. "Are you the Incinerator?"

Her laughter alternated between Deigh's icy tinkle and Teine's heated gales. "You are still not looking in the right direction. Open your eyes, *mo dragon*."

Then she was on her feet and sprinting away from him. Torque ran after her, closing the distance between them. Ahead of them, he could see bright lights, noise and people. If Teine headed that way, he would lose her. Worse, she could do untold damage in a group of mortals. He wasn't prepared to force her into a confrontation in a crowd and risk a demonstration of her powers.

As they drew closer, he saw it was a fairground. There were a few rides and stalls. To one side, an old-fashioned, steam-driven calliope wheezed out an annoyingly repetitive tune. As Teine darted into the throng of people, Torque lost sight of her.

Slumping against a wall, he pulled out his cell phone. His mind was reeling from what he'd just learned, but his first thought was for Hollie. Hopefully, she was still with Alban, and if Teine came for her, he would be able to protect her. If they were already back at the hotel, Torque could tell her to go to Ged or Khan and wait with them until he arrived.

He stared at his cell in fury as her number rang, then went straight to voice mail.

* * *

Although it was after eleven when Hollie and Alban got back to the hotel, once she reached her room there was only one thought on her mind. No matter how late it was, she was calling Dalton.

When she tried the number she had stored in her cell phone for him, she got a message that it wasn't recognized. Frowning, she tapped the digits in from memory. The message was the same. Of course, there was nothing to stop an FBI agent changing his number in the middle of an investigation. It was just…odd. And the prickling feeling of dread running down her spine intensified.

Calling the twenty-four-hour number for the Newark field office, she explained her problem to the operator. "I'm trying to get in touch with Agent Hilger."

Did she sense a slight hesitation? "Who's calling?"

"I'd prefer to speak direct to Agent Hilger. I just need his cell phone number."

"Agent Hilger is no longer on active duty—"

Hollie ended the call fast, her heart thumping out a mad, new rhythm. What the *hell* was going on? How could Dalton be in town as part of the Incinerator investigation if he was no longer on the team? And what had happened to get him taken off active duty? Her head was spinning out of control when her cell phone rang.

She experienced a wild moment of hope that it might be Dalton calling her to explain the misunderstanding. It was Khan.

"Hollie? I hate to ask you this so late at night, but Sarange is really ill. She's been throwing up nonstop for hours. I need to get her to a doctor friend of Ged's so he can get some fluids into her…"

"I'll stay with Karina." She was on her feet, placing her cell on the bedside table as she spoke.

"You're a lifesaver."

Khan and Sarange had a suite just along the corridor. When Hollie arrived, Khan was already waiting by the door. He drew her into one of his signature hugs. At his side, Sarange looked like a pale shadow of her usual self.

"Thank you." She kissed Hollie's cheek. "We can't go to the emergency room. Shifter DNA makes everything that bit more complicated. But we'll be back as soon as we can."

"Karina and I will be fine. You go and get well."

After they'd gone, Hollie checked on the baby. Karina was sound asleep in her crib. Going back into the sitting room, she paused, realizing she'd left her cell phone in her own suite. Wanting to let Torque know where she was, she called down to reception.

"When he returns, can you let him know I'm babysitting in the Colorado Suite, please?"

With a restlessness fueled by the information she'd been given about Dalton, she wandered the luxurious suite. It was almost identical to the one she and Torque were in, except this one had different views. Standing on the balcony overlooking the perfectly manicured hotel gardens, she drank in the mountain vista, trying to make some sense of her disordered thoughts.

When she had seen Dalton at the aquarium, there had been nothing in his demeanor to make her suspect a problem. He had been evasive, but otherwise he had appeared to be his usual self. *No longer on active duty.* That could mean so many things. Was he ill? Oh, dear Lord, was Dalton *dying*? She took a breath, getting her disordered thoughts under control. It was probably less dramatic. He could be on a misconduct charge. If that was the case, why would he be here, pretending to be part of the investigation? Could this all be a terrible mistake? Maybe the operator she spoke to had gotten the name wrong. Dalton was the most dedicated agent Hollie had ever known. The FBI was his life. She couldn't imagine he would allow anything to jeopardize that.

But those words had been so final. *No longer on active duty.* Not "unavailable" or "out of the office." Something drastic had happened, and it had happened fast.

Her musings were interrupted by a cry from the bedroom and she left the balcony with a feeling of relief. At least dealing with the baby would give her a break from her other problems for a while.

"It's okay, sweetheart, I'm here—" She walked into the bedroom and stopped in shock. Dalton was standing beside the crib holding Karina.

"She scratched me." Dalton cradled his hand against his chest, staring at the baby in horror. Blood was already running down his wrist and soaking into his white shirt.

"Good. I hope it hurt." Shock took second place to the need to care for the baby. Hollie strode forward, taking Karina from him and holding the sobbing child to her shoulder. Stroking her hair, she felt a fierce pride in the little shifter. "There, there. It's okay. I've got you now."

"What kind of baby leaves marks like that?" Dalton held up his hand, showing the deep cuts in his flesh.

One who has a tiger-shifter for a dad and a werewolf for a mom. Hollie decided not to mention Karina's parentage. "One that's scared out of her wits because you woke her up and she doesn't know you. What were you thinking? Why are you even here?" Trying to keep her anger and outrage under control so she didn't alarm Karina was proving difficult. "And how the hell did you get into this room?"

As she spoke, Dalton started to smile. Then she saw the gun in his other hand and everything fell into place. All at once. Horribly and easily. Hollie raised a shaking hand to her lips. "*You* are the Incinerator." Her voice refused to rise above a whisper. "Why, Dalton?"

His smile twisted, becoming something that made her glad Karina's face was still turned away from him.

"Why? Because, even when we were together, you wanted *him*. Do you know how it feels to be second best to an album cover? Well, now you've made your dream come true." He gave a mirthless laugh. "Only I'm going to turn it into a nightmare, Hollie. For both of you."

Torque had never wanted to shift so badly. His inner dragon was making a strong case for just forgetting convention and taking flight across the city. So what if he was seen? He'd cope with the wild speculation about dragons over Denver once he knew Hollie was safe. In the end, his human common sense prevailed and he ran faster than he had ever done. By the time he reached the hotel, his lungs were on fire. If Teine, or Deigh, or whatever the hell she was calling herself right now, had gotten there before him, it would only be because she'd found a way to teleport since the last time they met.

He was about to dash across the lobby to the elevators when the desk clerk called out to him. "I have a message for you from Ms. Brown. She asked me to let you know that she's babysitting in the Colorado Suite."

Calling out a quick word of thanks, Torque headed up to Khan's suite. As least he knew where Hollie was, although he didn't know why she was with Khan and Sarange. He also had no idea why she wasn't answering his calls.

Leaving the elevator at a run, he hammered on the door of the Colorado Suite…and was greeted by silence.

"Khan, open the damn door." Even as he shouted to his friend, he already knew the suite was empty.

The fury that surged through him was so powerful it took everything he had to contain his inner dragon. *Think. Focus.* He couldn't accept that there had been enough time for Teine to reach the hotel and snatch Hollie before he got here. And where the hell were Khan and Sarange? He was pulling his cell phone out of his pocket, ready to call everyone he knew, when the spots of blood on the carpet just outside the door caught his attention.

Squatting to get a closer look, he saw they were fresh and his heart ricocheted wildly against his rib cage. As he started to call Alban, his cell rang. He didn't recognize the number, but he answered it with a feeling of dread.

"Lost something?"

Torque was instantly disoriented. Having expected to hear Tiene's fiery voice, or Deigh's mocking tones, he was thrown off balance by the man's voice. "Who is this?"

"You don't get to ask the questions. I have Hollie and the baby. If you want to see them again, go alone to the Denver Image Company. It's a disused copy shop on Stockton Street."

"Let me speak to Hollie—" He was talking to dead air. The caller had ended the conversation.

Alone. For Hollie and Karina's safety, he would follow that instruction, but there was no harm in having backup waiting nearby. As he headed back toward the elevator, he was calling Ged.

"Get the guys together and head over to Stockton Street, but stay out of sight until I give you a signal. You'll need to track Khan down. He's not in his room."

After he ended that call, the next person he spoke to was Alban. "This is a long story and I don't have time to give you all the details right now. Teine and Deigh are the same person and she's loose in the city. Find her."

His friend was still spluttering out a series of confused questions when Torque cut him off. Having reached street level, Torque was about to exit the building when he realized he was missing a vital piece of information. Turning back, he walked over to the reception desk. "Stockton Street. Walking distance, or a cab ride?"

The clerk looked startled. "It's probably a ten-minute walk, sir. But it's not a great area."

"That's okay." Torque's smile was grim. "I'm not in a great mood."

The ten-minute walk took him five, during which time he recalled Hollie's words about accelerants. *Copier toner.* That was one of the things she'd said the Incinerator looked for in the buildings he burned down. And now the arsonist was in a copy shop...

Bright needles of pain danced across his forehead and his skin felt too hot, too tight. He forced the surge of panic back down inside himself. He was no good to Hollie and Karina if he gave way to the tumult of emotion that was threatening to overwhelm him.

Stockton Street was a short street comprising a number of commercial units on one side and a weary looking high-rise block on the other. Several of the streetlights were out and Torque took a moment to catch his breath as he approached the boarded-up storefront of the Denver Image Company.

He paused before he drew level with the darkened building, some instinct warning him to stay back. His intuition was telling him he would know if Hollie was inside that place. She was his mate. He would feel her. He didn't.

Now he had to weigh his options. Walk into what was probably a trap on the chance that Hollie and Karina were inside, or turn away, not knowing where they could be?

For a dragon, there was only ever going to be one answer to that question. Torque strode toward the door of the empty store.

Chapter 18

The streets were quiet as Dalton drove them away from the hotel. They had taken the back stairs down from the suite, leaving by a service exit to avoid crossing the lobby.

Hollie tried desperately to fix on something during the journey so she knew where they were going, but Karina was restless. Hollie had managed to snatch up a blanket from the crib and wrap Karina up in it as they left the suite, so at least the baby was warm.

"She needs something to eat and a diaper change."

"Too bad." Dalton kept his eyes fixed on the road.

He had ensured her cooperation as they left the hotel by keeping the gun pressed tight against her ribs. "I have enough bullets for the baby, as well."

Dalton, the scratches on his wrist still bleeding, ushered Hollie from the vehicle and into a run-down apartment building. All she noticed as she left the car was the fairground on the square opposite the building.

When they got inside, the elevator wasn't working and Dalton pushed her ahead of him up the stairs. She focused on counting. *Fifth floor. I don't know where I am, but I know how high. And that calliope music is already driving me crazy.*

She was still struggling to come to terms with what was happening. She had always believed the Incinerator fires were either a tribute to Torque or an act of vengeance against him. Now it turned out Hollie was the target. Yes, vengeance was the motive and Torque was the trigger. But this had been about *her* all along.

I was hunting a man who was pursuing me. And he was doing it in plain sight.

She remembered how Dalton had always joked about her fondness for Beast and her liking for Torque in particular. Back then, she hadn't seen it as a big deal. If anything, it had been a source of amusement between them. How had it come to this? A tear slipped down her cheek. How had it turned into this hateful obsession? And how had he committed these crimes while holding down his job as a federal agent? There were so many things that didn't add up.

Dalton kept the gun trained on her as he unlocked the door of one of the apartments. As he thrust her inside, the open-plan space was lit by a single overhead bulb. Hollie's gaze took in the piles of newspaper and cans of gasoline. Although she was confused about many aspects of what was going on, one thing was clear. She wasn't meant to leave this place alive.

Thankfully, Karina had fallen asleep again. Dalton gestured for Hollie to sit on an old sofa. As she did, he went over to the window, looking out at the street below. When he took out his cell phone, he turned to look at her.

"I'm going to call your boyfriend. If you make a sound while I'm talking to him, I'll shoot the baby. Understand?"

This couldn't be happening. It couldn't be *Dalton* saying those words. Dalton liked comics and computer games. He gave money to wildlife charities and would go to great lengths to avoid killing a spider...

"Understand?" He pointed the gun at Karina as he raised his voice.

"Yes. I understand."

"Give me his number."

With the gun still trained on the baby, Hollie stammered out Torque's cell phone number. Her whole body shook as she listened to Dalton speaking to Torque. There was a slight smile on his face as he ended the call.

"What happens now?" Hollie managed to get the words out despite the quivering of her lips.

"Now we wait." He threw himself down in a chair opposite her, his gaze fixed on her face.

"Why did you kill McLain?" She had so many questions, but that one bothered her most. Why did an innocent woman, one they had both known for years, have to die a horrible death?

He was silent for so long she thought he wasn't going to answer. Eventually he shrugged. "She wouldn't tell me where you'd gone."

"That was her job. I was working undercover and she was protecting me."

He didn't seem to be listening. "When you didn't come into the office and no one knew where you were, I tried asking McLain politely where you'd gone. She treated me like I was a kid in school. She actually had the nerve to tell me to back off and stay on my own side of the line. Guess she didn't realize who she was dealing with." His expression switched from a scowl to a smile. "She found out later that night when I followed her home. It took me a long time—she was one tough cookie—but I got the information I needed. Eventually. Of course, I couldn't let her live after that. So I took her to your apartment. Once she was dead, I made sure the place burned so good no one would ever know how she died."

The images of him torturing McLain to get the information about Hollie's whereabouts were sickening. *She died because she tried to protect me.*

"And Vince King? When I asked you to find his number, you said there was no one of that name in the New Haven office. Was that a lie?"

He laughed. "Yeah. I didn't even look for his number."

She swallowed hard. "Is Vince King dead, too?"

"Of course. They'll probably never find him. I tipped his body into a Dumpster and set fire to the whole thing. It was miles from his home and it burned for hours."

Hollie swallowed hard. "So when I spoke to you and you told me to come in so the Incinerator team could look after me, the truth was that you already knew where I was. And the only people who knew I had gone undercover were dead."

He grinned. "Clever, wasn't it? Of course, after I'd killed McLain and King, there was no need for me to keep turning up at the office each day. I knew where you were, so I followed you. The only times I needed to pretend that I was still on the team was when you called me and when I saw you at the aquarium."

Hollie shook her head in confusion. "But for the last

four years you *did* turn up at the office each day. How could you be the Incinerator if you were also working for the FBI? You didn't have the time to travel across the country—across the *world*—to start those fires."

"It always amazed me that no one came up with the possibility of an accomplice. Even you, Hollie, with your databases and analytics, never once suggested that there could be more than one Incinerator." He shook a finger at her. "You're not as clever as you think you are."

Hollie's mind went into overdrive. An accomplice? It was an explanation that opened up a whole range of new possibilities. But who? And why? She supposed the obvious motive was money, but Dalton wasn't wealthy and paying someone to start those fires, as well as buying another person's silence…well, that wasn't going to come cheap.

Dalton laughed as he watched her face. "I can see you're trying to guess who it is and I'll bet you're thinking about it all wrong. I'd like to tell you the whole Incinerator thing was all my idea, but my partner came to me with the plan just after you and I split up."

Hollie was starting to feel that familiar trickle of dread down her spine. "But I don't understand. If this is about me and Torque, we didn't meet until I went undercover. No one could have known that was going to happen."

Dalton hunched a shoulder. "I don't know how it works. Something about a destiny foretold. Gold, emeralds, rubies and a dragon hoard. Anyway, my partner told me Torque would find you eventually. Looks like it was a pretty accurate prediction, doesn't it?"

As far as Hollie was concerned, that cleared up any doubt about who the accomplice was. It must be Teine. Who else could have engaged in such destructive forward planning? She could see into the future. Five years ago, she had set this trap. Preying on Dalton's weakness and his jealousy, she had begun this devastating series of arson attacks, escalating the stakes when Hollie and Torque met.

The odds were already stacked against us, but this? We never stood a chance.

"Dalton, she is dangerous…"

"She? I never said my partner was a woman."

The door to the copy shop was unlocked, a clear signal that it was a trap. *Too easy.* Nevertheless, Torque stepped inside. The place smelled of disuse. Of dust, old newspapers and something unpleasant. Like maybe an animal had crawled in there and died.

Torque stood still, his finely tuned senses seeking any sign of life. Any sound or scent that would tell him Hollie and Karina were in this building. There was nothing. His eyes adjusted swiftly to the gloom and searched every corner. He couldn't see anything out of the ordinary. There were abandoned copy machines and computer monitors, a stack of old chairs and a desk with three legs and a pile of bricks in place of the fourth. On top of the desk Torque's attention was caught by a cell phone.

It was out of place in this run-down environment and there was enough light for him to see that the area around it on the table was dust free. Which made it look like the cell had been left there recently. But that wasn't the most noticeable thing about it. The most important, glaringly obvious feature by far was that it was taped to a bottle of clear liquid…

As the cell phone rang, the explosion hit. Blinding white light was accompanied by a sound like the roar of an express train approaching at tremendous speed with a loud whistling, wailing noise. The blast hit him at chest level, like an ocean wave, lifting him off his feet and powering him backward. Helpless, Torque let it take him, carry him back and slam him into the wall. With the breath driven from his lungs at force, he slid into a sitting position on the floor, feeling like a broken marionette.

But he wasn't broken. If that had been the intention, it had failed. Although he was shaken, he was undamaged. Whoever had planted that bomb hadn't known what they were up against. His inner dragon strengthened his mortal. He wasn't superhuman, but he was close. Pushing himself away from the wall, Torque staggered to his feet. His ears were buzzing, his head was pounding and his legs felt like they belonged to someone else. But his spirit was intact. And he was angry. Tail-swishing, wing-beating, fire-breathing furious.

Come for the dragon, would you? Best not miss.

He looked around him. Part of the ceiling had fallen in and the windows had blown outward. A pipe overhead had burst, allowing water to gush into the room. Several small fires had broken out. Ignoring the devastation around him, Torque stalked through to the back of the store. There was a locked door at the rear and he dealt with it by giving it several swift kicks. The panels of wood soon gave way under his onslaught and he barged through the ruined structure and out into the night air, taking in great gulps as he walked.

What now? He had walked away from a pathetic attempt at a trap, but he had done it with no way of finding Hollie and Karina. Breathing hard, he was trying to think what the hell to do next when his cell phone buzzed.

"Did you enjoy my little warm-up activity?" It was the voice of the man who had claimed to have Hollie and Karina.

"If that was the best you've got—"

"Best? I wasn't even trying."

Torque could hear a noise in the background. He forced himself to concentrate on that, trying to identify it. He had heard it before, very recently.

"Let's see how you like what comes next."

If this guy thought he was sending him on some sort of hunt… Torque had lived through a time of quests. In his opinion, they were mostly a waste of time and energy. Going straight to the main prize was so much easier.

"Head to the storage depot next to the railway station."

As he listened to the instructions, Torque focused on that noise. Jangling, discordant music. The wheezing of ancient pipes. It made him think of cotton candy and children's laughter. And he knew exactly where he had heard it.

"There is a container with a green door."

"Are Hollie and Karina there?" He knew damn well they weren't. They were near the calliope machine he'd heard earlier when he was chasing Teine.

"You'll find out when you get there."

"I hope you're prepared to die a horrible death when I find you."

The response was an amused chuckle before the Incinerator ended the call. Torque resisted the impulse to crush his cell phone underfoot. Instead, he considered the situation. All he had was an idea of the area where Hollie and Karina were being held. He didn't know the precise location. But he knew someone who might be able to help.

Ged answered his call on the first ring. "Are you okay? We saw an explosion."

"I'm fine. Any news on Khan and Sarange?"

"No. They're still not answering my calls."

That news was both good and bad. Sarange would have been the best person to track Karina, but she might have been distracted by concern for her daughter's welfare. But there was another werewolf on the team, and Karina was half wolf. Torque was hopeful Finglas would be able to pick up the baby's scent. And the Incinerator had left another trail for him to follow.

"Send Fin back to the hotel. Tell him to start at Khan's suite. I don't care how he gets in there. I want him to track Karina, so he needs to find something of hers to get her scent. The guy who is holding Hollie and the baby is likely to have taken them in a car, so he won't be able to follow the smell through the streets, but I know the area where they're being held."

I hope I do. He was pinning everything he had on that damn calliope. Torque paused to draw breath, aware that the words were spilling out too hard and fast. "They are near the fairground close to the Rooftop Restaurant."

"We'll meet you there." Ged's calm tone was as reassuring as ever.

"One more thing…there was blood on the carpet outside Khan's suite." Torque clenched a fist against his thigh, fighting the wave of emotion that hit him. *Let it not be Hollie's or Karina's.* "Fin may be able to use that as an additional way of tracking them."

He ended the call to Ged, aware he had one more thing to take care of before he headed over to the fairground. There was a booby-trapped container near the railway station. It was intended for Torque, but an innocent person could stumble across it at any time. He had to find a way to make it safe. Luckily, he wasn't the only fireproof person in Denver that night.

He made another call. "Where are you?"

Alban sounded mildly annoyed at the question. "Chasing around the streets of the city trying to find Teine, just as you asked me to. It's a big place and she's a small woman. If you could narrow the search area, I'd appreciate it."

"Forget that. Go to the storage depot next to the railway station and find a container with a green door."

"Any particular reason?" Alban asked.

"Yes. It will probably blow up as you enter."

Even on the fifth floor of the apartment building, the bright lights of the fairground and the calliope music were jarring. Hollie could feel a headache forming behind her eyes, but maybe it was unfair to blame the entertainment on the street below when there was a man with a gun sitting opposite.

"Your pet dragon is running around town obeying my every command." Dalton's gloating tones made her feel slightly sick.

"What do you mean 'my dragon'?" She tried to console herself that Dalton couldn't know the truth about Torque. No one could.

"I was there, remember? When he rescued you from the burning bus, I saw it all. That explosion wasn't meant for you. It was supposed to be for him. But you were wearing his clothes and I was too far away to see. It was your fault you got caught up in it, Hollie. But what came next, that was a revelation. A rock star who is also a dragon? I was too shocked to film what I was seeing, but I won't be so slow next time."

His next words chilled her.

"Soon the whole world will know the truth about Torque."

"Please, Dalton. You are angry with me. I understand that. But Torque hasn't done anything to hurt you." She hugged Karina tighter. "And let the baby go. She needs her parents."

He barked out a laugh. "He's done nothing to hurt me? How can you say that when he took you from me?"

The words frightened her even more than the gun that was hanging loosely from his fingers. If Dalton believed Torque had stolen Hollie from him, then his mind had become unhinged.

They had split up four years ago. Yes, Hollie had been a Beast fan back then, but she hadn't met Torque and there had never been any hope or prospect that she would do so. She hadn't even been an overzealous follower of the group. She had always written that strong pull she felt toward Torque off as imagination. She had certainly never spoken of it to anyone. If Dalton had somehow become convinced Torque was the reason they broke up, it was a problem *he* had; it wasn't anything Hollie had done.

"Dalton, you know that isn't true. I only met Torque recently…"

"But it was meant to be. You would never have stayed with me. Not when he was waiting for you." His teeth clenched in a tight, unpleasant grin. "You had a dragon in your destiny, Hollie. I was never going to be able to compete with that."

This mysterious partner of his, the other half of the Incinerator team, must have gone to work on him. Preying on Dalton's minor insecurities and jealousies, magnifying them until they became this huge, festering resentment. *For five years.* They had worked together, laughed together, been friends. And the whole time he was harboring this terrible secret.

Yet, even though he talked about destiny, his insistence that his accomplice wasn't a woman perplexed her. Who, other than Teine, could have seen into the future?

"And the baby is my way of making sure you behave. I know how feisty you can be, Hols."

She gritted her teeth. *Hols.* The man who used to call her that had been her friend. Whoever this was, he wasn't the Dalton Hilger she had known. She had to face up to that. This was the Incinerator. The enemy. He looked and sounded like Dalton, but she had to be prepared to fight him if she was going to get herself and Karina out of this alive.

"If you know who Torque is, you must know you won't be able to kill him," she said.

"There are worse things than death for his kind."

The words triggered a memory. What had Torque said? *There are worse things than being slain.*

"Once I expose him, once the world knows what he really is, he'll lose everything. Money, fame, freedom… you." He grinned. "When he's a circus exhibit, he'll wish he *was* dead. Better still, there could be a fortune to be made. Can you imagine how much people would pay to hunt a living, breathing dragon? Big-game hunting would be nothing in comparison. I could set up a company. Of course, I'd have to make sure he wasn't killed outright first time. Maybe the hunters could take trophies. A few scales at a time. The longer I let him live, the more money I'd make."

Hollie felt sick at the images he was conjuring. "You used to care about every living creature. Who did this to you, Dalton?" Tears burned the back of her throat as she asked the question. "Who made you into this person?"

For a moment, Hollie thought she saw a flicker of regret in his eyes. Then the mask came down again. "You did," he snarled.

His cell phone buzzed before she could say anything more. Dalton's expression changed as he looked at the screen. Anger became fear and something more. She'd have said it was awe, but he moved too fast for her to be sure. Getting to his feet, he went over to the window to take the call.

He was talking in an urgent undertone. No matter how hard she strained to hear, Hollie couldn't catch what he was saying. Whatever it was, she got the feeling something had gone wrong with his plan. Hope flickered inside her like a tiny star in a midnight sky and she tried not to pin everything she had on it. That little light was too small and insignificant to guide her out of this dark place, but for a brief instant, it felt good. And wouldn't it be wonderful if it was Torque who had somehow messed up Dalton's cleverly laid schemes?

When he finished speaking, he was breathing hard and his skin had taken on a waxy hue. He tried out a snarl, but it didn't quite work.

"Change of plan. It looks like the dragon boyfriend will have to die, after all."

Chapter 19

Karina woke up again and was weepy, clinging to Hollie and crying louder every time she caught a glimpse of Dalton.

"Can't you keep her quiet?" Dalton was pacing the small room. Hollie could see he was struggling to keep it together, and his earlier threats toward the baby terrified her.

"She wants her mommy. Maybe if I take her to the window, the lights will distract her."

He regarded her suspiciously for a moment or two, then shrugged. "Just don't get any ideas."

Bouncing the little girl against her shoulder and murmuring words of comfort to her, Hollie went to stand at the window. She wasn't sure what sort of ideas Dalton thought she might have, but jumping from this height with a baby in her arms wasn't on her agenda. The only reason she had come to look out at the view was to genuinely try and divert Karina from her distress. She supposed there was a vague hope at the back of her mind that she might catch a glimpse of something—anything—happening on the ground to reassure her. Maybe she would even see a muscular, flame-haired dragon-shifter striding to her rescue.

She didn't see Torque, or anyone she recognized, but the sight of life going on as normal had the effect of grounding her. Torque would be doing everything he could to find her and he wouldn't be using conventional means. He also had a formidable team around him.

Dalton had said Torque would have to die, but he also knew Torque was a dragon. Hollie couldn't make those two pieces of information add up. At first, she had believed that Teine was the person responsible for changing Dalton from her friend into a ruthless criminal. That would have made sense. Teine had the power to kill a dragon. She had already done so, murdering two whole dragon-shifter clans back in the Scottish Highlands.

But Dalton had insisted that Hollie was wrong. His partner was not a woman. That made her blood run cold. Because it meant the other half of the Incinerator team was a man with the same powers as Teine. And there couldn't be many of *them* around.

Her thoughts were interrupted by the buzzing of Dalton's cell phone. That half fearful, half worshipful look crossed his face again as he gazed at the screen. Grasping Hollie's arm, he dragged her toward the bedroom.

"In here." He pushed her across the threshold. "And stay there. No matter what you hear."

He slammed the door closed and she was left staring at it in shock and fear. What now? Was this part of the plan, or had something changed? She had thought she was operating at the highest level of anxiety, but this new development kicked her stress levels up a notch. Panic was like a silent fist tightening on her throat. Her eyes widened, darting around the empty room. Racing heart, brain on fire, nerve endings misfiring like a faulty car engine, thoughts that were a cluster bomb inside her brain, each new idea triggering a series of explosions…any attempt to function normally failed.

Karina wriggled in her arms, reminding her that she had to get past this. She *had* to calm down and think rationally. Hugging the baby close, Hollie pressed her ear to the hardwood panel. The silence was broken by three heavy knocks, presumably on the front door.

There was a murmur of voices and she strained to hear. She couldn't make out the words, and it might have been her imagination, but she definitely heard a wheedling note in Dalton's speech. He sounded like a child trying to make excuses for his behavior to an angry parent. There was obviously a seniority within the Incinerator partnership, and if she was right and the person who had just arrived was the other half of the team, Dalton was scared of his ally.

Then they passed the bedroom door and what she heard next rocked her back on her heels. One tiny word. Not even a word, more a sound, an unmistakable colloquialism. It was meaningless and out of context, but it told her everything.

Dalton's companion said, *"Och."*

Opening the bedroom door, she was face-to-face with Alban before she had time to think about the danger. "So that's why you kept your passport up to date. You needed to follow Beast around the world, starting fires in their wake when Dalton couldn't get time off from his day job." She was pleased with the way her voice remained perfectly calm as she confronted him.

"And that's why you said time settles all scores. You've been waiting a long time for this."

Unfazed by her words, he smiled. "Hello, Hollie. I didn't expect to ever see you again." His piercing gaze shifted from her, and the smile faded. "But I suppose I should have anticipated Dalton would screw this up."

Dalton's face went an ugly shade of red. He turned on Hollie. "I told you to stay in the bedroom."

"You told me a lot of things." Her panic was fading now and anger was bubbling up in its place. Alongside her renewed courage, she felt Karina's tears subsiding. It was as though the little girl was sensing Hollie's mood and drawing on this new surge of bravery. "Like how you were still investigating this case and you weren't a criminal."

She turned to Alban. As she did, her attention was briefly caught by the fact that the front door hadn't fully closed. Thoughts of escape flashed through her mind and were quickly quashed. There was a dragon standing between her and freedom. "You pretended to be Torque's friend."

He shrugged. "All's fair in love and dragon warfare."

"No, it's not." She practically stamped her foot at him. "You are the person who told me dragons are honorable. You said the feud between the Cumhachdach and the Moiteil was over when Teine imprisoned you and Torque together. Now I find out it was all a pretense and you were working behind his back all this time. That doesn't sound like the dragon way."

"He stole from me." Alban's expression was sullen.

"This is about *money*?"

"No. It's about dragon hoard. That which we value most. What the Cumhachdach stole from the Moiteil in the height of battle *was* treasure. The gelt we had accumulated over many centuries," Alban said. "Now the time has come to take from Torque that which he esteems most. That is no longer a material possession... It's you."

"No." Dalton's voice shook. As Alban cast a furious glance his way, he backed down from his initial protest. "I mean...you said you would let her live."

"Oh, come on, Dalton." Hollie turned the full force of her scorn on him. She swept an arm around her, indicating the piles of newspaper and gasoline cans. "You didn't seriously expect me to believe that?"

"This was another trap for your dragon boyfriend. I was to let him believe you died in a fire here." He cast a nervous look at Alban. "But Torque knows where you are."

Her heart gave a wild bound of delight. "He does?" *Then why isn't he here?*

"I hate to wipe that look of joy from your face, but he only has a vague idea of your location. That's why we're leaving right now," Alban said.

"And I hate to be the one to disappoint you."

Hollie gave a little cry of delight as she heard the beloved voice she had been longing for. Swinging around, she saw Torque standing in the doorway with Finglas just behind him. Fury burned in the opal depths of Torque's eyes. "But you are not going anywhere."

Rick had managed to get Finglas into Khan's hotel suite with a story about lost keys. Once there, the werewolf picked up Karina's scent from a soft toy he had found on the pillow of her crib. He had also found a patch of fresh blood on the carpet nearby.

Powered by anger as well as his wolf instincts,

Finglas led Torque to an apartment block close to the fairground.

"You're sure they're in here?" Torque looked up at the building in dismay. It was ten floors high. If the Incinerator got a hint that they were after him and started a fire in there, the outcome would be catastrophic.

"Positive. Karina is only half werewolf, but her scent is strong. And my tracking instinct, even as a human, is powerful."

"Do you know whose blood it is?"

Finglas shook his head. "It's not Karina's. That's all I can tell you."

That meant there was a possibility it was Hollie's blood. The thought that she had been injured while he wasn't there to help her chilled Torque to his soul. This was the side of loving no one had warned him about. That giving his heart to another so completely meant she had possession of his soul, as well. That if anything should harm his mate, it would come back and hurt him double, leaving him unable to function, barely able to breathe.

He had to take those feelings of helplessness and loss and turn them around, force them to become actions, or he would be useless. He pictured Hollie's face, her sweet, warm smile. Keeping her image before him, drawing strength from it, he pulled himself back from the abyss.

They were standing to one side of the building, away from the fairground and out of sight of any of the apartments and the front entrance. The whole team, apart from Khan and Sarange, was together awaiting Torque's orders. He hadn't heard from Alban since he'd sent him to check out the storage depot. It was infuriating because he needed confirmation from his dragon friend that he had neutralized the trap.

There was no time to waste. The Incinerator would be expecting to find out that his rigged explosion in that container had been successful. If Alban hadn't triggered it, or if something had gone wrong, he would get suspicious and that would put Hollie and Karina at risk.

"Finglas and I will go into the building," Torque said to Ged. "Hopefully, Fin can follow Karina's scent and lead me to the right apartment. The rest of you wait out here until I send for you."

"Be careful," Ged warned. "It could be another trap."

Torque turned to Finglas. "What do you think? Are you ready to walk into a trap?"

The young werewolf tilted his face upward. "Khan's daughter is in that building. Hollie is probably at her side. I'm with you."

The words summed up the spirit of Beast and powered Torque forward. Although he allowed Finglas to go slightly ahead of him, he was ready to surge in front at the first sign of trouble. If there was any fighting, a werewolf would be useful, but a dragon would be better.

There was an out-of-order sign on the elevator, but Finglas bypassed it and went straight to the stairs. Confidently, he led Torque up to the fifth floor. When they got there, he paused outside one of the apartments.

He sniffed the air before giving a nod of satisfaction. "This is the one."

The door wasn't fully closed and Torque could hear voices from within. One of them was Hollie's, and his whole body flooded with relief at the realization that she was safe. After listening for a moment or two, he could hear that she was alive, well and angry enough to be arguing with her captor. He spared a second to admire his feisty scientist. Then he recognized the answering voice and his blood froze.

Alban? Reality hit him hard, leaving him momentarily questioning everything he had believed about himself and his life.

Then the fire and fury of a centuries-old dragon feud crashed over him. Every slash, bite and flame-filled breath of Cumhachdach against Moiteil flashed before him and he knew what had happened.

He pushed open the door in time to see Alban seal his own death warrant by taking hold of Hollie's arm.

"Torque!" She wrenched herself free of Alban's grip and ran to him. The feel of her warm, trembling body was like heaven. A sweet, brief reminder of what he thought he'd lost. He dropped a swift kiss on the top of her head. And another for Karina, who, recognizing him, managed a tearful smile.

"Go with Fin. Wait for me outside." He looked over the top of Hollie's head at Alban. Met a pair of unflinching blue eyes. "The Moiteil and I have unfinished business."

"But I need to…" Hollie raised fearful eyes to his face.

"Tell me later." He placed a gentle hand in the small of her back, signaling to Finglas to go with her. "We will have all the time in the world when I'm done here."

"What about the guy?" Finglas jerked a thumb in the direction of a man who looked like he was trying to blend into the peeling wallpaper.

"I'll deal with him later."

"That's Dalton Hilger. He was working with Alban all this time because he somehow knew, even five years ago, that you and I would get together." Hollie cast a glance over her shoulder toward Alban. "Please be careful, but also make him pay."

"I intend to." His jaw was aching with the effort of talking while his teeth were so tightly clenched.

Alban seemed unnaturally calm. He had felt the force of Torque's anger before, but this? The Moiteil was about to discover what it was like to be caught up in the eye of the most violent storm the Cumhachdach could unleash.

Hollie carried Karina out of the apartment and Finglas, grabbing Dalton by the arm as he took his gun from him, marched out after them. Torque took a step closer to Alban. He had never felt fury like this. It was like molten lava building up inside him, creating a pressure so intense that, when the time came for release, it would scorch everything in its path.

"We were forged from the same fire, you and I. Enemies and friends. We hate each other and love each other with equal passion. But when we do it, we do it face-to-face." Torque's jaw was so tense he was having trouble getting the words out. "This? Hiding in the shadows is not the way of the leader of the Moiteil."

He could see his words had stung. Throughout the centuries of dragon clan warfare, the two sides had clung to their identities. The Cumhachdach were the mighty, the Moiteil the proud.

"Och, would you lecture me about dragon ways?" Alban attempted to regain some of his swagger. "You, the great Cumhachdach, who has been hiding himself away behind the swaggering rock star instead of facing his fears—"

The punch Torque swung missed its mark. Instead of connecting with Alban's nose, it caught him on his cheek, but it still rocked his head back. It provoked

Alban to come swinging back at him. A balled fist caught Torque in the stomach and he doubled over. Alban used his advantage and kicked his legs out from under him, getting him down on the floor and straddling him.

Torque had lost count of the times he had fought this man. Of the beatings, the broken bones, the blood and the dust. Each time, they had fought with honor and shaken hands at the end. This time it was different. Alban had threatened Hollie. There was no going back from that.

As they traded blows and swapped places, they knew there could only be one outcome. They were both breathing hard when Alban asked the all-important question.

"To the death, Cumhachdach?"

Torque jerked his head toward the window. "To the skies, Moiteil."

Hollie sank onto the grass at the side of the building. It was a warm night and the shivering that gripped her had nothing to do with the temperature. Nearby, Finglas stood guard over Dalton.

Ged came to kneel beside her, draping his jacket around her shoulders. "Torque will be okay."

"They are both dragons." She wished she could make her teeth stop chattering. "Both Highland clan leaders. They are equally matched and they are both fighting for a cause."

"But Torque's motive is stronger. He is driven by love," Ged said.

Hollie brushed away a tear, resting her cheek on Karina's head. "Have you spoken to Khan or Sarange?"

Her words were accompanied by a cry of relief from

the open window of a car that pulled up on the street nearby. Sarange leaped out and darted over to them. Scooping Karina up from Hollie's arms, she smothered the baby's face with kisses before checking her over. Karina chuckled with pleasure and waved her plump arms. Khan wrapped his arms around them both, holding them as close as he could.

"Oh, Hollie. How can we ever thank you for keeping her safe?" Sarange turned to her with eyes that were bright with tears. "When we were finally able to check our messages and realized what was happening, we were frantic with worry."

Hollie made an attempt to answer her. It was a miserable failure. Her voice didn't work and all that came out was a gulp. It was followed by a sob and soon she was weeping uncontrollably on Ged's shoulder as the full horror of the past few hours hit her.

When she could finally talk, she gestured toward the apartment building. "Torque." It was the only word she could say, the only thought on her mind.

"Torque can take care of himself—"

Khan was interrupted by the sound of breaking glass from high above them. Hollie got to her feet, covering her mouth with a shaking hand as two figures tumbled from the window of the apartment she had recently left.

The scene was perfectly illuminated by the lights from the fairground. Torque and Alban were in free fall, heading for the ground, arms and legs windmilling wildly. Hollie's every sense seemed heightened. The screams of the people watching from the attractions were overloud and the breeze in her face became an icy wind. For an instant she could almost have sworn Torque looked directly into her eyes. His gaze pinned her in place, searing into her mind, blazing into her heart.

With only feet to go before they hit the ground, there was a sudden upward rush of air. A ricochet of force that sent Hollie reeling back. In an almost choreographed move, both men stretched out their arms, shifting in the same instant. Two giant dragons snorted twin plumes of smoke, banking around hard as they rose above the apartment building.

"Son of a…" Khan threw back his head, watching the spectacle above him openmouthed.

The dragons circled the building in a tight arc before facing each other across the roof. The ground shook with the depth of a single dragon roar. Hollie knew for certain that Torque was the challenger. When Alban's answering bellow came, it was equally thunderous.

All around her, people were gathering to watch the spectacle. Cell phones were raised to capture the scene for all time.

"Do something," she begged Ged. "He will hate this." *If he lives.* She shook the thought aside. He *had* to live. She couldn't think about the alternative. It was hard to watch the scene above her, impossible not to.

"I can't stop other people from filming. I can only try to limit the damage." Ged didn't take his eyes off the two winged figures in the sky as he drew his own cell phone out of his pocket.

Above them, Torque, distinguishable to Hollie because of his red-gold scales, launched a stream of fiery breath toward his opponent. Alban jerked violently as he absorbed the impact of the flames. Tilting his nose to the heavens and streamlining his body into an arrow shape, he took off with Torque just behind him.

Twisting and weaving to make himself a difficult target for his pursuer, Alban kept going until he had gained sufficient altitude. Then he pulled up abruptly. Seeing his intention, Hollie cried out a warning even though there was no chance of Torque hearing her.

Alban seemed to hang in midair before starting a nose-down strike. Torque, coming up beneath him, was flying too fast to turn. One of Alban's long-clawed feet hooked into his lower left flank and he spun away with a roar of pain.

Sarange handed Karina to Khan and came to stand next to Hollie, placing an arm around her shoulders. "I don't know much about dragon fights, but I know about good guys. We always win and Torque is the best there is."

Whirling back on course, Torque dove after Alban. From the ground, the next few minutes were a blur of aerial wrestling as they engaged in a tooth and claw battle. Straining to see what was happening in the eye of the dragon storm, Hollie glimpsed Torque's lethal talons tearing into his opponent. The hit to his upper right shoulder sent Alban reeling from the blow, knocking him off course. He fell, hitting one wing on a corner of the apartment building.

Alban emitted a high-pitched screech of pure fury and veered away. Torque was too fast for him. Lashing out again, he inflicted a long gash on Alban's already injured wing, limiting his ability to maintain height.

Gripping his victim in his claws, Torque opened his powerful jaws wide. Clamping on to Alban's muscular neck, he used his huge fangs to tear through the thick dragon hide. Although Alban struggled, he was powerless to break free of the excruciating grip and Torque gave him a final shake before sending him plummeting to the ground.

Chapter 20

As he landed and shifted, Torque could see Ged doing what he did best. Crowd control and public relations.

"Nothing to see here, guys." Ged was signaling to the other members of the band to help him out. They were working as a team to keep people away from the point where Alban had crashed to the ground, shifting into human form as he fell. Forming a human barrier against prying eyes, everyone was giving the same message.

"That's right. It was a promotional display for Beast's new album. Glad you enjoyed it. Realistic? That's what we were aiming for. Spread the word to your friends…"

Incredibly, Alban was still alive. Just. Torque knelt beside him.

"It was a good fight, Cumhachdach." The words were barely a wheeze. "Best dragon won."

Torque took Alban's hand, and his clasp was returned. "You did the Moiteil proud."

"No." A shadow crossed the other man's face. "You were right. What I did to you…to Hollie…that was not the dragon way. I guess it was jealousy. It affected my ability to think straight."

"Jealousy?" Torque frowned.

"Teine once told me your most precious treasure would not be gold coins and jewels, but a human woman you would love. I never gave it much thought until five years ago when I got a letter telling me you would soon find her and, unless I could stop you making her your mate, the Cumhachdach would rise again. I believed Teine was dead, so I did'nae know who sent that letter. I know now, of course." A spasm of pain crossed Alban's face. "Even though I didn't know it was Teine who sent the letter, it named Hollie…told me where to find her. I tracked her down, and once I knew what her job was, I came up with the Incinerator plan. Jealousy is the only word for my motivation. I couldn't stand the thought that you would have all the things that would never be mine. A mate. A clan. A new life."

"I can't have those things. I'm a dragon-shifter. We can't convert our mates."

"Och, you can do anything you choose. You are the last of the Cumhachdach…believe in yourself, man." As he spoke, Alban's voice faded, his clasp on Torque's hand loosened and his eyes drifted closed.

Torque remained on his knees with his head bowed, only vaguely conscious of someone placing a blanket around his naked body. This man—this dragon—had been part of his life since he was born. All his memorable moments, good and bad, had been shared with Alban. The Cumhachdach and the Moiteil. The names were ingrained in Highland legend. Now the Moiteil were no more. The last of their name was gone.

Dragon honor. It was the code by which Torque lived, the one by which Alban had died. The leader of the Moiteil had brought dishonor on himself, but that didn't make it any less painful for the one who had been forced to strike the death blow. To a dragon-shifter the shedding of dragon blood was the greatest offense one of their kind could commit, permissible only in battle, or for the punishment of high crimes.

The stupidest part of all was no matter how much he hated what Alban had done, Torque would mourn him for the rest of his life. Not this man, the warped criminal whose mind had conceived the Incinerator plan. The other Alban, the brave warrior, loyal friend and sensitive intellectual. The man who could make him laugh until he had tears in his eyes had now made him cry for an entirely different reason.

He lifted his head as a hand slipped into his.

"I know you loved him." Hollie's face was wet as she raised his palm to her cheek.

"I love you more." He gained strength from the words.

She clung to him. "When I saw you fall from that window, I thought I'd lost you."

He wrapped the blanket around them both and held her until his heartbeat was restored to normality. "Are you okay?" He looked around him to where Dalton Hilger was sitting on the grass with his head in his hands. Renewed anger pounded through him. "Did he hurt you? There was blood in Khan's hotel suite…"

She gave a shaky laugh. "It was Dalton's blood. Karina scratched him."

"She did?" Khan, who was standing nearby, overheard. "That's my girl." His face hardened as he looked at

Dalton. "What's happening with that guy? He kidnapped my daughter…and you, Hollie. But…*my daughter.*"

"Maybe we should hand him over to the FBI. Let the human forces of law and order deal with their own," Torque said. "He can try and explain his involvement in the fires by telling them his partner was a dragon. Who knows? They may even listen."

Dalton took his hands away from his face. Across the distance between them, Torque could see the fury in his eyes. "You did this." Dalton's voice shook. "If it wasn't for you…"

Reaching behind him into the waistband of his pants, he withdrew a hidden gun. He aimed it at Torque, but two shots rang out almost simultaneously. The one Dalton fired missed Torque by inches.

A look of surprise replaced the furious expression on Dalton's face and he toppled forward. Behind him, Finglas held the gun he had taken from Dalton in the apartment.

"I thought he might try something like that," Finglas said. "I decided not to wait around and see if he was bluffing."

Ged stepped forward to check Dalton. "Dead." He looked around. "Which leaves us with an issue. We have two bodies here and I'm guessing the authorities may want to know what the dragon story that will be hitting the media any time now is all about. If they don't, the press will. Even if my claim that it's promo for the new album holds, it will draw a lot of attention our way. We should probably get out of here and do something about these bodies."

Torque got to his feet, clutching his injured side. Alban's claws had cut deep and the gash was still bleeding. "Alban may not have earned an honorable departure from this world, but I choose to give him one. His ashes must be scattered on the soil of our homeland."

"For the time being, would you settle for going back to the hotel so Hollie can tend to your wounds? You can trust me to deal with Alban's body with sensitivity and also leave this scene free from any trace of our presence," Ged said.

Torque nodded. "Very well."

Khan drove Torque, Hollie, Sarange and Karina back to the hotel. Ged, Finglas, Dev and Diablo remained at the scene of the dragon fight. Torque didn't know the details of what they were doing, but he knew Ged would be true to his word. When he had finished, there would be no trace of the dragon fight or of Beast's presence. The following afternoon, they would leave Denver and set off on the final stage of the tour.

Hollie's head flopped wearily against Torque's shoulder as they completed the short drive in silence. When Khan pulled into the hotel's underground parking lot, she stretched and yawned.

"You haven't told me what happened when you took Deigh out to dinner."

"Ah, hell." Torque ran a hand through his hair. "I'd forgotten all about her."

Hollie bit her lip as she knelt on the floor and studied the wound in Torque's left side. "This needs stitches."

"I can't go to a hospital." He was seated on the bed and he flinched as he moved his arm. "But there is a medical kit in my suitcase."

She attempted a smile. Given everything that had happened, she thought it worked pretty well. "You bring along a suture kit just for this sort of eventuality?"

He grinned. "It happens more often than you'd imagine."

Her lip wobbled and she took a moment or two to get it under control. "I've never stitched anyone's skin before, Torque. I don't want to hurt you."

He used his right hand to grip her chin, tilting her face up to him so he could drop a kiss onto the end of her nose. "I need you to help me heal. And once you stitch me up, I'll heal fast. Shifter DNA," he explained in response to her look of inquiry. "It works quicker than the human kind."

Torque explained where the medical kit was, and once she had it, Hollie took it through to the bathroom and arranged its contents on the counter beside the sink. Returning to the bedroom, she took Torque's hand and he leaned on her as she helped him through to the other room.

"This will sting." The gaping cut in his side looked even worse in the harsh fluorescent light.

Torque gripped the sink hard as she poured antiseptic onto a swab and cleaned the wound. Beads of sweat broke out on his brow and he trembled violently.

Hollie bit her lip as she cleared the blood away and viewed the damage. It was even worse than she'd thought. The razor-sharp talons had penetrated deep, tearing through flesh and muscle as Alban had sliced into Torque's side with full force. It was a devastating injury.

Having thoroughly cleaned the wound to prevent any infection, she turned to the suture kit, checking the instructions carefully. The pack included a syringe and a local anesthetic. Taking a deep breath, she injected this into the area around the wound in Torque's side.

Forcing herself to remain calm, she prepared the

needle and suture material. "Okay. I'm going to stitch you up now."

Torque smiled. "You say the nicest things."

"You do not want to make me laugh while I'm approaching you with a needle in my hand," she warned. Bending over her task, she managed to complete it quickly and effectively. "There. It may not be the neatest, but you no longer have a hole in your side."

Torque studied his reflection in the mirror. "Looks fine to me."

Hollie placed a dressing over the stitches and secured it in place. Then she gave Torque two painkillers washed down with a glass of water, before helping him back to the bedroom.

"I'm not completely helpless." He was torn between laughter and frustration.

"So you can get your own underwear on, can you?" She faced him with her hands on her hips, a teasing smile on her lips as she studied his naked body.

He held up his right hand in a gesture of surrender. "Um…maybe not."

Having helped him into his boxer briefs, she led him to the bed, drawing back the bedclothes so he could ease himself down.

"Where are you going?" he asked as she walked away. "I need you next to me."

"Give me two minutes. I just have to dispose of the medical waste."

He nodded sleepily. Having tidied up in the bathroom, cleaned herself up and stripped down to her underwear, Hollie slid into bed. The sound of his rhythmic breathing told her Torque was already asleep. After the events of the day just gone, she didn't expect to join him, but as she turned out the bedside light, slumber was already tugging at the edges of her consciousness.

The beat was so loud Torque could hear it in his teeth. A slow, heavy pounding. Half-time, slower than a human heartbeat, maybe more like that of a whale. Every light went out, plunging the huge arena into darkness. Screams and cries from the audience filled the night. Slow, lazy guitar chords joined the drumbeats.

Above the stage, a single beam became a whirling series of colored lights. Flashing, red-green, yellow-blue. Within the indistinct patterns, a shape began to emerge. Pure, pulsing light became a creature of fire and scales. As the beat picked up and the guitar faded, the dragon in the sky roared once, shooting a stream of fire over the heads of the stunned crowd.

Blackness reigned once more, and then the lights focused on Khan as he screeched out the opening lines of the final number. Los Angeles. Seventeen thousand people. The last night of the tour. The dragon special effect was Ged's way of answering the media frenzy that had followed the Denver dragon fight.

We are Beast. We gave you werewolves, tigers and other shifters in Marseilles. Now it's time for dragons.

As they bounded off the stage, Torque didn't feel his usual sense of elation. This time there was only relief. He was thankful the performance was over and was experiencing a sense of freedom now that this nightmare tour was finally at an end.

The whole band was staying at Khan and Sarange's luxury Beverly Hills mansion. Hollie and Sarange had left the performance as soon as it finished so they could prepare a celebratory meal. There had been times during this tour when Torque wondered if they would ever make it to this point. Now his thoughts were on the future and what it might look like.

There hadn't been any police backlash from the events in Denver. Ged had ensured that the scene was scrupulously clean. The following day, he had drawn Torque and Hollie's attention to an online news report about a body found in a fifth-floor Denver apartment. The man, identified as former FBI agent Dalton Hilger, had died from a single gunshot wound. The room in which he was killed had been prepared as though for an arson attack. Investigations were ongoing and included the possibilities that Hilger, already under investigation for the killing of a senior officer, was responsible for a series of fires over a number of years and that he had been shot by an accomplice.

There was, of course, the issue of the bizarre dragon fight that had gone viral on social media. In Marseilles, Ged had done everything he could to play down the incident, assuring fans that it was an experimental special effect and there would be no repeat performance. This time, so many people at the fairground had filmed the spectacular beasts in the sky above Denver that he had been forced to take a different approach.

Refusing to name the digital geniuses responsible for the aerial display, Ged had given several interviews, simply stating that it was a promotion for Beast's new album. Luckily, he already had a reputation for being enigmatic and Beast was known for its commitment to its privacy. Ged had then arranged several other dragon-themed displays, including the one at the performance they had just given. They were intended as a distraction, but he suspected the questions would remain about how the animation in Denver had been achieved.

When they arrived at the house, Sarange had already

sent the caterers away. If the team she employed to provide food for the party found anything strange in the
meal they were asked to provide, Torque guessed they
had been too professional to comment. Or too well paid.
Meat, fish and salad—and plenty of it—was arranged
on tables at the side of the swimming pool. The elegant
gardens were the perfect place to unwind.

He sought out Hollie, who looked delectable in a
flowered sundress, and wrapped his arms around her,
lifting her off her feet. Although the wound in his side
twinged, it was already healing. "The tour from hell
is over."

"It wasn't all bad." Her smile sent electrical currents zinging through his bloodstream. "I can think of
a few memorable moments. Some of the hotel rooms we
stayed in will always have a special place in my heart...
and so will some of the forests."

"Let's take a vacation." He hadn't thought about the
immediate future until now, and it was a spur of the
moment suggestion. "Where do you want to go? Anywhere in the world."

"I may have some thoughts about that, but I'll tell
you later."

When he pushed her to elaborate, she shook her
head mysteriously and led him to the drinks table. At
least Hollie hadn't said the words he was dreading. She
hadn't told him that tonight would be their last night
together. But at some point soon they would have to
have that conversation about the future. About how they
could be together as humans, but how they couldn't have
forever. And they would have to talk about children.
He had watched her with Karina and seen how much
she loved the little girl. Hollie would be a wonderful
mother, but dragon-shifters would never accept those

who were not pure of blood. Unless their parents were both dragon-shifters, their children would be outcasts. Torque was not prepared to bring a child into the world knowing he, or she, would be a misfit. He didn't think Hollie would do that to a child, either. Would she be prepared to face a future without a family of her own? It was yet another shadow hanging over them.

Even as he took Hollie's hand and enjoyed the prospect of a vacation during which they didn't need to look over their shoulders, his heart was heavy at the thought that this happiness could be on borrowed time.

Khan and Sarange made their announcement about the new baby to laughter and jokes.

"Did you think we hadn't guessed?" Dev raised his glass, anyway. "All that running out of the room and the sound of throwing up was kind of a giveaway."

While everyone was crowded around their hosts, Hollie approached Ged, who was standing slightly apart from the group. "Can I ask you a question?"

He smiled down at her. "Always."

She took a deep breath. "In your alpha-male world, have you ever heard of a dragon-shifter being proposed to by a human?"

"Now, that's a question." His gaze went over her head to where Torque was standing with Khan. "And the answer is no. No, I have never heard of that."

"Oh." Hollie considered his response in silence. She wasn't entirely surprised, but she had hoped there might be a precedent.

"Why are you asking me this, Hollie? Torque already approached me about the dragon mark."

"You told him I would have to walk through fire to receive his bite, didn't you?" Ged nodded. "That's the problem. It's the whole alpha-male thing. No matter how much Torque wants us to be together, he won't do anything that puts me in danger."

"I see. So you are planning to take the initiative away from him."

"Yes. Of course, he may just refuse."

Ged regarded her in fascination. "What would you do then?"

She smiled. "Walk into a fire, of course. Then he'd have to rescue me and he could bite me while we were there. But it would be so much easier if he'd just accept my proposal. Don't you agree?" He started to laugh and she watched him with a bemused expression. "What did I say that was so funny?"

"Nothing. I was just thinking that the dragon has finally met his match."

Torque came over to them then. "Are you two hatching secrets?"

"You could say that." Ged kissed Hollie's cheek. "Good luck."

"Good luck?" Torque watched as Ged walked away. "Why do you need luck?"

She took his hand. "Let's go somewhere private so I can tell you."

His expression was somewhere between confusion and trepidation as she led him to their luxurious bedroom. When she closed the door and turned to face him, her heart was trying to hammer its way out of her chest. Telling herself she had to go for it, she launched into a speech without being entirely sure what she was going to say.

"When you said you'd find a way for us to have forever, why didn't you tell me about the dragon mark?"

He muttered an exclamation. "I suppose it was Ged who told you about that?"

She shook her head at him. "Don't try to change the subject. And don't do that dragon frown at me, Torque. I asked you a question first."

His sigh seemed to come from the depths of his soul. "Did Ged explain what the dragon mark entails? That, unlike when another shifter species asks their mate to convert, it is much more than just a bite. Before you received my mark, you would have to walk into a pit of fire to demonstrate your allegiance." His voice was tortured. "I could never ask you to do that."

"When the Pleasant Bay Bar was on fire, you walked through the flames to rescue me. If I stepped into a fire pit, surely the effect would be the same? You would be there to protect me."

"That was different. Your life was in danger and I had no choice. This time I would be asking you to do it." Torque's expression was anguished. "I can't do it, Hollie. I can't send you into a blaze not knowing for certain I can get you out of it."

"Then I'll make it easier for you." Slowly, with her heart pounding out a wild tattoo, she went down on one knee.

"What are you doing?" The words were a growl, originating somewhere deep in his chest.

"Well, if we were both human, I'd be proposing marriage. But since you're a shifter, I'm asking you to give me your dragon mark." She swallowed the constriction in her throat. "Be my mate, Torque. Give us forever."

"Hollie, you don't know what you're asking." He stepped closer.

"I do. I'm clear on the details. Fire and fangs." She took his hand, holding the palm against her cheek. "If you don't say yes, I may as well walk into that fire pit, anyway. You don't want eternity without me, but I don't want a human future where I have to watch you hurting. I don't want half a life."

He gave a shaky laugh. "Are you trying to blackmail me?"

"I'll do whatever it takes, my dragon…" She gasped as he hauled her to her feet, crushing her tight to his chest.

"You win." Torque's lips were hot and hard on hers. "I'm going to throw you into a fire. Then I'm going to bite the hell out of you."

"That's what I love about dragons. You are so romantic." Hollie melted against him, returning his caresses with a fervor that matched his own. "That answers the question of where I want to go on vacation. Take me to Scotland. We can scatter Alban's ashes and then have ourselves a honeymoon."

"We'll leave in the morning."

Chapter 21

Deep in the heart of the mountain, the fire leaped and twirled in a fiery dance, its glowing embers twinkling like stars in the heated atmosphere. Each time Hollie tried drawing a breath, the air was hotter and her chest grew tighter. This was the place where it all began. The pit where the Cumhachdach and the Moiteil were born.

Flames licked close to her bare feet, crackling playfully at the edges of the rock. Flaring higher toward the center, they flared and spat, showering sparks like a fountain, hurling plumes of gray smoke high into the air. Ash flew up high before showering the ground like great dirty flakes of snow.

"It's like a living creature." Hollie wrapped her arms around her naked body, gazing into the inferno. "A great hungry serpent, ready to devour everything in its path." She turned her head to look at Torque. "Ready to consume me."

His hands gripped her shoulders even tighter. "I'm here."

She let herself feel the fire's force, using her fear to drive herself onward. The blaze was regal and proud. Well, Hollie could hold her head up and stare into its yellow heart. For the sake of her future, she could take its hissing, spitting challenge. "Will it hurt when you bite me?"

"Yes." Torque's lips brushed her ear. "But the pain won't last."

She nodded. There were natural steps carved into the rock, and Hollie moved onto the next one, sucking in a breath as the scorching heat kissed her flesh. How beautifully the flames swayed and danced, reaching for her, inviting her to join them. She was so close now that her pale flesh had taken on a bluish tinge.

"It will be like walking into a river." Her voice was dreamy. "Waters of fire."

Behind her, Torque wrapped his arms around her and they took the last few steps together.

The blaze welcomed her with a brilliant display of color. Reds, oranges and purples bloomed all around her, bursting into life and fading to golden embers. As it heated her blood to boiling point, Hollie had a moment of perfect clarity. This was a mirror on her new life. Glowing bright and fading, only to be renewed seconds later.

Behind her, she could feel Torque shifting. His body was growing, his hands leaving her shoulders as his wings wrapped around her, his skin on hers becoming scales. Instead of the fear she'd anticipated, the fire acted as a balm, calming her nerves, warming her body and emptying her mind of care.

This moment, this commitment, they were all that

mattered. Tilting her head back against Torque's shoulder, she exposed her throat to his mouth. His sharp fangs closed on her neck and shoulder and Hollie hissed out a breath.

The searing pain was like a knife blade being driven deep into her flesh, but the agony quickly dulled to a throb. Time ceased to exist and she had no idea how long they stayed that way, his wings enclosing her, his teeth marking her. Slowly, he pulled away and shifted back. His human body was hard and strong against her, his lips tender on the skin of her neck. Sensation rushed through her, and her body became boneless. Hollie sagged against him, feeling Torque lift her off her feet as her vision darkened.

When she regained consciousness, she was on a ridge, close to the summit of Càrn Eighe. A warm blanket covered her nakedness and she was wrapped in Torque's arms. Both of those things felt just fine. She raised one arm, studying her unblemished flesh with a sense of wonder.

"No burns."

"How do you feel?" Torque's expression was concerned.

She felt for the tender spot on her neck and shivered. It wasn't painful. It was…delicious. "Different. And very turned on. Is that normal?"

His laughter held a note of relief. And something more. Her gaze traveled down his body, her eyes widening as she identified what the something more might be. "This is all new to me, as well. But I'm willing to learn."

"We should probably go with our instincts, but maybe find some privacy." Getting to her feet, she led him back into the cave.

Whatever had happened to her in that fire, she was

now aching and raw with desire. As soon as Torque pushed her up against the rocky wall and kissed between her breasts, Hollie was squirming and panting.

"Please, Torque. I can't wait."

He swirled his tongue over her diamond-hard left nipple several times before taking it in his mouth and sucking. Pleasure shot through her and she moaned. He reached up and began caressing the other nipple between his thumb and forefinger. The restless longing spiraled out of control.

"Need your mouth on me now." It was hard to talk, but she managed to gasp out the words.

He obliged by kneeling in front of her, pressing his face to the apex of her thighs. Hollie couldn't believe how close she was to orgasm already. Using his thumbs to hold her outer lips apart, he ran his tongue along the length of her sex. Hollie's whole body jerked wildly.

"Keep still." Torque used one hand to hold her hip, keeping her pressed up against the cave wall.

With the other hand, he continued to keep her open while he covered her with his mouth. Finding her clit with his tongue, he flicked the tiny bud before sucking it hard. Hollie gasped. Throwing her head back against hard rock, she instantly succumbed to a thunderous orgasm.

"Want you in me. Right now."

Torque threw the blanket down on the cave floor. As soon as they were lying down, Hollie pulled him on top of her.

"No condoms." He ground the words out just as he was about to enter her.

"We don't need them anymore, my dragon."

He gazed into her eyes, and she felt the strength of the connection between them more powerfully than ever. This was what they craved. This was forever. Torque pressed forward, pushing into her, and the pleasure that streaked up her spine made her cry out.

"Mine." It was a growl.

Hollie wound her arms around his neck. "Always."

As she arched her back and lifted her knees around his hips, he sank fully inside her. They both moaned at the exquisite feeling. Torque held himself still and Hollie closed her eyes, reveling in the delicious sensation. Before long, it became too much and she gripped his arms.

"I need you to move now."

In response, he pulled right out and plowed straight back in. Hard and fast. Hilt-deep. Hollie cried out with pleasure. He filled her completely and she instinctively squeezed her muscles around him. Torque repeated the movement, drawing out and thrusting in, over and over. Each thrust tipped her closer to a second orgasm. She could feel the familiar tingle building even though it felt impossible after only a few minutes.

When Torque began to tease her with shallow movements, she arched her back, and dug her nails into his shoulders. This time, when her release hit, there was no warning. She was thrashing wildly, flung into the most intense climax of her life. The fire she had walked through had entered her body, filling her veins and rushing through her bloodstream. Dragon pleasure. It was almost too much. As her vision grayed and the pressure inside her skull triggered a series of sunbursts behind her eyes, she clung to Torque as he continued to drive into her sensitive flesh.

His thrusts triggered a series of exquisite aftershocks and her muscles clenched tight around him, pulling him deeper into her.

"Ah, Hollie." His head dropped onto her shoulder as he gave one final thrust before holding himself still. She could feel his own release shuddering through him.

After a few minutes, the reality of lying on the rocky ground intruded and Hollie sat up. Something more began to tug at her consciousness. It started out as a need, a hunger that filled her whole body, and quickly became a craving so strong she couldn't ignore it. She hugged her arms around her upper body, unsure how to express this new sensation.

Torque, who was lying on his side watching her, started to smile. "You need to fly."

She regarded him warily. "I do?"

"Trust me, I know exactly what you're feeling. And remember—" He got to his feet, holding out his hand. "I'll catch you if you fall."

Torque watched Hollie closely as she stood on the ridge. She was trembling all over, her expression a combination of trepidation and exultation.

"I don't know what to do." It was a wail of frustration.

"You are trying too hard. Shifting is a natural process." He tried to find the words to explain it to someone who had never done it before. "You are part dragon now. A creature of legend, born to fly, to hunt, to mate, to breathe fire, to bring up your young as part of a clan. Reach deep inside yourself and feel your inner dragon rippling in the depths of your muscles, and simmering in your bloodstream. Hear the call of the Highland skies beating in time with your heart."

As he spoke, Hollie closed her eyes. Her breathing slowed as she lowered her head and stretched out her arms. And slowly—oh, so slowly—she shimmered. He caught a brief glimpse of her dragon. Then a gasp left her lips and Hollie came back into view.

"Let it happen, Hollie."

She gulped and nodded, her expression becoming determined. "I felt her."

A second or two later, she shifted. A beautiful, graceful dragon stood poised on the edge of the ridge. Her scales were the color of shimmering aquamarine and she shyly unfurled new wings. She blinked as if waking from a deep sleep, and her eyes were like emeralds catching the light of the morning sun. As she raised her head toward the sky, white smoke drifted from her elegant nostrils.

Torque shifted quickly, wanting to be at her side when she took her first step off the mountain. Nudging her lightly with his snout, he swooped from the ridge, watching in delight as Hollie followed him. They soared together over the slopes and valleys, camouflaged against prying eyes as Torque showed his mate her Highland home.

Swooping over one dark loch, he hovered above a gaunt gray house that nestled among the tall pines. The exterior was as dour and unprepossessing as all Scots mansions of the same age tended to be. They had been built, after all, with the intention of repelling invaders, rather than welcoming guests.

When they returned to the ridge some time later and shifted back, Hollie was laughing with delight.

"I did it." She threw her arms around Torque's neck. "I really did it."

"Yes, you did. Now get some clothes on, or I won't be answerable for the consequences."

They dressed quickly in the hiking gear they'd left inside the cave and started the long walk back down the mountainside. By the time they reached Inverness, it was evening.

"I'm so hungry I could eat two charred steaks," Hollie said. "Maybe three."

"There speaks a dragon after my own heart." Torque pushed open the door of Kirsty McDougall's and stepped aside to let her enter.

Kirsty bustled forward to greet them, her face breaking into a beaming smile. "Have you brought that reprobate Moiteil back to us?"

Torque took her hands. "I have some bad news for you, Kirsty." He led her to a quiet table and the three of them sat down. "Alban is dead. We scattered his ashes on the slopes of Càrn Eighe this morning."

"Och, no." She burst into noisy sobs. "I suppose it was all his own stupid fault?"

"I guess you could say that." Torque decided to keep it diplomatic and say as little as possible about the circumstances surrounding Alban's death. "How's the insomnia situation?"

Kirsty dabbed at her eyes with a corner of her apron. "All cured. The remedy Deigh recommended worked like a charm." She gave a watered-down version of her chuckle. "Which is good, since I suppose it *was* a charm."

"And has anything been seen of Teine or Deigh recently?"

Kirsty shuddered. "Not even a glimpse of the whites of either of their eyes. Tell me it will stay that way?"

"I hope so, but I can't make you any promises."

Kirsty sighed heavily. "We'll live in hope. Now, can I get you some food? Neeps and tatties?"

"We'll have steak. Well done," Hollie said firmly. "No sides."

Kirsty looked from her to Torque and back again with interest. "Like that, is it? Well, I hope you'll both be very happy." A dreamy look came into her eyes as though she was looking beyond them and into the future. "Aye, I can see it. You *will* be happy, although your hands will be full in about nine months' time with the twin dragon-shifters that are coming your way."

"Twins?" Hollie gave an exclamation of surprise.

"Och, did he no mention that twins are common in the Cumhachdach clan?" Kirsty chuckled to herself as she disappeared into the kitchen.

"Twins." Hollie pressed a hand to her flat stomach. "Do you think we just…?"

"It's possible." Torque smirked. "We Cumhachdach are very virile."

She started to laugh. "We haven't even talked about where we're going to live."

He took her hand. "I showed you my ancestral home."

Hollie's brow wrinkled.

"When we were flying."

"That house beside the loch was your home? Torque, that place was incredible."

He nodded. "Home to the Cumhachdachs since my birth. Of course, my commitments with Beast mean we'd have to spend time in America, but we have the house in Maine and the apartment in New York."

"I'd be quite happy with just one home."

Torque's cell phone buzzed as she spoke, and he experienced a fierce desire to throw the damn thing against the nearest wall. *Just leave us alone.* Surely nothing else could happen? When he checked, it was a message from Ged with a link to a news report.

Might want to check this out.

The article was short. Denver police were appealing for help in identifying a woman whose body had been recovered from the South Platte River. Although there were no signs of violence, the medical examiner had released the information that her body appeared to have been frozen for some time prior to entering the water. The unknown woman was described as petite with pale coloring and unusual, silver-white hair that was natural. At some point in the past, she had suffered severe burns to her upper body.

Torque held his cell phone out to Hollie so she could read what was on the screen.

"Deigh won," she said when she finished.

"It looks that way. She finally defeated Teine, even though it was at the expense of her own life." He placed a hand under her chin, tilting her head up so he could look at her face. "Are you crying?"

"Only because I'm so happy. I can't believe, after everything that's happened, it's all going to be okay." She smiled through her tears. "You will no longer be the last of the Cumhachdach."

"And you, my beautiful dragon mate, need to start planning our wedding."

"But we had our ceremony." She blushed. "Up on the mountain."

"That was for us." He raised her hand to his lips. "But I want the world to know the truth. Next time I say it, I want it to be in public. You are mine, Hollie. All mine."

* * * * *

COMING SOON!

We really hope you enjoyed reading this book. If you're looking for more romance, be sure to head to the shops when new books are available on

Thursday
12th July

To see which titles are coming soon, please visit
millsandboon.co.uk

LET'S TALK

Romance

For exclusive extracts, competitions
and special offers, find us online:

 facebook.com/millsandboon

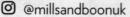 @millsandboonuk

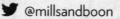 @millsandboon

Or get in touch on 0844 844 1351*

For all the latest titles coming soon, visit
millsandboon.co.uk/nextmonth